CHAPTER ELEVEN

Kissa
Corporate
Bankruptcy Ka

AF663382

Amit Shankar

Vitasta
Let Knowledge Spread

Published by
Vitasta Publishing Pvt. Ltd.
2/15, Ansari Road, Daryaganj,
New Delhi - 110 002
info@vitastapublishing.com

ISBN: 978-93-80828-33-6

© Amit Shankar 2011
Reprint 2013
Edited by Sonithaa J Kapoor

All Rights Reserved.
No part of this publication may be reproduced, stored in a retrieval system, or transmitted, in any form, or by any means—electronic, mechanical, photocopying, recording or otherwise—without the prior permission of the publisher.

All the names and the characters in this book are fictitious. Resemblance to anyone, living or dead, is purely coincidental

Cover design by Deepak Jain
Layout by Vitasta Publishing Pvt. Ltd.
Printed by Vits Press, New Delhi

I dedicate this book to

Late Dr Vishnu for giving birth to this present, and to

Vishu, the present that holds the key to a splendid future.

Also, to my loving sisters–Manju and Ranju di–who

initiatd me into the habit of reading.

Thank you and More...

My Guardian Angels for helping me through this journey; My Goddess and God for being so kind and giving; Vagmi Kumar for the insights and the steady inflow of suggestions; Suren Chawla for the nuggets of information, stories and fillers; Prashant Rana for his faith and trust in my skills; Siddharth Narula for his unconditional help and support; Sanya for yet another brilliant cover design; Amit Mukherjee for the cover layout and creative support; Prakash Baghri for his valuable suggestions, support and feedback; My friends in the IT sector—Ashish Dhawan, Manish Arora, Shubhankar Dhar, Sukhvinder Ahuja, Sanjay Singh and many more, who inspired me in some way or the other; Shayantani Datta Sen for always being there as a friend and advisor; Surbhi Dubey for inspiring me with her honesty and courage; Sana Talwar for her honest feedback and review; Renu, Sudesh and Santosh for bringing this story to you; and my Maa, for her unflinching, unconditional and undying love.

Thinking Loud

Life, for some, is to traverse the labyrinth and maze of years in a robotic haze. Whizzing past years, the alleys remain a blur. While for some, it is more of a saunter, pausing to smell a flower or stroke a puppy and simply arrive at the destination without realizing the journey just got over. Mulling over this, I realized that my generation belongs to the first lot.

We have carried on our shoulders the luggage of excessive expectations and speed. From living through times of no television to the jet speed of communication; from commuting in just two car brands to a choice of dream brands with mind boggling number of zeros in their price tags, we have been inundated by the choice of dressing, eating, networking. No wonder, the entire orchestra of life has done a complete three-sixty-degree whirl.

To keep up with the speed of life—with distances, with the ever demanding relationships, most of us are bleeding the basic values—the simple goodness and ethics.

The entire establishment seems to be rotting within the shining exterior. One push and the entire structure might just crumble.

But when did this happen?

Did the decay start setting in with the advent of consumerism? Did the plethora of choice and the need for instant gratification at every bend, coupled with the fast changing technological landscape, affect our social tapestry? Was that the moment when the 'intelligence quotient' became more important than the 'emotional quotient'?

Well, today it is fashionable to read anything about neo-fad topics—*karma, dharma, moksha,* the art of living, yoga and the yogic way of life, and also discuss the same over glasses of wine in chic parties. However, when it comes to embracing the truth, the simple way of life, simplicity of thoughts, we get cold feet. Why? Are we too greedy or is it our insecurity that makes us cling to that part which is anything but the real us?

This novel, *Chapter 11,* is built on the framework of a decaying organization. It not only digs into the impacts of the Chapter 11 phenomenon, but also tries to trace the human reasons, which ate its way inside the robust establishments. The story is not only about the slick Sandy versus the conscientious Shubhankar, the small town upbringing verses the metro life or duty versus love. It is an X-Ray of our own world and times. Is our society too becoming a lumbering headless giant, like CommTech? With the heart still in its place, but the severed head renders all connections between the head and the heart useless.

I know this book will annoy many and please many more. But neither of the reaction is the reason which drives me. This story is just a humble attempt to mirror me and myself, who in turn mirrors this society and to connect with you, urging you to look beyond the obvious and engage the soul to elevate the present times beyond the bankruptcy of society, hearts and minds.

I am no teacher or a preacher, therefore there is no *gyaan* in this story. It is about introspection as it is time we did that. The world does not need prophesies of the Mayan calendar to bring it to an end. So let us open our eyes now, adjust our navigation tools and re-chart the direction of travel, or else, very soon we may be walking into self-devastation.

— **Amit Shankar**

Carte Blanche

The beautiful city of Hong Kong looked distorted and hazy. He gently used the left sleeve of his white, soft cotton robe to dab at his misty eyes. This spread the tears even more, distorting his vision even further. He wiped his eyes again, this time using both the sleeves, forcefully. His effort was rewarded.

He inhaled deeply, trying to focus on the geometric, black, imposing structure, just across the street. Maybe, he assumed that this would shield his mind from an onslaught of thoughts. Tears welled in his eyes again, clouding his vision. This time he did not bother to do anything about them, and on finding no attention, they silently escaped the confines.

From his 20th floor, Hotel Mandarin Oriental room, the view was splendid. He pulled back the thick drapes, further from the wall-sized glass window, letting the skyscrapers stare at him, directly. They stood there; silent, tall, in all shapes and sizes. He pulled out a pack of

Marlboro lights from his robe's pocket and used the sleek, red hotel matchbox, with a Chinese inscription on it, to light the cigarette. Warm air curled up from his lungs, arching towards the white ceiling. With every upward inch, the smoke lost its color and intensity. Was this true of humans too? Do they also lose strength—of conviction and character, with every step on the corporate ladder? Or was he just overreacting to a new way of life?

New way of life? My foot! He turned back to scan the room. The white bedsheet, bedcover, pillows and cushions were all strewn around. The feeling of nausea and repulsion again hit him and the momentum to throw up started building up. He turned back to the glass window, but as he turned, his eyes caught the condom pack lying on the side table. He cursed himself and hurriedly walked towards it, crushing the pack with all his might. How could he have done this? How could he cheat on Ambica? Didn't he love her? Wasn't she the only one whom he really cared for? How hurt she would be if she ever knew that he shared his bed with a hooker, irrespective of the circumstances? Was he any better than the middleaged, graying CommTech bastards who went to any extent to appease their male egos? Fuck, why did he get into this mess?

A train of thoughts exploded within, which was laced by the previous night's vodka shots and a heart cramped with guilt. Was he missing something? He walked towards the glass-paneled, sliding door and moved it to reveal a wardrobe. He unzipped his newly bought red suitcase and searched for something inside. As his hand hit the object of his desire, his tense face relaxed. Hurriedly, he pulled it out. It was a Rubik Cube. His hands started rotating the rows and the columns, trying to solve it, while his mind was playing a different game, trying something more complex than the cube—LIFE!

"I am sorry, Ambi. Please forgive me," with a heavy heart, he tendered an honest apology. He put the cube on the side table, lit another cigarette and surrendered himself to the comfort of the stylish pristine white recliner. The 32-inch LCD screen, on the wood-paneled wall, displayed his name and announced how pleased the hotel was to have him as a guest. A guest? Were guests supposed to use their host's place as a hump house? "Fuck these Chinese. What do they know of hospitality in any case." He went to the window and looked at the magnificent skyscrapers again, while his mind tried to figure out the chain of events that led to this guilt assault.

He could vividly remember the dinner after the channel partner meet. Everything was fine, well almost. He was nattily dressed in a black suit and a flaming red silk tie. Going by the compliments his outfit generated that evening, he had every reason to feel happy about himself and his existence at CommTech. After all, during his entire life; the twenty-six springs that he had seen, he had never come across something as grand, lavish and ostentatious as the Get, Set, Go—CommTech's Channel Partner Meet for the year 2010. Three hundred people were flown into Hong Kong—two hundred and fifty channel partners and fifty CommTech employees. They were put up at the most fashionable hotel, The Oriental Mandarin. Everything was on the house—food, booze and some other privileges, too. The last bit, though, was the sole prerogative of the tier I-channel partners. These privileged channel partners sold a lion's share of CommTech's range of switches, routers and solutions, turning CommTech into a fat cow, enabling the senior CommTech executives to milk it.

As per the much-debated and discussed agenda of the three-day extravaganza, the dinner for Day One was under way when Sandy spoke to him.

"VVS, had your grub?," Sandy enquired. His voice had a sense of urgency.

"Well, sir, tell me if you want me to do anything," he played the unctuous junior.

"No, no, have something first," Sandy insisted.

"Sir, don't worry, I will. I am sure you remember that since college days, I never mixed food with booze."

They both laughed.

"You tanker, how can I forget that you used to polish off almost one bottle daily. And then this asshole Sandy," he pointed towards himself, "used to take you to that God forsaken, hospital campus of Bara Hindu Rao for your favorite *aanda-bread*."

Nostalgia hung thick, making the silence awkward.

"Now now, don't you get lost in your thoughts, young man," Sandy patted VVS.

"Sir, I miss those days," his voice was heavy and slurred, with emotion and vodka. Maybe his sixth drink was getting the better of him.

"Listen, VVS, I need you to do something for me." Since college days, VVS was the ever-ready junior.

"I want you to visit the reception area, where you will find some girls waiting. Escort them to my room. And here is the key."

"But sir…," VVS was clearly confused.

"You just escort them to my room. I will join you in the next five minutes."

"And listen, if someone at the reception asks you about the girls; tell him that they are from our Hong Kong office, here to attend the event. Right, dude?"

A junior never questions his senior—college senior or the seniors at workplace. To VVS, Sandy was both, and more. A God-sent savior, who pulled him out of his insignificant existence at Udaipur and gave him a chance to prove his calibre.

As VVS escorted the motley group of girls towards the elevator and then down the long corridor to room number 2111, he was quite surprised at the assortment—Chinese, Russians and even Europeans, of all shape, size and color. Were they hookers? He chided himself for letting even such a nasty thought cross his mind. Surely, Sandy Sir; though manipulative and unpredictable, would never stoop so low, playing a corporate pimp. After all, Sandy was the one he looked up to. A father figure, who protected, provided and cared for him.

He swiped the card and ushered the girls in. Once the twelve girls were seated in the brightly-lit room, he tried to inspect them. His eyes did not know where to stop and what to inspect. There was too much flesh on display. The taut pair seeking attention from beneath the tube-top, the ripe ones highlighting their story while peeping from the plunging neckline, the cute ones firmly encased within the four walls of a shirt. For the first time he noticed that even something as innocuous as calves could be of different shapes. The slender ones, the athletic ones, the plump ones, the round ones, the bony ones. From various shaped navels to different shapes of lips, he was spoiled for choice.

The moment they were ushered into the room, they assumed it to be their own. The Chinese group hit the bed; the Russian brigade went for the mini bar and the three, of suspect nationality, lit cigarettes. He was confused, as he had no experience in managing such an unruly crowd, especially of women. However, there was nothing much he could do. He just stood there, like a zombie, trying to decipher the Chinese rock song, blaring on the 40-inch LCD.

With such a crowd, surely Hong Kong office would be rocking. But weren't they a little too garish to be working in any office? But then, the boss is always right and especially if the boss is someone like Sandy.

Ding-dong ding-dong. He hurried to answer the door. It was Sandy. He thanked his God for ending his ordeal. To his surprise, the girls from their Hong Kong office did not even bother to acknowledge Sandy's entry or presence. He knew that one could either hate or love Sandeep Khandelwal—Sandy, but there was no way one could ever ignore him. At six feet plus, he was built like a true swimmer—long limbs, powerful arms and a broad chest, which were a result of braving the numerous laps in the pool. His curly hair, thick moustache and a deep voice made him look less of an executive and more of a movie star. No wonder, during his college days, he was nicknamed *Jaggu Dada* because of his resemblance to a famous film star of those times.

"VVS, do me a favor. Go downstairs and find Neel Sir. Tell him that the *kebab* platter is ready."

"I didn't get you?," VVS had no clue about the message, which he was meant to deliver to Neelesh Dang, VP, Enterprise, and the man second in command at CommTech, India.

"Dude, it's a simple message. Tell Neel Sir that the *kebab* platter is ready. Now run."

On his way to locate the recipient of the message,

VVS tried hard to think what the five-foot-some, frail, almost delicate-looking Neel Sir could have to do with these raunchy, ill-bred girls. Surely not discussing strategy. He was also sure that the articulate, suave and well-respected Vice-President, Enterprise, CommTech, could not be having paid sex either. It's a different story that Neel, who was the most senior executive at the channel partner meet and, therefore, assumed that the funds for the event were coming out of his own pocket, walked upstairs and chose two girls—a Russian and a Chinese. The last thing VVS heard him saying while he walked out of the room, with two long-legged, gaudily-done, stilettos clicking women by his side, was, "Love you darling. I miss you too." Even someone as naïve as VVS could tell that Neel was talking to his wife, back home.

More myths were shattered and more vodka was gulped—out of embarrassment, shame, betrayal, hurt and helplessness. As the night progressed, and the tier I channel partners took their pick, one girl was left. Being the large-hearted senior that Sandy always was, he insisted that she went with VVS. He still stood there, in his 20th-floor room, repenting, wondering, and introspecting. It all seemed like just yesterday....

***

Blow Hot and Cold

CommTech

Jasmine Plaza, 17th Floor,

Gurgaon–Haryana

www.commtech.com Phone: 0124-2460 5467, Fax: 0124- 2460 5555

June 4, 2010

Virendra Vikram Singh,

32, Panchratna,

Udaipur - RAJASTHAN

OFFER LETTER

Dear Mr Singh,

CommTech is pleased to offer you a job as a Senior Web Communication Specialist. This position is based out of the Gurgaon office. We trust that your knowledge, skills and experience will be among our most valuable assets. Should you accept this job offer, per company policy, you will be eligible to receive the following beginning on your hire date.

- **Salary:** Annual gross starting salary of Rs 10,20,000.
- **Performance Bonuses:** Up to five per cent of your annual gross salary, paid quarterly.
- **Benefits:** Standard, CommTech provided benefits. Please see the attached sheet for the same.

As he read it, repeatedly, he could not believe his eyes. In sheer disbelief, Virendra Vikram Singh—VVS to his friends; moved the cursor on his 21" computer screen and zoomed in. Yes, finally, his long-awaited break was there! That too, with an American, Fortune 500 company—CommTech.

Out of sheer jubilation, with his closed fist, he made a semi-circular arch in the air. "Corporate world, here I come. *Bana* boys, fuck you guys. I am off for good. Far from you—the bumbling, conceited and narcissistic fools. To make a career, to be part of the corporate world. To rub shoulders with the polished and suave, IIT and the IIM types, to be seen flaunting a Blackberry and sleek laptop," he rambled in his mind. He grabbed the Rubik Cube kept on his workstation and twisted it at random. He analyzed the formation and started working on the puzzle. Twisting it, looking at all the sides, his mind working on the complex string of moves and there he was with the solved cube. He smiled and looked at the computer clock. Five minutes. Not bad. He placed the cube back. Solving the cube acted as a stress-buster for him. During these five years, at Web Link, this was the only thing he had learnt.

He got back to the offer letter and smiled. It was his key to a better life. The much-awaited corporate exposure would give him a chance to do something worthwhile by getting away from Udaipur and *Rawla* Akhepur—his ancestral village, fifty kilometers from Udaipur. To him, both these places were nothing but a cesspool where he was disintegrating, seeking refuge in the bottle of Old Monk, repeatedly arguing and defending the past glory of his forefathers and being just another, faceless '*bana*' who mumbled '*hukum*' and '*khamaghani*', out of sheer habit rather than any respect.

"Thank you, Shree Naathji," he closed his eyes and as if automatically, his hands went up in a folded *namaste*, out of reverence, for his revered deity. This gesture was a pointer to his traditional upbringing, where God and deities were the focal point of every single action. Though Maa Ambe—the Goddess of *Shakti*—was their *kuldevi*, but for some incomprehensible reason, when as a child, he had visited Shree Nathdwara, the holy abode of Shree Naathji, he felt a strange fascination towards him. Ever since that day Shree Naathji became his Lord, Master and Confidant. Whatever he had was a gift from him and whatever he aspired for would also manifest due to his blessings.

Seeking assistance from his Lord, in making his dream of joining an MNC come true, he had provided him with a special incentive—eleven consecutive

Mondays' fasts. However, deep down, his logic made him wonder what Shree Naathji would gain with his eleven or twenty-one fasts. Therefore, he thought of replacing them with something better—maybe eleven kilos of *laddoos*. However, owing to the mean and revengeful portrayal of our Gods; who wrecked havoc and stopped at nothing if a promise made to them was broken; he decided to stick to his original one. As this dream was too special, he made the offer better by adding the eleven-kilo *laddoo* clause to it. But weren't eleven Mondays too long? The devil in him surfaced again, whom he silenced immediately.

Casually, yet cautiously, he looked around, just to make sure that his petty officemates were nowhere in sight. He knew well that even if a whiff of this unexpected news found its way to the much-feared cabin of Neeta Madam, it would create a furore that would end in a loss of full one-month's salary. Moving his cursor to the bottom right hand panel of the desktop, he checked the date. It was 04.06.2010.

Damn it! Six more days to go before the salary cheque would be in his hand. He knew that his absolute silence was the only protector of Rs 26,780— his salary. To ensure this, he promised to himself that he would not share the news with anyone in the office—Sakshi included. Receptionist and PA to Neeta Madam, Sakshi was the only bright spot in the office for him. After the initial formal 'hi' and 'hellos', somehow, the relationship gradually progressed to regular smooches and fondling sessions. Now, when it came to the CommTech news, the smart man in him knew that being the woman that she was, she would never take kindly to his leaving Udaipur, as it would leave her high and dry. Therefore, like a jilted woman, she would surely act mean, to settle the score. In this case, by sharing the news with Neeta Madam. "Sorry baby, even you cannot be a party to this secret."

VVS shifted his focus from Sakshi to the other woman in his office, Neeta Madam—the tyrant, his boss and the owner of Web Link. He tried to figure out her reaction. Being the self-centered, egoist and 'no heart behind her big breasts' woman, she could never take kindly to anyone leaving her—husband, client and employees alike. Maybe the trauma of a bad marriage, which resulted in a messy divorce, had still not healed. He could almost visualize her, standing in a tight deep-neck *kurta,* her obnoxiously large breasts sticking out, her *dupatta* nowhere in sight, nostrils flared and her authoritative tone spewing venom. "VVS, how dare you? Whatever you are today, it is because of this company. I taught you everything. Remember, when you walked in you were just a loser. I invested time and energy in turning you into someone worth four lacs per annum."

The intimidating imagery of her and the scary thought of facing her wrath sent shivers down his spine. Nervously, he licked his lips and rubbed his chin. Why was he scared?

After all he was a *bana*—a *Rajput* by birth, hailing from supposedly one of the most gallant and fearless marshal clans. If he believed the folklore, his ancestors took on the mighty *Moguls* head on during the historically archived and the much-talked about *Haldi Ghaati* battle. Considering all this, surely, at least genetically, he was programmed to handle more than a weak, single, middle-aged and, that too, a *Baniya* woman.

His mind started conjuring up plots to avoid the dreaded encounter with the ferocious and devilish Neeta Madam. He hated her for many reasons. But most of all for her repetitive stories of having introduced the 'City of Lakes' to the ocean of opportunities, via the world of internet. Though not a native of Udaipur, for the past twenty years or so, she had been there, almost like a permanent fixture. With her little knowledge of technology and internet, she had taken the onerous task of putting the tourist destinations of Udaipur on the World Wide Web and had largely succeeded. No wonder, the hotels, the handicrafts showrooms and travel agencies, literally anyone and everyone who had anything to do with foreign land, tourists and promotion, hitched on to the dotcom wagon. Within no time, her influence and contacts multiplied—from Udaipur to Delhi, from owners of hotels and travel agencies to chief and cabinet secretaries. Though the locals doubted and scoffed at her business ethics, but he knew that she was a successful woman who dined with the who is who, drove a Honda Civic and had a palatial bungalow in the upmarket Panchratna Society, where he could afford just an outhouse.

He looked around and, after seeing no one in sight, again opened the offer letter.

"To accept this job offer:

1. Sign and date this job offer letter where indicated below.
2. Sign and date the enclosed Non-Compete Agreement where indicated.
3. Sign and date the enclosed Confidentiality Agreement where indicated.
4. Sign and date the enclosed At-Will Employment Confirmation where indicated.
5. Mail all pages of the signed and dated documents listed above back to us by 7 June 2010. A copy of each document is enclosed for your records."

The lines, though written in English, made no sense to him. He had been working for almost five years now and not even once had he come across words like 'At Will Employment Confirmation' or 'Non-compete agreement.' As a matter of fact, his first and only job at Web Link came without a formal offer or even an appointment letter. After all, Neeta Madam's words were more honorable and sacrosanct than plain words typed on any A4 sheet. It was only when he applied at CommTech was he told that, if shortlisted, he would need the formal appointment letter and salary slip. Out of sheer embarrassment, he could not mention that instead of an appointment letter, he had Neeta Madam's word and, in place of a salary-slip, his bank's passbook.

Thanks to Google, the format of a salary slip and appointment letter was just a click away. Aided by his knowledge of imaging software—Photoshop and Coral Draw—in less than two hours, he had both the documents ready. While he looked at the two documents, he was proud of himself. After using the most downloadable format, there were few chances of going wrong.

He read the document further.

> "To decline this job offer:
> Sign and date this job offer letter where indicated below."

*D*ecline the offer? Only a jerk would. He looked around again to check if there was anyone around. He knew that for the day office would be deserted as Neeta Madam and her two business development guys were out for a tender meeting and Sakshi was on leave. But it was better to be safe than sorry, especially when a full month's salary was at stake. He continued with the offer letter that detailed further the consequences of joining vis-à-vis not joining.

> "We at CommTech hope that you will accept this job offer and look forward to welcoming you aboard. Your immediate supervisor will be Nick Doe, Head-Web

Communication. Feel free to call Nick if you have questions or concerns. Call the main number in the letterhead above during normal business hours."

Sincerely,
Ajay Jasra
Hiring Coordinator, Human Resources

He vividly remembered the day when he had come to see Neeta Madam some five years back, with just a file carrying his marksheets, web designing and some obscure software development certificates.

"So you have done your college from the Delhi University?"

"Yes Madam, Shriram College of Commerce." Guilt hit him, right in his guts. A north zone CBSE topper, who went to the best commerce college in Asia, was sitting in the non-descript office of some obscure web agency, and that too with a recommendation letter. He had no hesitation in accepting the fact that, if he got lucky with the job, it would be only because of the recommendation.

"Hmmm", she scanned his certificates.

"How do you know Akhilesh *bana*?"

"He is my uncle." For the first time, knowing a *bana* was working for him. He knew it well that it would be Akhilesh *bana's khaki* credentials, rather than the genetic factor that would get the deal sealed.

"What all web technologies you know?"

"Dreamweaver...," he was cut short.

"For the backend bit, can you do programming?"

"Yes. I can work on...."

"There is this small eight-page website for a travel agent. Design it and host it. If I like the work, you are on. That is the computer. 'WebLink' is the user name and 'loveneeta35' is the password. Any questions?"

There were none and he was hired. Of course, sans any offer or an appointment letter.

His eyes caressed every word of the CommTech's offer letter. It was his passport to moving back to a big city again, working with a big company, doing something constructive in life. It was long ago; during his college days, that he had realized the futility of the whole concept of being a *Rajput* and basking in the past glory. In a city like Delhi and a college like Shri Ram College of Commerce, no one really bothered about a *bana* or any other prefix until he or she was loaded and had something to offer. He knew that the world was changing fast. This made him pity people like *Daata*—his father and *Dadosa*—his elder brother, who were still obsessed with a false sense of feudal pride and superiority. Displaying self-designed coats of arms with a clichéd and convoluted imagery of the Sun God, lions, swords, eagles and more, putting it on the grille of a dilapidated jeep that badly needed servicing, flaunting bush coats, scarves, twirled-up moustaches and ear studs did not make any sense to him. As he knew, it did not make any sense to the real world either.

For him, the world—right from the feudal times to the present, needed and respected money, as money was the source of power. The offer letter of CommTech promised him the same. From a meager four lakh CTC, he would straight reach the ten-lakh bracket. More than a hundred percent jump! Thank you, Shree Naathji, he folded his hands again and bowed his head in front of the picture of a black-stone idol, covered with garlands.

He longed to share the good news with someone, someone close. But he knew that his parents would never understand the importance of this news, as back in Akhepur, Web Link or CommTech evoked the same emotion—of disdain and contempt. His wife, Rajeshwari, was too naïve to be anywhere close to his dreams or aspirations. Her world was confined to the four walls of their crumbling, ancestral *haveli,* which, if sold, would not fetch even a 2BHK flat in Delhi.

Of all the places, why did his father have to choose to live there? Being the village head—the *Rawla*, taking up a regular job was out of question. Being addressed as '*hukum*' was all that he had to feed his ego on. His penchant for wine, women and horses, not necessarily in the same order, was not doing his financial status any good. No wonder, the landholdings were shrinking fast and now they had only twenty *bighas* left, barely enough to feed them. The sight of *Daata,* his father; the village chieftain, a frail man, sitting on his dilapidated chair and smoking *beedis* in the verandah of his ancestral *haveli*, gifted by the then ruler of Mewar principality, appalled him.

Shifting his focus back to his mobile; an obsolete Nokia model, he dialed Sandy. While the overloaded network beeped to connect him, the urge to smoke made him walk out of the office. Sandy alias Sandeep Khandelwal was his college senior and one of the smartest people he had known so far. He was a living example of the fact that success in the real world and educational degree had no co-relation, whatsoever. Without any management degree from any top institute, just by using his soft skills, he had reached where any MBA from a top B school would be. Born into a refugee Punjabi family, from an early age, he had started helping his father at the family shoe shop. This taught him that one pair did not fit all. Tossing pairs of shoes and sandals, wiping them on his sleeves and trousers for that extra shine, letting the waiting patrons slip their feet into them, he had learnt how to win and influence people. Building on his survival genes, he developed an uncanny comprehension and understanding of people. No wonder, in no time, he had the world eating out of his hands—at his shop, college and later in his professional life. His early salesmanship stint, which inculcated the desire to please and serve, made him a favorite junior to every boss he worked for. Soon, he was going places and his transition was phenomenal. He crossed barriers, which no one else would have dared to. From being a sales guy in a car showroom to debuting as a client-servicing executive in a PR agency, from fixing journalists to his subsequent bosses he went places. Sandeep Khandelwal *aka* Sandy was a phenomenon. The one who always said, "you don't walk your way through, you talk your way through."

"Afternoon sir, finally I have got the offer letter."

"You lucky bastard. Congrats. Today itself we have received a circular which puts a freeze on all hiring." An exuberant Sandy gave out a hearty laugh.

"Sir, hope that does not…," VVS sounded apprehensive.

"No no. It will come into effect from the next week and you have already been hired."

"Thanks, sir," VVS managed to smile but the uncertainty lingered.

"What's your joining date?"

"21st June."

"Good. Ok, listen, with this circular thing, I mean the hiring freeze shit, without wasting any time, print the forms, which you have got in your mail, sign them, scan them and mail them back to the same mail ID."

"Thanks for everything, sir. I know that, without you this offer would never have been possible."

"Shut up, asshole. Thank you and all, eh? When I am in Delhi the next time, you can set the score right by treating me to car 'O'bar session. Done?" The euphemism for drinking in the car made VVS nostalgic.

"Sure sir. Only problem is that for car 'O' bar, I don't have a car."

"Don't worry, dude. We will hire a cab. Long live CommTech."

They both laughed.

"Once you have sent the forms, you should call up the board number, speak with the HR guy and enquire about your accommodation. We have a guest house in Gurgaon. Also, we have apartments for single execs. Ask the HR to put you up at the guest house until the time you can move into one of the company apartments. Then ask him to transfer you to the Admin guy. Ask them to send a cab to pick you up from the airport."

"I can take the night train, sir. Why waste money?"

"Because after an overnight journey, walking into your office, on your first day, wearing a crumpled *kurta-pyjama* is a bad idea. Book the air ticket now and do as I have told you. Don't forget to tell the Admin about the flight number and its arrival time."

"Don't worry, sir, I will manage. I have been in Delhi for a good four years."

"Trust me when you land this time, you will be shocked. It has changed big time. Moreover, you have to go to Gurgaon. In our times, it was just a sleepy town, a place from where we got our beer and booze after Delhi vends pulled down their shutters. But now, courtesy the multinationals, that God-forsaken place is touted as the city of the future."

They both laughed again.

"Ok VVS, I will be travelling around that time. I will speak to a colleague of mine, Sanjay, who sits out of the Gurgaon office. He is the SMB leader, a nice guy. Once you reach the office, get in touch with him. He will show you around. In addition, I will also put in a word to Ashish Tandon. He is the Data and Voice Leader, kind of branch head for Gurgaon. Align yourself with him. A very resourceful guy."

A wave of fear hit VVS. He felt confused, scared and exposed. Whatever Sandy told him seemed to be a big task. For all these five years, he had been walking to the office of Web Link, ordering a cup of tea from the small tea-stall, located across the street, bending over to switch on the grimy computer switch under the table and then following the deluge of orders from Neeta Madam. Words like HR, Admin, and SMB were like an alien language.

"Sir, are you sure that I will be able to adjust?," his innocent and honest question was filled with apprehension.

Sandy laughed. "You will rock. Trust me. This place is infested with *haramkhors.* Just be there, do your work and that's it. You do not worry. I will take care of everything."

He lit another Navy Cut and thought about the positive changes, which were just around the corner.

***

"Leaving our ancestor's place to make a living?," Raj Rajeshwar Singh's statement was filled with disdain and disapproval. A frail man of about five feet seven inches, he looked a lot older than his actual years. Attired in a bush coat and a bright-colored scarf, with his white twirled moustache; amidst the crumbling surroundings of his ancestral legacy, very much like his *haveli*, he too looked in a desperate need of restoration.

"At least listen to him," his wife, who was mother to VVS, intervened. She was a pretty woman who displayed the generous bounty of a rich genetic pool—glowing skin, shiny black hair and almost child-like innocent eyes. Thankfully for VVS, he had inherited her looks. Also, she looked too young to be the mother of a twentysix-year-old. This could have been due to the customary and rampant child marriage during her time.

"He is doing fine here. The job here is just like a permanent one. We know Neeta Madam. Out there, God only knows...," Raj Rajeshwar continued.

"*Daata*, it is the world's largest telecom company,

a Fortune 500 company." Having said that VVS knew that his stubborn father did not know anything beyond horses, stories of *haka* and *shikar* and the stories of his splendid past.

"You think that your father is the biggest fool. Don't you?I know these multinationals well. They use and throw people," he looked towards his wife, VVS's mother. "Rudrapratap's son was working in Bangalore, with an American software company. One day, for no rhyme or reason, he was asked to leave. Poor thing went into a depression and committed suicide."

"*Daata*, you are taking things too far," VVS interrupted.

Raj Rajeshwar continued with what he had in mind. "I did everything to give you the best education, but ..." VVS's mother knew well what was coming and immediately came to his rescue.

"Now don't you start cribbing again. Didn't he do you proud by topping the entire Rajasthan and then by joining the best college?"

The unrelenting father in Raj Rajeshwar was in no mood to give up. "I let you pursue something as feminine as designing. But then there are times when I have to say no. You are going back to Udaipur." He walked out of the verandah, into the courtyard, which blended with the darkness.

VVS looked at his mother, who was back to stirring

the pot. Knowing there was nothing he could do, he also walked out. Before stepping out, he stopped and asked, "*Bai ji,* where is *Dadosa*?"

"Don't you know him?," she sounded irritated. "Only *Maa Ambe* knows when he will mend his ways. He and his political ambitions," she complained. "He has gone to Jaipur to organize some rally."

VVS walked out of the makeshift kitchen, which was housed at the far end of the long verandah. As he crossed the courtyard, he looked at the imposing walls with peeling plaster. He stopped by the stable to pat the two horses—Khudabaksh and Khudanoor. Akhilendra Vikram Singh, his *Dadosa,* elder brother, had bought them, as a part of his ambitious heritage tourism project which never took off. In the process of making a fast buck by turning a hotelier; another great fancy of the *banas,* he lost whatever little he had. Apart from causing a serious financial setback, his dream was also a huge blow to the emotional quotient of the entire family. They had to move to the older part of the *haveli,* as the rest of it was refurbished, to offer the visiting foreigners a close encounter with the lifestyle of a medieval *Rajput* chieftain. Matching Akhilendra *Dadosa's* moustache, his plans were also towering and lofty. With horse safari, jeep safari, cultural evenings, village outings, his dream destination promised to give everything that a *phirangi* dreamt of when he thought of Rajasthan. Unfortunately, the dream of his was never to see the light of the day. Midway through the project, owing to his mismanagement and high handedness, the financer, who was also his partner—a Gujarati, backed out. With no working capital, Akhilendra Vikram Singh had no other option but to shelve his long-cherished dream of fleecing dollars and Euros from the *phirangis.*

As VVS strolled out of the courtyard, walking towards the high, imposing iron gate, he tried to figure out his next step. On the one hand, answering his life's calling; immediately after his conversation with Sandy, he had immediately printed all the forms, signed and scanned them and mailed them back. To safeguard his salary, he had taken special care in clearing the temporary file folder from his hard disk, as he knew that Neeta Madam was in the bad habit of snooping around. Here, on the other hand, his obstinate father was all set to anchor his dreamboat.

***

"*Bai ji,* have you spoken with *Daata*?," his question had strong overtones of a request. She was busy concentrating on getting the dough right and did not bother to look up.

He insisted, "Please make him realize that this job will give me whatever I have always longed for. My life will be secured. Apart from the salary, they are also giving you, *Daata* and Rajeshwari, an insurance cover of five lakh each. Plus LTA and other benefits too."

"What can I say? I just want to see you happy. Do not worry. I will speak to him tonight."

"Where is Rajeshwari?"

"She has gone to attend *Sandhya-Vandan.*"

VVS knew that it was time to incentivize every single God and Goddess. After all, everything was fair in love and war… also in getting your dream job.

***

"How was it?"

"Why do you always have to ask this?," Rajeshwari put up an acerbic smile.

"As your husband and partner, I need to know if it worked for you as well. For a happy and healthy married life, physical compatibility is necessary. Isn't it?" He kissed her lips.

"And what would you do if I told you that it wasn't?," she taunted, looking into his eyes.

VVS pulled her closer and looked into her dark-brown and deep eyes, which were overflowing with love. She could also clearly see his eyes, overflowing with testosterone. As her lips quivered, he nibbled on her lobes and whispered, "I would request to grant this novice one more chance. This time this slave to her highness will work harder and faster and will deliver an earth shattering, divine experience." She closed her eyes as he took her in his arms again and set off on a long journey.

Standing by the window, inhaling deep on his favorite Navy Cut, he turned towards her. She was standing at the far end of the room, with her back towards him, getting dressed. His eyes scanned her 5'3" frame. Still naked, she had just the right amount of flesh coupled with perfect tautness. His eyes caressed her naked back and slithered down her waist, stopping at her round and wide hips, which were God made to bear sons. By any standard, she was beautiful. No wonder, *Daata* had agreed to the marriage of his Delhi-returned, English-speaking son, without much fuss.

As his eyes lingered a little longer on her, he could feel the surge again. He controlled himself and inhaled the nicotine. "Raj, do you think you will be happy if I moved to Gurgaon?"

As she clasped her bra, she turned around, casually and replied, "For me Udaipur and Gurgaon are more or less the same. While you are here, you ask me 'was it good' once a week, there you will be asking the same maybe once in three months."

The sarcasm in her statement was evident and hit the bull's eye. He threw the cigarette out of the window and turned towards her. "What do you mean? Do you think I only come here to have sex with you?"

She was buttoning up her blouse and did not even bother to look at him. "If it were love, you would have taken me to Udaipur with you, not leave me here with your sadist parents who keep on cursing me for not giving them a grandson."

VVS knew what was waiting for him.

"At times I feel like asking them if they even know that it takes two to make a baby. Why can't you tell them…," she continued.

An agitated VVS barged in. "What should I tell them? Tell me? Do you think I can walk up to *Daata* and *Baiji* and tell them about my low sperm count? Do you think they will hold me in very high esteem after knowing that, least of all, I don't even have my sperm right?" Anger turned his face a shade of amber. He looked up at the ceiling fan, which failed miserably to provide any respite from the scorching heat. The office was better. At least it had an airconditioner.

She put the *chunni* on her head and walked out, to take care of the last round of household chores or maybe to hide her tears.

***

Action Items

The big glass door was imposing. More so was the view on the other side of it. The spotless designer marble flooring added another dimension of grandeur to the already colossal and magnificent lobby. Tan, leather-upholstered sofa sets punctuated the vastness and were arranged in clusters, in a formal setting, interspersed with large vases with artificial plants. In the center of the hall, behind the big black granite table, with embossed 'CommTech' in stainless steel letters pasted on the front of the table, sat a young girl.

As VVS scanned the view, he could not see any reason for the receptionist to be wearing a headset and have a flat screen monitor in front of her. After all, this was not one of the famous five-star hotels of Udaipur, where the receptionist needed a computer to facilitate guests' check-in and check-out. But then how did it make a difference to him, he thought as he was more interested in life on the other side of the door—his dream corporate life.

He checked his watch. Still five minutes to go. He adjusted his tie and checked his black, shiny new, Liberty leather shoes. For years, he had been eyeing them. But for want of an event where he could flaunt them, without sticking out like a sore thumb, he had resisted buying them.

In his mid-twenties, almost six feet, fair with short-cropped hair, his deep-set sharp eyes and robust build made VVS look quite attractive. His new beige trousers and indigo shirt formed the perfect partner for the new sky and navy blue striped tie.

He checked himself in the glass for the one last time and pushed the door. Surprisingly, it did not budge. He pushed it again. Nothing happened. He gave an awkward glance around, slightly embarrassed. He pushed the other half, gingerly looking for PUSH/PULL options. It moved a little but it did not swing open on its hinges. Gawkiness swept all over him. He looked around to see if there were people watching. Thankfully, there were none. He looked inside, towards the hi-tech, headset-wearing receptionist. She was staring at him and he broke into a sweat under the indigo shirt. He pushed it again, this time with all his might. Suddenly, the receptionist got up from her seat and rushed towards him. Something told him that he had goofed up big time. As she reached the door, her hand went to the side of the door, on to the door panel and the door clicked open.

"Can't you see that white switch and the signage above it which says press here to open?," she was furious.

He looked sheepishly at the switch, placed right there, on the granite wall. The white plastic tag placed above the big white switch had 'Press here to open' written in big and bold. He cursed himself for his negligence.

"Sorry, Ma'am," he tendered an apology, mortified to his core. The receptionist did not even bother to accept it. She walked across the hall, back to her table, the leather-capped metal in her stilettos softly adding some life to the stillness of the lobby. Following her, he walked to her desk, crossing the long hall. For the first time he realized that his feet, used to wearing sandals, were feeling horribly uncomfortable in the new pair of leather shoes. He tried to wriggle his toes, inside, trying to make them feel better, but the cramped feeling just increased, with every step.

The receptionist slithered behind the large granite table and put her headset on. He stood there, waiting for her attention. In the meanwhile, he pulled out the small piece of white paper on which he had noted the names of various people whom he was supposed to meet today—the HR guy for his joining docket, the Admin guy for his cab badge, the IT guy for his laptop and many more. He scanned the list and moved closer to the table.

"Ma'am, can I meet Mr Sanjay please?"

Without even bothering to acknowledge his existence, she replied curtly, "which one, Singh, Kumar, Dhar or Bagchi?"

He looked at her, confused, trying to remember if Sandy had mentioned anything about the surname bit. He really was not sure. Why hadn't he asked him for his full name, he cursed himself.

He knew that the answer was simple as he could never anticipate that one office could have more than one Sanjay or, for that matter, more than any one name. However, going by his past interaction with the receptionist, he did not dare to let her know that he had no clue to the surname.

"Just a moment, let me confirm," he pleaded. His heart was pounding, loud and fast. He took out his phone and dialed Sandy's number.

"This facility is not available on this number."

He cursed himself again.

"Ma'am, my phone is not working."

"Is that my fault?"

"No, no, certainly not. But do you mind calling up Sandeep Khandelwal at your Bangalore office to confirm Sanjay's full name?"

"His ESN?," she shot back.

"His mobile number is …," he blundered

"I am asking for his ESN?," she repeated her question.

"ESN... well...."

After a couple of minutes of further embarrassment, finally he got it sorted. While he waited for Sanjay Singh, who had not come in until then, he wondered if like Web Link, CommTech also deducted salary for coming in late. He looked around and could see people walk in, elegantly dressed, carrying their sleek laptop bags. Until a few minutes before, he never thought that someday he would be in an office where everyone carried a laptop. Just the mere thought of a laptop bag on his shoulder seemed to be so exciting. Would he too be lucky to get one?

With nothing better to do, he again looked around the five-star lobby of CommTech. He could not help but remember the day, when during a trip to Connaught Place with Sandy, he had gone to a five star, Le Meridian, to answer his 'out of nowhere' nature's call and was stopped by the hotel security for questioning. The random thought of the good times spent with Sandy and his out-of-the-way help made his face gloss with gratitude. He owed everything to him. Sandy was so aggressive, so focused and so clear about the priorities in his life. No wonder he was the Head, Marketing and Communications, for CommTech India, Sri Lanka and Bangladesh, making pots of money.

"And you are here to see Sanjay Singh in what context?," the enquiry from the receptionist caught him off-guard.

"Well, I am joining from today."

The scorn on her face multiplied. "Don't you think you should have informed me the same?"

"But you never asked," he fumbled.

"And how do you think Sanjay Singh will be able to help you with your joining?"

"Sandy errr Sandeep told me ...."

He was cut short.

"Fill in your name here, collect your visitor pass and walk down straight to the end of the corridor, to the HR station. Meet Sumit there... and welcome to CommTech."

***

Wearing the blue-colored CommTech visitor's pass, he walked down the long-carpeted passage. On his way, he could see smart workstations, on both the sides. Unlike the shabby workstations in his previous office, where grime accumulated at all the fingerhold spots, these looked almost new. Each one of them had a three-tier red tray, a complicated-looking big telephone set, a laptop docking station and a penholder. To his surprise, none of them had picture of any deity or God. At Web Link, between four workstations, various Gods jostled for the prime space on each of the soft boards. Also, he could not see any woman. He calculated that, on a rough estimate, there would be around two hundred people. The remarkable thing even with such a high head count, the area was as silent as a graveyard. As he walked past the graves, none of the grave residents even bothered him with a look.

He reached the small room with a glass door marked HR.

"Can I see Mr Sumit Sahay, please?," he enquired, standing there, holding the half-opened door.

"And you are?," a man in his late twenties, with a sharp trimmed moustache, shot back.

"Well, I am Virendra Vikram Singh."

"Hey, the new joinee?," he smiled. "Come on in." The man got up from his chair and shook hands vigorously. VVS was pleased to see the first smile since the time he had set his foot on the premises of CommTech.

"I am Sumit, Sumit Sahay. Care for some tea or coffee?"

"Well, some coffee should be fine." He wanted to sound corporate like. After all, tea was meant for employees of Web Link, not for people who carried laptops, chatted over their Blackberry and worked for Fortune 500 companies.

"Well, Mr Singh, here you are," Sumit handed over a glossy docket with CommTech printed on it. "Your seat is on the sixteenth floor, B-9. We have an identical office on that floor, too. Go through the papers and annexure and you will get to know more about us. Could you please sign in here?," Sumit pushed a letterhead, which was a duplicate copy of his joining letter. As VVS signed with a pronounced flourish, using his new Parker pen, he felt a surge of excitement. Finally, he was a part of CommTech. Bye bye Udaipur, Web Link and *banas*. Thank you Shree Naathji.

Sumit took the signed copy and smiled, "welcome to CommTech." VVS smiled back.

"And on your way back, on your right, you will find the pantry. You can get yourself some coffee, wafers or biscuits. Please make yourself comfortable," Sumit smiled.

Sitting in the cafeteria, which was at least ten times the size of Web Link's office, sipping coffee in a CommTech branded mug, he wondered if even the warm drink could take away the coldness of the people he had met during the past hour or so. Back in Udaipur, hospitality was a way of life. Was Udaipur more hospitable due to its roots in tourism, or were CommTech people extra cold to all small town people like him? Thoughts played on his mind while he watched the elegant waiters, dressed in smart jackets, ties and white gloves.

From the pantry to his sixteenth floor seat was hardly any distance, but the guard at the reception of the sixteenth floor kept on asking for his GID. He had no clue about

GID and looked aimlessly in the docket for the same. All efforts to contact Sumit, the HR guy, proved abortive as he was not in his seat. Only after a good hour or so, when Sumit returned to his seat, did he tell the guard to escort him to his designated seat. As he entered the office, he realized that the sixteenth-floor office was a replica of the seventeenth floor. The same cubicles, same flooring, same workstations, even the same eerie silence. As he sat on the expensive, executive chair of his designated B-9 cubicle, he noticed that the small holder on the workstation was already displaying his name and his seat number. He was very impressed at the efficiency and planning of this amazing 'too good to be true' company.

The first drawer of his workstation had a brand new set of markers, a stapler, a box of pins, pencil sharpener, eraser, cello tapes, a glue stick, a post-it notepad, a writing pad and colored magnetic holders. He longed to show all this to Neeta Madam, just to watch her go green. A big landline phone was there on his table. He could not believe that his own workstation had a separate phone. After five long years of using the phone kept at the reception of Web Link, and that too when Neeta Madam was not around, had made him lose hope that some day his table would have his own phone and his own number.

He picked up the receiver and he could hear the dial tone. Bingo, his phone was even working! He closed his eyes and thanked Shree Naathji again. That reminded him that he had to start the fasts from the coming Monday.

Some hundreds of pages, stapled in different bunches, greeted him as he opened the docket handed over by Sumit. The first page was the index and, as he glanced through it, his head almost wobbled. The offer letter, terms of employment, copyright, privacy protection, intellectual property right, termination clause, HR policies, sexual abuse clause, training and the topics just went on to reenforce his conviction that he had finally arrived. The next two hours or so were spent answering various calls from IT, HR and Admin. He also collected his much-awaited laptop and laptop bag. It took him sometime to figure out that GID was nothing but an acronym for 'Global Identification'. This number allowed CommTech employees to log on to their computers, the network, to access official mails, to open the doors across CommTech offices, to book a cab, to order stationery, to claim insurance, to open a bank account and for a zillion other things.

As a privileged owner of the GID, he logged on to his official email, vvs@commtech.com. To his surprise, the email engine–MS Outlook–started pouring mails like a torrent. He could not figure out, if his ID was a newly-created one and if he was logging on for the first time, how could he receive emails? A closer inspection revealed that most of the mails were the customary welcome messages from various departments and people.

It was already lunchtime. People were leaving carrying their lunch boxes. He had no clue what to do. Feeling lost, he checked some more faceless email messages. One was from his line manager, Nick. It said that he would call him at 2 pm, Indian time. During the few calls he had received from the IT, HR and Admin, he had figured out that everything, every action had a time attached to it. No wonder, Nick called him at sharp 2 pm

"Hey, welcome on board."

"Thank you, sir."

"Oh come on, call me Nick and save that sir thing for some other old man," he laughed.

"So tell me, how are you finding it there?"

"Well…."

"I know the first few days could be a little unsettling. But trust me, within a week you will feel that you belong to this place."

"I am sure, Nick."

"As your line manager, I welcome you again and hope that you have got your life figured out there."

"Yes I have."

"Good."

"So what work do I have today?"

"Work?," Nick burst into laughter. "I mean people always tell me that Indians love to slog, but this early, I mean on your first day?"

VVS was surprised. He could not think of any

reason why he should not be working on his first day. After all, the company was paying him. Neeta Madam ensured that not even a single minute of their paid time was wasted. "I mean, Nick...,"

"Have you got the HR dossier?"

"The what?" He could not get Nick due to the strange twang to his heavy accent. Nick laughed. "I mean the HR file."

"Yes," he replied.

"Have you gone through it?"

"Well...."

"I am sure you haven't. Cause if you had, on the second page, you would have seen what you are supposed to do on the first three days."

He panicked. How could he be so careless and miss the instructions spelt on the first few pages itself? What if Nick got a wrong impression? What if before getting confirmed, he was sacked? No, he could not afford to lose this job.

"I am sorry, Nick. I will go through it immediately and follow the same."

Nick laughed. "Please follow them Mr Singh. Have a good day."

As he hurriedly scanned through the first few pages, with every passing line, he was more and more convinced that he had wasted his five years at Web Link. As per the instructions listed, for the first few days he was just supposed to adjust in the new environment. Everything was spelled out. How the first three days should be used finding out things like the coffee-vending machine, the lunch room, the washroom, familiarizing oneself with the laptop and the logging process, collecting the swipe card, getting a picture clicked for the card, placing order for the visiting cards and the list was exhaustive. He could not believe that someone wanted him to take three days to do things, which required not more than an hour or so.

"VVS?," a voice made him swivel. A man in his late thirties, tall, dressed smartly in a pink shirt, black trousers, was standing there, smiling. VVS got up from the chair.

"Sorry, I got late in a meeting. I am Sanjay Singh."

They shook hands.

"You had your lunch?"

"Well...," he fumbled.

"Come on, let's rush downstairs and grab some. Once we are through, I will show you around."

"But what if Nick calls and...."

Sanjay laughed and patted his shoulder. "Firstly Nick is not one of the guys who will ever bother calling someone and, secondly, Singapore is two-and-a-half hours ahead of us. By this time, CommTech Singapore would not have even a single soul."

As Sanjay got into a conversation with the waiter while ordering the typical executive lunch—grilled sandwich and clear chicken soup, VVS looked around the restaurant. Sanjay told him that, as it was situated on the ground floor of their office building, it was patronized by CommTech employees. No wonder, it offered a discount of twenty-five per cent to them. Over sandwiches and soup, Sanjay told him that he was from Mirzapur, a small town in UP. VVS was quite surprised at his revelation as Sanjay's persona and confidence did not betray any shortcoming of a small-town guy.

"So what is your plan?," Sanjay enquired.

"Well." He had no clue.

Sanjay figured out his confusion and offered a solution. "In that case, let us go upstairs and let me show you around."

Sanjay turned out to be quite a helpful guy. He showed him how to make the complex telephone set work along with the multifunction printer and scanner. He also introduced him to the people in the mailroom, the utility room and the pantry on their floor. He showed him the coffee vending machine and told him how it worked. He also introduced him to the most important person on that floor: Abhishek Saxena, the accounts head.

"He is the *baap* of CommTech India, so be in his good books. He will pass your salary, all your vouchers and bills." While Sanjay cautioned him, his Blackberry beeped. Sanjay took the call and gestured VVS to follow him as he walked down the corridor.

"Hi Sir," Sanjay chuckled.

VVS pulled out his Nokia handset and dialed a number, just to check if the roaming had been activated. No luck.

"What?," Sanjay exclaimed.

VVS looked at him trying to figure out the reason for his loud outburst.

"You cannot be serious. Fuck, man! This was the last thing that we expected."

The Sanjay he had seen in the past hour or so was very soft spoken and balanced, therefore such extreme reaction coming from him indicated something calamitous. However, VVS tried to look busy with his phone, as he did not want to appear inquisitive.

"So then it means the grapevine was right and our top management took us for a ride. I never trusted that mother-fucker Buck right from day one."

VVS tried to make sense out of the one-sided conversation. As they walked down the long passage, for the first time, he noticed that the decibel level in the cubicles was going up and there was some kind of unrest, though still tame. People were huddled in small groups and curse words were gaining momentum.

"Sanjay, got the news?," someone shouted from one of the cubicles.

"Yes just now. We are screwed."

"They are downsizing the teams, too." The guy from

the cubicle updated Sanjay.

"Fuck," Sanjay got back to the conversation on the phone.

"Sorry, sir. I am sure you must have heard what Shubhankar just said."

The reply from the other end just made Sanjay more furious. "How can they do this? Just last week, in his official mail Buck had assured us that the rumors doing the rounds were just a figment of fertile imagination. If we had enough cash surplus, then how come we are standing here?"

With every step down the aisle, VVS could sense the commotion build up. He could see people standing around their cubicles, expressing their disbelief over the news. What could be the news, which was potent enough to shake the entire office? With his limited exposure, all VVS could think of was a bounced salary cheque, some client stopping the payment or the death of some senior executive. After all, with Web Link as his benchmark, these were the only issues, which could cause such a mass hysteria. Finally, Sanjay was off the phone, only to dial another number.

"So you know it. Damn! I cannot afford to lose this job. The recession has already squeezed the market bad. Finding a new one would be real tough."

As they entered the coffee area, VVS noticed it was buzzing with gossip, four-letter words, extreme reactions and disbelief. Holding his mobile precariously between his ear and shoulders, Sanjay managed to get two mugs of coffee.

"Bad day and bad news," he looked at VVS apologetically.

"Why, what happened?," VVS tried to maintain his nonchalant composure.

"Well, we have filed for Chapter 11, in North America and parts of Europe."

VVS stared slightly agape, waited for an elaboration of the statement which was full of unfamiliar words. Sanjay dialed another number as he walked out for a conversation. VVS stood there, looking at people and sipping his coffee. It was only then he realized that every conversation had the same words—Chapter 11, North America and Europe. There were two guys, standing right in front of the vending machine, arguing over the legality of Chapter 11. One believed that there was a difference between filing for bankruptcy and bankruptcy protection whereas the other argued that they were more or less the same. And then it hit VVS hard! Had CommTech gone bankrupt?. But the next moment he rubbished the thought. After all, how can a company with such a big office, gloved waiters, go bankrupt? His middle class mind knew that when cash became sparse, expenses were immediately reduced. If CommTech knew that they were not doing well, they would have reduced all the frills to tighten the cash outflow. However, since morning, he was a witness to the fact that money was in excess.

"Sorry, VVS," Sanjay apologized as he reentered the cafeteria.

"That's ok. All well?"

"I don't know. No one knows anything for sure. But in a few hours we will know the facts," Sanjay sounded apprehensive.

"If I may ask, what is the exact problem?," VVS tried being upfront about it.

"Well, to cut a long story short, CommTech has filed for Chapter 11, which is a step taken, especially by American companies, when they run short of cash. By filing for Chapter 11, the financial management of the company goes into the hands of the court and the court decides how much and in what priority to pay to the creditors." VVS was still confused as he could not understand if it was good news or bad.

"Well, how will it affect my…errr… I mean our jobs?"

"For all I know, before you even get your visiting cards, you could get axed."

***

Zero Tasking

"*Khamghani Daata.*"

As soon the roaming facility on his mobile was activated, he called up home.

"Have the *goras* given you a place to stay? Do not trust anyone there. I know these *goras.* Rascals of the first order." His father was still living in the era when the British ruled India.

VVS wanted to disconnect the call immediately. The inconsequential question and apprehension of his father was a constant irritant to him. He wanted to share the Chapter 11 episode; rather the news with him. But then he wanted to avoid his father's 'Didn't I tell you' mode.

"*Daata,* I am doing well here. The office is very big and good. Worldwide, there are more than fifty thousand workers." He could hear *Bai ji* reprimand *Daata* for hogging all the conversation.

"Ok, ok. Your *Bai* is creating a ruckus as usual. Speak to Rajeshwari and take care of yourself." He handed the phone to Rajeshwari.

"Yes," Rajeshwari squeaked. VVS knew that she was upset with him for leaving her and going away so far.

"Everything is fine. The office is very good. I wish you could see it. It is so big. My office is on the sixteenth floor."

"Don't you feel giddy looking down?"

He laughed.

"You stupid woman, no I don't." At times, he loved her simplicity but then life was more than about being simple.

"I am staying at the company guest house. I will be here for a week. After that they will shift me to a company house. Maybe then I will call you to spend some time with me."

"I know you are just interested in asking 'how was it' and nothing else."

"What is wrong with you? Why are you always so sarcastic?"

The call dropped or maybe she disconnected it.

***

A good breakfast of boiled eggs, milk, toast and sausage served at the company guest house made VVS feel like a king. However, the fear of Chapter 11 stopped him from thanking his stars. What the fuck, live for today and be happy. He thought as he got into the office cab.

It was a normal day with nothing much on his plate. He got his access card and Nick called up again to enquire about his well-being.

***

"You need not to worry about anything."

Sandy's voice always had something very comforting about it, at least for VVS.

"Chapter 11 is not about a roadside shopkeeper going bankrupt." Sandy shared his point of view. "You there?" He wanted to be sure that the news, which for VVS had come at a very wrong time, did not perturb him.

"Yes sir, I am with you." VVS held the black ESN handset closer to his ear. As his eyes scanned the base of the handset, he could see COMMTECH written on it in blue. The handset itself looked like a piece of technological marvel. No wonder, on his first day, when he tried deciphering the numerous buttons, a lot many red lights started to flash and like a scared kid, he silently placed the receiver back on the hook.

"Dude, it's just legal terminology, nothing else. If I were to articulate, it is a corporate way of reorganizing things while seeking protection from creditors. Every big corporate does it. And it is only North America and Europe, which have filed for Chapter 11. We are under

APAC and our region is sound and growing."

"But, sir, with headquarters going bankrupt, I think… I mean, don't you think that India will also get affected?" By any logic, his doubts were justified.

"Remember, recently General Motors filed for Chapter 11 in America? Did they shut shop in India? On the contrary, GM India did launch two new variants—Spark and Beat. There are more GM cars on Indian streets than ever before. Please correct me if I am wrong."

Well Sandy had a point there and VVS could see some merit in the argument.

"So you just chill, dude. It is just a corporate move to get rid of some flab. In any case, India is a focus country. They can never touch us."

Sandy's confidence gave VVS some hope. After all, he was his super-boss and senior, rolled into one. In addition, he had an access to the higher-ups. Therefore, for sure, his information could be relied upon.

"You just try to settle down asap Don't let anyone notice that you have no work. Look busy."

"But Nick has told me to go slow."

"Jackass! His parents should have named him Dick." Something infuriated Sandy and VVS had no clue about what or why. However, the good part was that, within seconds of venting his anger on Nick, he got back to his normal self— poised, and always in control.

"Dude, though I just told you that everything is fine,

please don't forget I also told you that they would use this time to lose some flab. So, for God's sake, just open your laptop, some web page, some PPT, just about anything, but keep your head down and keep looking at the laptop screen. That is the only way to avoid the flab status."

Scared after Sandy's warning, while staring at his laptop screen, VVS checked Sandy's statement with the only reference point in his life—Neeta Madam. He could not figure out how she would give salary to her business associate, who was sitting in Delhi, if she had no money in Udaipur.

***

Nick seemed to be a chilled-out guy. Actually more than what VVS wanted his boss to be. A quick Facebook search showed him as a man in his early forties—a lean, mean machine, with golden hair. An Australian by passport, he had been with CommTech for over eighteen years. His passions were surfing, white water rafting, trekking, scuba diving, bungee jumping and every other activity that VVS had only watched in Mission Impossible or in some James Bond movies. With a penchant for the outdoors, no wonder, Nick sounded so constipated within office surroundings.

Nick kept on calling VVS, enquiring about his process of settling down, things around, just about everything but work. This upset VVS even more. Under no circumstances, he wanted to be seen as the flab, which the company could do away with. Therefore, he tried spending most of his time staring at his laptop screen with some PPT frozen in there, which Sandy was kind enough to lend him.

Amidst this entire quandary, his bay-mate Manish Kumar was the only redeeming feature. Manish, in his late twenties or maybe early thirties, was with the 'project management' team. He was responsible for something called 'transition' and VVS had no clue what it meant. All he saw him do was to remain glued to his seat, with the headset on; making the black contraption a part of his existence, trying to explain some complex PPT slide over numerous conference calls, which never ceased to exist.

Manish introduced him to a completely new world of possibilities that VVS thought only existed in the sci-fi movies. For instance, when Nick asked VVS to fix a call with the Indian web vendors, like a true uninitiated corporate foot-soldier, he sent out a mail with this mobile phone number in it. On receiving the mail, Nick, who was also marked on the same, laughed his guts out. With fear and hesitation, when VVS asked him the reason, Nick, the true sadist, never bothered to explain or help. Before he hung up, amidst hysterical guffaws, he told VVS that he should seek help from anyone around—his bay-mate or even the coffee machine guy.

Still feeling the acute humiliation, with flushing ears and cheeks, he approached Manish. Like a good bay-mate and a hard-to-find 'helping *Dilliwala,*' Manish told him about the novel concept of a 'Voice Bridge'. It was a virtual bridge that facilitated internal conference calls at no extra cost and was a common feature in any large-format organization. He also told VVS that it provided ease, security and economy. VVS nodded his head in bewilderment while Manish took him through the small demo. He explained how the person who set up the call was supposed to be the 'chairperson' and how as soon as the chairperson logged on to the bridge, at the designated time, everyone invited to the call; with a logging bridge number and a password, could have a conversation at the same time. On his enquiry as to why this could not be done using a normal telephone or a mobile phone, Manish told him that with a global operation and a virtual team spread over vast geographies, the costs got prohibitive, not to forget about the security concerns.

***

With a technical bent of mind, though setting up a call required none, within no time VVS was setting up calls left, right and center. He realized that his boss, Nick, was not only sarcastic, opinionated and whimsical but also lazy to the core. No wonder; he started passing on his errands to VVS. As his 'Man Friday', VVS would set up his calls, reformat his PPTs, draft mails, work on XLS, everything but the web work for which he was hired. For the first few days, VVS was excited as it kept him gainfully employed. However, soon it started getting repetitive though there was nothing he could do about it.

After politely enquiring about some real work and being playfully reprimanded for the same by Nick, VVS knew that it was like being stuck in a bad marriage—could not live in it, could not walk out of it for fear of financial implications.

***

His morning breakfast got larger—toast, ham, sausage, bacon, cornflakes, porridge, butter, jam, milk, coffee and tea. It was the only bright spot of his entire day. For almost five years, the time that he spent at Web Link, this course of the meal never existed for him. After long nights of drinking spree with *banas* and owing to a conspiracy between the clock and God, morning meant just a shower and shine. At the office reception, Neeta Madam waited, praying for him to show up late, as that gave her an excuse to deduct his salary. It was only after signing the register and having his first cup of office tea that he would feel the need to use the WC, around noon.

Life at CommTech was good. With no real work,

he would be back on time, drink on time, eat well, sleep on time and get up the next morning with ample time to use the WC.

Thank God for small mercies and for not making him an actor. He would have reeked of overacting right from the very first scene. No wonder, he got so conscious while essaying the role of an overworked executive. He wondered how the entire office portrayed the same, so naturally and with so much of ease and aplomb. His Rubik Cube kept him gainfully employed. From his last best of five minutes, he had moved to the four-minute mark.

After his first dream gadget, the brand new HP laptop, within the next few days, he got his second one too—a brand new Blackberry Bold. He could not believe that he was actually holding one. Most of his office time was spent reading the lengthy manual that came with it and he was awed with its features—real-time mail, surfing, chatting and GPS. He spent hours, filling forms, getting Nick's approval and submitting them with the Singapore office for the server authentication code. Finally, it happened! His Blackberry was in-sync with the CommTech server. It meant real-time access to his official mails. He knew that the *banas* would turn a shade of green seeing his messenger status as 'On my Blackberry.'

Thank you Shree Naathji!

Courtesy Manish, the coffee machine and the extended lunch breaks, he did manage to befriend a couple of guys. After his initial round of embarrassment over his previous organization's name, which of course no one had ever heard of, he realized that his family background fascinated the corporate urbanites. Living in cramped apartments and driving their EMI-fuelled cars and lives, stories of *hukum, khamghani, haveli, rawla,* horses, guns and glory enthralled them. When he invited them to his desk to share his Facebook album, which had his pictures in riding breeches, boots, straddling the gorgeous Khudabaksh and the handsome Khudanoor, they were in awe of his entire persona and being. This was further accentuated when they got a slide show of his crumbling, but huge *haveli,* the walls studded with guns and swords, the hunting trophies mounted on the walls and his handsome *Dadosa* sitting in his open, left-hand-drive Willys jeep.

Watching their jaws drop and eyes pop, for the first time VVS was proud to be a *bana.* No wonder, before the slide show was over, the group nicknamed him *Thakur.*

***

Wild Assed Guess

They were seated in the cafeteria. It was a huge hall. The walls had huge pictures of smiling Indian faces—rural women, a kid with a bright red kite, green and yellow mustard fields and many more. The warmth of the pictured walls was offset by the tiled floor, which imparted the hall a sterile look. The gleaming steel counters, placed on both sides of the hall, were lined with bone china mugs and saucers. Blue and red plastic trays placed on the counters had expensive-looking cutlery. Huge tea and coffee dispensers stood around the shining counters.

"Boss, I tell you, RC is negotiating hard for his cabinet," Aditya sounded emphatic. He was the Group Manager for the Enterprise Sales Team. In his early thirties, he was a typical *Punjabi* MBA. Fair, good-looking, clean-shaven, with a mop of thick hair. The expensive frame resting on his long nose imparted him the intelligence quotient. Always dressed in a black trouser-shirt combo and patent leather, pointed shoes, he never blushed when someone complimented him on his good looks.

Rakshit Chaheil, better known as RC, was the Managing Director of CommTech, India. He ruled over his empire, assisted by his cabinet, which had twelve members. Most of them were the zonal sales heads and a few were from other departments too. Sandy was also a part of his cabinet. RC reported to Jules Crompton, Head, APAC.

"But, tell me something, who is he negotiating with? Aren't we all in the same boat?," Ashu raised his doubt. In his early thirties, short-statured and with a receding hairline, he was just the opposite of Aditya. An Account Manager, with the Pre-Sales Team, he was not too fond of flashy dressing and was always in his favorite shades of blues, greys, and whites. Both, Aditya and Ashu, were a part of the north-zone sales team and reported to Shailender Bajwa.

"Boss, let me tell you something. This place is going down and it is going down fast. So please don't be fooled by the 'H mails' which keep on popping up like the love letters you had stashed away from the prying eyes of your wife." Aditya was referring to the periodic mails sent from the mail ID of CommTech's CEO, Buck Howard. These mails were branded as the 'H mails'. Black font on a shocking yellow made them stand out. Within CommTech system, it was the only communication, which did not use the customary blue color. Apart from the symmetry in the color and font, there was something else, which never changed—its boring content.

"Irrespective of who acquires CommTech, RC wants some sort of an assurance that his cabinet will be safe and untouched," Aditya answered Ashu's question.

"And no wonder, a jackass that Crompton is, he would surely give in to his demands. These guys should be whipped," Ashu reacted strongly as now he could see the bigger picture.

"No, you should call the cops, get them handcuffed and publicly cane them. They are the ones responsible for all this mess," Aditya was furious.

VVS sat there silently, listening to the IIT types who knew it all.

"*Thakur,* what do say?," Aditya wanted to know his point of view.

"Well, since I don't know much, I am in no position to comment. But I cannot understand how an individual or even a group of people can bring down this big a company? I mean even to get a pencil here, one has to fill triplicate copies of request and send a mail marked to different departments."

"Hi guys!" It was Shubhankar, standing there, holding a coffee mug. In his mid-thirties, he was the APAC Prime—Systems and Process. Built like a bull, his short, weed-like hair gave him the typical wrestler look.

He wore half-sleeve shirts, which highlighted his powerful forearms and the bulging biceps. Contrasting with his physique, his face always had a gentle smile which was never fazed by any situation. People liked him. He pulled a chair and joined the gang. "So whom are we going to slander and rape today?" All of them laughed.

"Well, *Thakur* has a question," Aditya told Shubhankar.

"And what is that?," Shubhankar was ready to take whatever was coming his way.

"*Thakur* wants to know how Crompton and his cronies managed to rape CommTech."

"Hmmm, I will try to do my best. Are you ready for some eye-popping facts?"

"Don't you worry. He is a blue-blooded *Thakur*, the brave heart," Ashu smiled as he quipped. VVS blushed and never bothered to correct Ashu that he was just the son of a village chieftain and not from any royal family. However, he did like the association with the word 'blue blood.

"It's simple. CommTech is a company ruled by the sales people. Right from the CEO to our regional and country heads, all are from sales. This holds true for most of the technology companies as sales is the most critical function." Ashu and Aditya both felt proud of their position in the sales team and bowed to accept the compliment. "Now, if you look at any other company, an FMCG giant, a pharma company or even an automobile company, it is never the sales guy who heads them. Think of Honda, HLL, HSBC...."

"Shubhankar, could you focus on answering the question, please?," Ashu helped in aligning his thoughts.

"Well, yeah. I was just trying to give a small background. You see, *Thakur*, what happens is that before a financial year, every regional head is asked to pick a target for his region. So Andrew picks up a target for North America, Crompton for APAC, Longwood for Europe and so on. Regional leaders pick their targets as per the forecast made by the country leaders. So in the case of APAC, Crompton asks RC to forecast the numbers which India is expected to achieve in the next financial year."

"This sounds like the right thing to do. I don't see any holes in here," VVS was trying to grasp and comprehend every single word spoken by Shubhankar.

"Yes, you are right. All this is perfect, assuming the leaders are upright and honest."

"You mean RC sir is not honest?," VVS was a little shocked.

"Well, it depends on how you see it. Excuse me," Shubhankar got up and walked towards the coffee-vending machine for another refill.

"Record him exposing RC. We can blackmail him throughout his life," Ashu laughed.

"If not throughout his life, surely for as long as he is with CommTech." They both gave a hi-five.

Aditya's eyes turned towards Shubhankar who was getting a refill, and then towards Ashu. "With that plastic smile plastered on his face, this bastard thinks he is some kind of Buddha or something. Man, you should have seen him in Vegas."

"You guys have been to Vegas?," VVS was impressed.

"Yeah, thrice," Ashu stated in a matter of fact tone. "On a sales training program. And there this Buddha was a transformed man."

"I know what you mean," Aditya supported him.

"Buddha with a perpetual hard-on," Ashu added and they both laughed.

"Horny bastard. Ogled at everything in skirts," Aditya explained the reason for the title, which was just shared with VVS. VVS was surprised at the level of backbiting. Until a few seconds ago, all of them were so friendly. All it took was for one of them to turn his back to start a volley of personal attacks. Would they be doing the same with him? Without straining his head too much, he got the answer.

They could see Shubhankar walking towards them, with the same smile on his face. VVS tried visualizing how Shubhankar would look with the smile on his face and.... Not a very appealing thought. He shrugged it away. Shubhankar sat down.

"Fuck. They are not serving the jasmine green tea

any more. I really loved it. I was reading the other day that green tea helps you lose weight."

"No wonder you have lost a lot." It was Ashu this time. Everyone laughed.

In the next hour or so, Shubhankar explained to VVS how RC, like a smart leader, projected and picked a target that was far lower than the going industry rate. He went on to put numbers to his explanation. He told if their nearest rival, Sailnet was doing a hundred and fifty in the switching and routing vertical, RC would pick eighty as his target. This would ensure that his sales team achieved the target easily and got their entire salary. Shubhankar also explained how the salary of the sales team had two components to it—fixed and variable. To get the variable component, achieving the allotted target was necessary. To the horror of VVS, this undersubscribing and overachieving entitled the sales guy to huge bonuses. Last year, Shailender had a brand-new Toyota Corolla as his bonus. Not to mention, sales leaders of east and central got a Rolex watch worth rupees six lakh each.

It all sounded bizarre. VVS was not ready to believe that such a practice could flourish within such a large, sound and process-driven system. How and why had no one noticed all this bungling? He vividly remembered that at Web Link, Neeta Madam signed every voucher, verifying the amount and the expense head. Now, after joining CommTech, he understood that it was not possible for the Buck to verify each voucher but surely he could appoint a few honest men to do the same. After all, the market growth rate and the industry trend were no secrets. Why couldn't Crompton cross-check the numbers given by RC sir?

For the entire day, VVS felt miserable. He tried his best to get away from all the negative talk but Shubhankar's conversation kept on haunting him. To him, these men, from the top engineering and management institutes, were his role models. He wanted to be like them, dress like them, converse like them, see the world, earn millions and lead an enviable lifestyle. But whatever little he had seen or heard was nothing he ever wanted to be. To him, all this was nothing but treachery and back home, where he came from, treachery amounted to only one punishment—death penalty.

Back at his guest house, three drinks down, he felt lonely. He called up Manish, who was out with his wife and kid, attending some birthday party. Sandy was busy socializing with RC and promised to call back. Rajeshwari was attending some *Sandhya Vandan*.

Everyone but him was busy. Was he missing *banas*? Nah, not at all. He was so happy being here, on his own, being treated like a prince—someone to do his laundry, someone to take his order for dinner, someone to make his bed. He loved every bit of it. Yes, he did.

***

Weighing the Pig

There were rows of houses; of various colors and shapes. Cars were parked on both the sides. Finding the address, D-55, was fairly simple. VVS opened the small iron gate and stepped in. There was a small lawn to the right. The dismal condition of the grass and the trees stank of crass neglect. As he crossed the lawn, ahead of him, he could see a flight of stairs. He sighed as just, in a few days, he had got accustomed to snazzy elevators and, therefore, the idea of climbing up two floors was not a very comforting one. No wonder, his lungs also failed to cooperate. By the time he was there on the second floor, he was panting. Maybe it was time to cut down on his quota of nicotine.

He looked at the iron door with a grill and, through the grill, he could see another white door behind it. He ran his fingers through his hair and licked his lips, as he wanted to appear presentable and get this apartment. Going by the mail from the Admin, due to the immediate cost cuts, they were closing down the guest house and the shared company apartment within ten days. So here he was, doing the most demanding and frustrating of things in a metropolis—looking for an apartment.

Ding-dong.

No reply. He waited.

"Maybe the guys are sleeping," he thought.

Ding-dong.

Still no reply. "Maybe they got sloshed the previous night." He cursed himself, as he could never come up with any better reason.

Ding dong.

"Maybe they have already left for the day." He patted himself for coming up with a better and a more logical reason.

Ding dong.

The wooden door opened. Through the honeycomb, fine iron grill, he could see a woman standing there, still in her nightgown.

"Well, apartment number 55D?"

"Can't you read the nameplate?" The reply was brusque.

"Sorry, the number on the nameplate is smudged... and I am here to meet Chaitali."

"And may I know the reason?" The voice was still business like, yet had a pleasant ring to it.

"Well, actually, I have come to have a look at this apartment." He clarified his intentions, as he did not want to appear like an obtrusive salesman or, worse, a stalker.

"And may I know who has sent you?"

"Well, Manish. Manish Kumar of CommTech."

"And you are?"

"I'm Virendra Vikram Singh."

"Where are the others?" The woman asked, peering behind him. The curtness in her voice still held its ground.

"I didn't get you?" Her question took him by surprise and the joke completely bounced off him.

She laughed finally.

"*Arre Baba,* I mean aren't you tired of carrying such a long and boring name?"

He smiled coyly. "My friends call me VVS."

"Hmmm but I think Veer would have been better. Don't you?"

Gosh, she was right. Veer sounded so much better and so contemporary. He strained his eyes to figure out the woman, behind the fine honeycomb grill. She would be about 5'5" and was fair. His eyes scanned her harder. She looked like a full-bodied woman, the kind always playing on his mind. Even after the initial round of not-so-pleasant conversation with her, he could feel her sight working on his libido.

"Mr Veer, act like your name and stop checking out an *abla nari.*"

He was embarrassed on being caught but was also

happy to have found his passion surging back.

"Well, actually, I was told that this apartment had a vacancy for a flat-mate, but it seems that I was misinformed." He channelized his thoughts.

"No, you were not. We are indeed looking for a flat-mate." The woman opened the meshed-grill iron door. It made a loud, squeaky noise. With the door opened, now he could clearly see the woman. In her late twenties or early thirties, she was tall, fair, with beautiful eyes. Her lips were full. With her tresses tied back, her face looked more oval. She had a little diamond pendant around her milky neck and the lucky diamond just nestled between her cleavage. Her floral pink nightgown, which was knee-length, made her appear a little plumper than she really was. He realized that since the time he had landed in Gurgaon, she was undoubtedly the prettiest woman he had seen.

But he was confused. "Well, I mean, when I was told by Manish I did assume that it would be guys looking for a flat-mate but…."

"Listen mister. I don't care what you assumed or were told. The fact is that there were three of us who shared this apartment. One of our flat-mates had to leave. With her gone, we are in no mood to bear an additional burden of ten thousand. Therefore, we are looking for someone to fill in. And I don't see any reason for you to get worked up if we are cool with having a male as an apartment mate."

"No, no, I did not mean that. But you know…."

While he defended his stance, a million thoughts hit him. Rajeshwari screaming blue murder. *Daata, Dadosa* knocking at the door of 55D, threatening the women with dire consequences. Gosh, the whole thought was scary. He stood there sheepishly with no clue.

"Hello, Mr Frozen Ice?," the woman goaded him.

He looked up embarrassed.

"So, would you like to have a look at the apartment?"

"Well, actually, you know...let me think it over and I will get back to you."

The door was slammed on his face.

***

"VVS, what's your problem?" Manish was puzzled.

"Nothing," he answered sheepishly.

Manish waved his hand and raised his eyebrows out of sheer desperation.

"Bro, finding a house in a metro is tough. Trust me."

"But how can I stay with a woman? And that too, two of them?," VVS clarified his stand.

"Are they going to rape you?," Manish was blunt. "And even if they do, would you mind it? I mean would anyone mind it?" His eyes had the naughty glint and he let out a mischievous grin. VVS was not amused.

"Manish, I mean, think of it. How can you dry your undies along with floral panties and lacy bras? Won't that be embarrassing?"

"Simple. Learn some project management skills from me. Dry your undies in your room or when theirs are not up on the clothesline," Manish laughed.

"Stop laughing. Won't they get scandalized seeing a man parade in the house, wearing shorts, scratching his balls?"

"Don't wear shorts if you feel gawky in them and don't scratch your balls there, do it here, at CommTech. Everybody does the same. Right up to the CEO. Scratch, scratch, scratch." Manish imitated the action, using both his hands and let out a throaty laughter. His demeanor was comforting, but also upsetting at times, as VVS did not know how under such stress of work, bankruptcy and uncertainty, he could laugh and smile.

"Go for it, bro. Take life as it comes."

VVS allowed himself a feeble smile. Somehow, he was still not convinced about staying with two women. How would Rajeshwari react if she ever discovered her horny husband sharing an apartment with two women? Her sudden thought made him yearn for her. For some reason, ever since he had come to CommTech, his libido had declined. Back in Udaipur, between Sakshi and Rajeshwari, he was always raring to go, looking for opportunities to score. And this enthusiasm was not restricted to these two women alone. The world was his harem, or so he thought. After all, he was a *bana* and a penchant for wine and women was embedded in his genes.

"I will find a house on my own. Thanks for your help." VVS shifted his attention to something more important than his libido—the house-hunting.

"As you wish," Manish got back to his headset.

VVS spent the rest of the day searching for property dealers' numbers and making calls to them. Every single call made him loose hope. His budget of ten to twelve thousand seemed paltry in the NCR. He also figured out that even if he was willing to shell out thirty to thirty-five thousand a month, no apartment-owner would let out his property without a company lease! And with the company itself going bankrupt....

***

Heads Up

It was another normal day for VVS—confused, apprehensive and nowhere to go. Nick was playing his normal role, that of a lazy boss. There was nothing to do but guzzle coffee and munch on the Good Day and Monaco biscuits, which still existed even after all the cost cuts. Everyone in the office had some story or a new rumor to share. He could not figure out why there was no effort to save the company if it were in the red. Why was everyone taking it for granted that it was end of the road and the story? How come everyone—right from the Global CEO to the management trainee, was still chilled out?

The rats had started deserting the sinking ship. The first one to jump off was Ashish Tandon, the branch head of CommTech, Gurgaon. Sandy had instructed VVS to meet him and to be in his good books. But ever since, Ashish Tandon had never stepped in the office. It was only after a few weeks that someone mentioned that he had quit.

One lazy afternoon, there was a sudden murmur, which started to build into something more serious. VVS got up to locate its source, "Check your mailbox." Shubhankar, who was standing in his cubicle, in the next bay, flashed his patent smile.

> Dear CommTech Employees,
>
> We all remember that for months Buck Howard, CEO, CommTech, kept on harping about the strong cash position of CommTech. Therefore, in my opinion, he made the filing a big surprise. Mr Howard appears to be unable to lead the corporation out of this difficult period.
>
> It was noticed that even after the tight financial spot that we are in currently, Mr Howard has been found using the CommTech Corporate Jet for commuting from his summer residence to CommTech's office. During my twenty-five years of employment with CommTech, I have never been paid for my travel to and from work. That means no gas money, no vehicle reimbursement, no maintenance costs! Using the corporate jet for commuting during a time that the company is in the worst financial position in its 100+ years history is an example of what a LEADER should NOT do.
>
> Thirdly, and the MOST egregious, outrageous and bold statement during Mr Howard's tenure at the helm of CommTech has been that the executives will share $55,000,000 US in 'retention incentives'. These incentives are nothing more than a bonus for poor performance.

Mr Howard, it is time for you to get real.

- Stop the talk of the 'retention incentives'. This is nothing more than a bonus.
- Lead by example and take a pay cut, or even better yet, show your confidence in the recovery plan by taking a salary of $1.00 until the company is profitable.
- Show that you truly value people, by reinstating the severance payments for those that lost out at the time of Chapter 11 filing.
- Lead by example, because so far, your leadership has received a failing grade.

Sincerely,
Disgruntled and mad-as-a-hatter
CommTech employee

Like everyone who read the email, VVS was also aghast. His simple, small-town mind could not figure out what was making even the most senior guys in Comm Tech behave in such an irresponsible manner. Coming from a martial clan, he knew that a leader always led from the front and had the motto 'my men before myself' embedded in his psyche. What kind of leaders did Comm Tech have? Why did everyone at Comm Tech believe in the philosophy of 'to each one his own'? What would have Neeta Madam done in such a situation? How would she have taken control of things? Would she be able to turn things around?

It infuriated VVS to realize that, in spite of all his hate for Neeta Madam, he really looked up to her. In his subconscious mind, she was an epitome of efficiency, leadership and dynamism. After looking at the mismanagement array at CommTech, he could now understand why she kept a check on every single thing—paper expense to salary deduction, travel vouchers to electricity bills. Without her checks, Web Link would have turned into another nightmare like CommTech.

Gosh, he needed a smoke break. Too bad, even this break was confined to an airconditioned, closed room with concealed chimneys and black leather upholstered chairs.

***

He read it again…and then again. Still the words did not make any sense. This could not be true. Rough weather could not strike so close to him.

Beep beep, beep beep.

His ringing ESN—the black and complex Comm Tech handset on his table, jolted him. The screen on the phone displayed Sandy's name. VVS picked up the receiver. Without the customary greeting or the informal chit-chat, Sandy went for the bull's eye.

"Dude, now listen to me carefully. Whatever I am going to tell you is highly confidential and it has to remain with you only." Sandy's voice was stressed and high-strung.

"VVS, are you there?," he sounded slightly agitated.

"Yes sir."

"The downsizing has started. Though it was expected, but no one expected it to start so soon, and certainly not in the APAC region."

VVS could feel a lump build in his throat and his feet going numb, a strange feeling which he had never experienced in his life. His heart was pounding like a drum and his face was flushed.

"I want you not to overreact when I tell you that in APAC the downsizing has started with the web team, with your line manager Nick. He has been asked to go." As instructed, VVS did not react. In any case, he was too numb for any reaction.

"But VVS, you need not to worry. I am responsible for getting you here and I will do anything to have you here. Just keep your calm, keep on pretending to work and do not let rumors affect you. In a day or two, you will start receiving mails from the HR, telling that the web division has been scrapped. Your colleagues, sitting out of the Gurgaon office will definitely walk up to you and enquire about your job status, advising you on how to find a new one. For God's sake, don't let any of this bother you. Just stay calm."

VVS had tears in his eyes. He felt miserable, as he never expected his dream to end so soon. He looked at his leather shoes, shining and new. His shirt, crisp white linen, the new dark-brown tie. He looked at his shiny black HP laptop, his new Blackberry. He was living every part of his dream and like any other sweet dream, he was afraid to lose it, and that too so soon.

"Jai Shree Naathji, please give me some more time," he prayed.

"Dude, I have already spoken with RC and also to my line manager Lawrence."

"Lawrence?," VVS could barely speak.

"Lawrence sits out of the Singapore office and is the Vice President, Marketing and Communication for the APAC region. He likes me. I have put in a word to create an opening in his team so that I can hire you here. To strengthen my proposal, I have asked RC to speak with him on the head count thing."

VVS did not know how to react as even the dark cloud had a silver lining to it. He could still see some hope. However, deep down, he was not sure if he could believe his college-time senior. Was Sandy really trying to help him or was he just trying to make his existence less painful by giving him some hope?

"Sir, that's ok. You need not to bother. I will go back to Udaipur." VVS's tone, speech and content made him appear to be a true loser; on his knees, seeking sympathy and ready to go down without even a fight.

Sandy identified the trait immediately. "Stop

sounding like a loser. If you think you have lost it, believe me even I will not be able to help then."

The strong rebuke from Sandy worked and VVS sat up, straight, ready to fight rather than go down like a coward. Hope gave him a new lease of life. Color returned to his face. Manish, who was on a call, turned. VVS smiled. Manish could sense that something was wrong, but the ongoing call was an important one, so he got back to it.

"Dude, send me your CV right now. Before that, modify the web technology part to web communication."

"But sir…," VVS protested.

"And stop this but-and-why thing. I don't know how you will do it, but I want your resume in my inbox in the next twenty minutes."

"But, sir…."

"You are an asshole, VVS," Sandy's voice had a deep, quiet annoyance. "For how long do you want me to spoon-feed you?"

VVS was hurt. He knew that Sandy had done a lot for him but saying it in so many words? Sandy immediately realized he had overreacted and also that VVS was the sensitive one.

"Ok, send me your resume and I shall make the changes. And you jack ass, you better pay me for this resume writing service."

Hope replaced anger and embarrassment and VVS smiled. For some odd reason, he always trusted Sandy. Maybe it was this blind trust that made the north zone topper in school, slip from 90.5% to 48.2% in college.

He shifted his gaze back to his laptop screen, where the mail from Nick was still open.

> "Dear Virendra,
>
> Before you hear it from anyone else, as a rumor or as an official release, as your line manager, it is my duty to share the same with you.
>
> I have been asked to go. I want you to take this news objectively. We both knew that with squeezed resources, the web department was slated to face the axe, sooner or later.
>
> I had a good 18-year stint here. I plan to go back to Australia and indulge in what I love to do the most—adventure sports.
>
> Keep in touch and God bless.
>
> Nick"

So straight, so honest and right from the heart. While an Indian would have taken the opportunity to crib and cry as to how he was cheated and taken for a ride by Comm Tech, Nick, like a man of character, took it with dignity and grace. VVS felt a strange kind of respect building up for Nick. Respect, which he hadn't felt for any man in a very long time. He wanted to reply but knowing his Indian way—emotional and subjective, refrained himself.

Shree Naathji, bless Nick with a new and a better job soon, he prayed silently.

***

It was hot as hell and the humidity was making it worse. After the emotional highs and lows, with fear and apprehension still resting in his mind and heart, VVS had no one but Manish to confide in. The efficient project manager that Manish was, he studied the situation, which was desperate and grim, identified the problem—lack of hope—and ordered a solution—an all-boys beer party at the all-time favorite *haata*, Machaan.

Machaan wasn't anything like what VVS had seen. During his college days, the *haata*—an open piece of land—adjacent to the liquor shops, used to be shabby joints authorized by the Haryana Government to prevent nuisance by drunkards in public places. These official drinking places were only patronized by rickshaw-pullers, petty traders, truck drivers and the likes. So, when Manish shared his plan, VVS almost revolted at the thought of CommTech executives, carrying their laptop bags and Blackberrys, drinking at a *haata*. But on the insistence of the entire gang—Manish, Shubhankar, Aditya, Ashu and Sanjay—there was little he could do but agree.

Machaan was placed right next to a swank, brightly-lit shop called Ganapati Wines. Poor Ganapati, VVS thought, from selling *ladoos*, he surely had come a long way. The entrance was guarded by a huge wooden door, which could have protected some ancient *haveli* either in Rajasthan or Gujarat. As VVS stepped inside, the scene hit him hard. The place was done up like a designer restaurant. There were thatched mud sheds to his left, which had rural motifs painted on them. The enclosure to the right side was a huge open kitchen with the latest gadgets—big freezers, electric chimneys, hobs, stainless steel counters and chefs sporting white uniforms. Damn this place! There was a bullock cart placed right at the center, sans the bullocks. People seated on the cart were enjoying their drink. The far end corner had a huge raised wooden platform, approximately ten feet high,. with a wooden ladder attached to it. On the platform there were people, the corporate kinds, as VVS could see their laptop bags too, enjoying life while being served by the skilful waiters who glided up and down the narrow rungs. VVS had only seen such a structure—a real *machaan*, in the middle of fields with crops, to keep the cattle and birds at bay. The place had around three hundred patrons. To add to his surprise, there were also girls and families hanging out there. How could a woman risk her modesty by sitting and drinking amidst some 300 drunkards was beyond the comprehension of the guy from Udaipur.

They got inside a small hut, which had the board 'air-conditioned' painted on its wall. The interior was basic, but again designer. Cane chairs, wooden crates decked up as tables, the mud walls with floral motifs and Continental, Italian, Chinese and Thai on the menu.

"So what are we having?"

"Of course some chilled beer," Ashu said.

"Kingfisher?," Manish clarified.

"Foster's please," Aditya intervened.

"*Thakur*, what about you?," Aditya enquired.

"Anything."

Manish ordered twelve bottles of Foster and some munchies.

Cheers! They all raised their glasses.

"But cheers to what?," Sanjay smiled.

"Well, to CommTech and Chapter 11," Aditya clarified.

The chilled beer along with the airconditioner, which was working hard to fight the soaring mercury and the humidity, had a soothing effect on their nerves. Soon, they were all three bottles down.

"VVS, I don't know if I should be telling you, but today, on one of the calls, there was some mention of scrapping the web division. Are you aware of this?"

VVS almost choked on his beer. He was under the impression that no one else would be aware of the news. But Sanjay's revelation, in public, made him feel so unwanted and small, almost worthless.

He decided to act normal and the best way to do

so was to counter Sanjay's question with another one. "Who told you?"

"Never mind," Sanjay grabbed a handful of salted peanuts.

"Hey, does that mean that our *Thakur*'s job is in danger?," Ashu was concerned.

"As if he is bothered. He will go back to his *haveli* and enjoy with all those *ghagra*-wearing hot babes. Won't you *Thakur*?," Shubhankar's smile was laced with sarcasm.

VVS smiled back. He wondered how incorrectly *Bollywood* had painted a rosy picture of *thakurs*. Living in palatial *havelis* with hardly anytime for anything substantial, except raping girls, enjoying the raunchy *mujras* and treating themselves to the choicest of whiskies.

"Getting Nick out of the system would be such a good riddance. Useless fellow," Sanjay voiced his opinion. "He has been here for God only knows how many years, and has done nothing at all."

"Ever worked with him?," Aditya quipped.

"Yeah, I was doing an SMB campaign. The typical small medium business campaign, which focused on saving. For the same, I needed a web-based application to let the SMBs calculate their electricity savings, using our switches. Nick took three months, only to tell me that he could not give the required application."

VVS chose to keep quiet and sip his beer.

"Fuck Nick. Tell me something Sanjay, you are a

part of RC's cabinet. Tell us which way are we headed?," Aditya enquired.

It had taken VVS a few days to realize that like a prime minister, the country heads of CommTech also had a cabinet. The cabinet was made up of various departmental heads, which met once or twice a month to brainstorm and plan the future course of action. No wonder, these brainstorming sessions happened at some exotic location. Going by what VVS was told, it was nothing but a royal waste of three days at CommTech's expense. Also, it was these cabinet meetings where the sales heads decided and invented new ways to hoodwink the sales pipeline and funnel, which at the end of the day decided the variable component of their salaries, along with hefty bonuses.

"Well, to be honest, the ship is sinking and it's just a matter of time. I was there at the cabinet meet in Ooty last week and the general atmosphere was that of apprehension."

"What is RC's take on this whole thing?," Ashu was keen to know the top man's perspective.

"He is the one who has got us screwed." Before Sanjay could respond, Aditya barged in.

"No, no, we can't put all the blame on him. He is a decent guy," Sanjay shielded his line manager.

"Boss, tell me something," Shubhankar, who had been silent for a while, finally spoke. "How can you absolve him of all the shit that is flying here?"

"Shubhankar, I get your point. I am just telling you that it is not fair on our part to blame him alone. He is not the one who is responsible for this Chapter 11 situation. It is a global thing, which is a result of decisions which have gone wrong globally," Sanjay tried to present the case in an unbiased manner.

"Boss, I am sure that you haven't forgotten the Zenith fiasco. Have you?," Shubhankar taunted. Beer was playing its role in loosening up tongues while fanning, fears and apprehensions.

"Shubhankar, there is no use going there again," Sanjay was in no mood to spoil his evening.

"There is boss. This son of a bitch, RC, and his right and the left balls, Neel and Rohit, screwed the entire Zenith deal, which cost us $500 million. A loss, which had global impact and repercussions. We could never recover post that."

"Shubhankar, please watch your lingo," Sanjay warned him.

"What if I don't?" The beer spoke and continued. "The project managers and the transition managers have to face the heat when the project gets into the execution phase because the motherfucker sales guys of CommTech leave nothing for a smooth project transition. Just to fulfill your targets and to flaunt your Rolexes, you undercut projects by almost eighty per cent. Don't you?"

"Shubhankar, let us not get personal," Manish intervened. "Chill dude. Let us order some more beer," Ashu supported Manish.

"I am only three bottles down. What do you think, I am drunk?" Shubhankar challenged.

"No one is suggesting that you are drunk but then…" VVS chipped in.

"You keep out of this, *Thakur*. You don't know a fuck about CommTech." Shubhankar was curt.

VVS got back to his glass, knowing well what was coming. After all, he had been a part of the same situation, many a time, right from his college days. But he never realized that even the polished and suave CommTech executives would stoop down to the same level. Maybe, destiny had entrusted Shubhankar the job of proving VVS right.

"Yes, Mr Sanjay Singh, so what were we discussing?"

"Shubhankar, it's quite late, I think we should leave," Manish got up. Shubhankar held his hand and pulled him down. "You better not leave. I am not finished yet. Hey there, get us more beer," he signaled the waiter.

"Mr Singh, weren't you also a part of the Zenith contract?," Shubhankar taunted. "How stupid of you guys. You could not even fill and submit a tender contract? Don't you know that after all the jet setting your *baap* RC …."

"Shubhankar watch your words." Yet another warning from Sanjay came in.

"Hear the whole thing, you piece of shit and then threaten me."

Sanjay, who was sitting on the other side of the table, got up to leave. But Shubhankar got up and gripped his hand.

"Won't you call up your *baap* and complain?, you parasite."

Sanjay lost his cool and hit Shubhankar right on his face. Under the impact, Shubhankar reeled back and landed on VVS. VVS could not handle the sudden momentum and the mass and fell down with Shubhankar. Sanjay rushed from the other side of the table pushing Manish, Ashu and Aditya and pounced on Shubhankar.

"You motherfucker, how dare you? Your CTC would be less than the money that I claim on vouchers. Just because I decided to have a drink with VVS and you guys, you assumed that I am a no one. You bastard, I can get you sacked even before you know it."

People sitting outside gathered at the door, trying to figure out the reason for the brawl. Waiters silently excused themselves.

As Manish, Ashu and Aditya were trying to pacify Sanjay, Shubhankar lay there on the floor, his face plastered with beer, peanuts, strands of onion and mud.

VVS walked back to his guest house, which was

close by, with his linen shirt crumpled, his tie stuffed in his pocket. His mind was too tired to think of anything. He just wanted to run away to a place far off.

Was he missing the small-town camaraderie? Was he missing *banas*? Was he missing Udaipur? Maybe he was.

***

With his line manager and immediate senior Nick gone, whatever little VVS was doing—playing the 'good junior'—also ended. Tired of looking at the same PPTs, out of sheer desperation, he requested Sandy to send him some new ones, maybe with better graphics. At least, graphics would keep him interested for a little longer. His Rubik Cube timing was showing signs of improvement as now he was clocking three minutes and forty-five seconds.

Manish, as usual, was always on some or the other conference call, with some overseas client, trying to facilitate the transition—whatever that meant. On a day when Manish was without his most important body part—the headset, just to kill time, VVS asked him about the exact nature of his work. Manish started by telling him that whenever a new client bought a product from CommTech—primarily switches or routers—to avail the service, the client needed to connect his equipment remotely. For this, a VPN—Virtual Private Network—

had to be established. Right from setting the network to helping the client add the processes and systems, which would help the NOC monitor and rectify alarms, was his duty and responsibility.

The mention of the word NOC got VVS curious. He was always fascinated by the big room, on the 17th floor, with a solid wooden door proclaiming 'Authorized Personnel only'. Manish, courtesy all the calls, on which with great dexterity, he handled more dim wits than VVS, elaborated that NOC meant Network Operating Center. He was also kind enough to ask the NOC head, a fat bald guy, whom VVS had never seen anywhere close to his favorite spot—the coffee-vending machine, to show VVS around.

It was a five-minute tour, which blew VVS's mind. NOC was a huge hall, straight out of Star Trek or one of those sci-fi movies. There were some hundreds of LCD monitors mounted on the wooden panel wall. The main control station was a huge semi-circular black-colored fiberglass table, approximately twice the size of a normal dining table. The table was studded with consoles, buttons and flash panels. The fat bald guy commandeered the chair. Wow! VVS was impressed. Near the wall, close to the monitors, were smaller workstations on which technicians, who surely were engineers from top universities, watched them and typed away furiously on their keyboards. The fat bald guy, whose name was Ramachandran, tried his best to explain to VVS how NOC, which was based out of Bangalore and Gurgaon, was the backbone of CommTech's Managed Services Portfolio. He further explained that NOC, which was part of the Managed Services Team, facilitated 24x7, end-to-end monitoring for Comm Tech's clients and helped CommTech earn precious dollars.

Still dazed by the hi-tech tour of the NOC, he could not believe that a company this advanced could have gone bust. Even if it had to go bust, couldn't it have waited for another year or two?

***

His ESN rang and the flashing screen told him it was Sandy. "Morning sir."

"RC will be in Gurgaon today and tomorrow. Speak with his secy, Murthi, and see what time you have been allotted." VVS was taken aback as he did not know of anything he had done to warrant an appointment with the MD. Sandy cleared his apprehension.

"Actually, I forgot to tell you that I have spoken with Lawrence. Remember, VP Asia, Marketing and Comms?" VVS nodded his head, "and he has given a go-ahead to recruit one more guy for my team. This new team member will handle the additional marketing activity, which this Chapter 11 situation warrants. In the same context, RC would like to interview you."

"But...," VVS stammered.

"Don't you worry, it's going to be an informal thing."

"But sir, how can I join marketing? I don't know anything about it."

"And who told you that I do?," Sandy countered blatantly.

"But sir...," VVS tried defending his stand.

Sandy cut him short. "Don't you know that I am plain B Com? Thereafter, I joined a car showroom and then the wretched one-room PR agency where my first designation was of Branch Head as I was the only head in the entire branch. Where do you think I learnt marketing?, tell me?" He was being honest and insistent.

"Well...," VVS was flabbergasted.

"Ok, leave my case," Sandy continued further, "What makes you think that Lawrence has any clue to marketing?"

"Sir, you ought to be kidding me. At his level, I am sure he would be from Harvard or ...,"

"Harvard, my foot. Fifteen years back, he was a desktop support technician at CommTech, China. And back then, computers were those 286 kinds which needed no whiz kids to fix the drive, driver, mouse or even the mother board."

"You mean, Lawrence Kilam is not an MBA?," VVS was shocked.

"That I don't know. What I know for sure is that after feeling stagnated in his role, he approached the then Marketing Head of China, who was a kind guy and hired Lawrence as he showed interest. Moreover, no top marketing brain was willing to be a part of a B2B set-up. Lawrence sucked up to his bosses and here he is, VP Marketing and Comms, APAC."

VVS was still in a state of shock. Was this what he had longed for? Mediocrity? If it were for mediocrity, then what was wrong with Web Link? If it were only for sucking up to your boss, then Neeta Madam would be the better choice. "So dude, you are as good or as bad as the VP, Marketing, APAC, CommTech," Sandy laughed. "Just chill and meet RC. I have arranged everything. Before the slow-moving HR guys can even type your sack letter, I will put an iron rod up their ass and make them issue your function-change order. And before I forget, all the best for your interview," Sandy ended his call laughing at his own wit.

Long after he placed the receiver on the cradle, words like Lawrence Kilam, desktop technician and VP Marketing kept on multiplying within VVS's head. He walked towards the gas chamber, the smoking room, but not before calling up Murthi to find the slot allotted for his interview.

***

Dear Friend,

We announced some tough but important decisions today–decisions that will significantly impact many of you. In a press release issued today, I have announced the reduction of an additional 5,300 positions. This is in addition to the reduction of roughly 1,600 positions still to be completed from previously announced plans.

You deserve as much clarity as possible, as soon as possible. For the same, at 12:00 pm EST, I'll address you in a global GIS session (details below). Joining me on the GIS will be Holster Gallup, our CFO, and Belinda King, SVP of Human Resources. Holster will walk you through the restructuring process we are in and where we stand today. Belinda will be there to cover some of the specific issues around the upcoming reductions. Please join us for the same.

Our company is in a difficult situation. The harshness of the economic reality and lowered-spend profile of our customers, combined with the worries associated with our filing are directly impacting our revenues. Therefore, we must act quickly to adjust our costs to the realities of our industry and of our business.

First, to achieve this, we have decided to keep the AIP in place. With one change–calculations and payouts will be made quarterly instead of once a year. This is a step forward and recognizes the immense task ahead, and the important role that all our people play in driving results.

We are making the tough decisions we must to restructure CommTech and work to successfully emerge from creditor protection. We are making progress towards that objective everyday.

Thank you all.

Buck Howard

VVS could not make anything out of the 'H mail', which had just hit his mailbox. Ever since he had joined CommTech, he had heard regular and heated discussion around the 'H mail'—the emails from Buck Howard. Not that he had seen many, but the 'H mail' with its garish yellow background and black font was surely one of the most ludicrous web layouts he had ever seen. Loaded with acronyms—GIS, which was nothing but a very large conference call where the top management addressed everyone at one go; AIP, which stood for Annual Incentive Program, the mail provided no hope for anyone.

VVS could not figure out why the employees were not being protected from being sacked if there was still money to be paid as incentive. It did not take an Einstein to figure out that at the given rate of bonus, ten to twelve per cent, for fifty thousand people, just by doing away with the bonus bit, jobs could be saved. But then maybe being professional, was all about number crunching and not worrying about real people and real emotions.

Would he ever be a true professional?

***

"I had enough of Akhepur. I cannot keep on answering the queries of your parents and relatives," Rajeshwari sobbed.

VVS knew that either *Daata* or *Bai ji* must have taunted her again for not gifting them a grandson. It was nothing new. Only when the taunts assumed a sinister proportion that he got to know about them, courtesy Rajeshwari's tears. To this date he was unable to fathom why he couldn't lead his own life. Why did he need to do everything the way he was expected to? Why did he have to choose a job according to his parents' convenience? Why was he forced to marry a girl of their choice? And now, for even something as personal as parenting! Wasn't he a man enough to make choices in life?

"Raj, I am sure that by this time you know *Daata* and *Bai ji* better than me. Don't you?" He tried donning the hat which, after marriage, every man is supposed to wear many a time during the day—that of a referee, moderating between parents and wife.

"Yes, I do. Therefore, I can see that things are getting worse. Why can't you tell them that it's not me who is responsible?" Maybe the hurt was too much as Rajeshwari was in no mood to relent.

"And do you think I should walk up to *Daata* and tell him that my sperm count is low? Or do you want me to go and tell *Bai ji* that her son isn't producing enough sperm for a grandson? Tell me Raj. Why are you silent?"

The pent-up frustration of CommTech was making him react more fervently.

"At least you can start with your medication and stop smoking and drinking. Didn't the doctor tell you that both these things are bad for sperm count?"

"Also, didn't the doctor say that I need to be happy?," he retorted.

"What more should I do to keep you happy? I am a married woman who is staying away from her husband, just to keep him happy. I have never cribbed about never having gone on a vacation with you. I slog all the day, in the kitchen, in your house. I take all the insults and scorns hurled by your parents for being infertile and what not! What else am I supposed to do? Tell me? Tell me now?" Her sobs turned into wails. A man can handle 32 caliber bullet, a cannon shot, but surely not tears and that too of a woman.

"Raj, don't do this. Please," VVS revealed his soft side. "I know you do a lot for me. It's me who has never done anything to make you happy. Not that I don't want to, but you know that times have been rough. I thought once I would join CommTech, everything would improve. But here also, my misfortune is a step ahead of me."

The wife part in Rajeshwari—caring and loving —took over the woman part—demanding, complaining and self-centered. Her sobs were immediately replaced by concern. "What happened? Aren't you happy? Are they not treating you well? Tell me please. Don't hide things from me. I am your wife. I will go and pray to *Maa Ambe* and you will see that everything will be fine. Trust me."

As VVS poured himself another large, he knew that with a staggering debt amount of $8 billion and a Desktop Technician as VP, Marketing and Communication, bailing out CommTech was not possible, even for the omnipotent God.

***

F2F

It was a big day for him. He was going to meet RC.

Rakshit Chaheil, better known as RC, the MD of CommTech India and a much-respected and revered leader of the corporate world. No wonder, the mere thought of facing the great visionary was making VVS nervous. He was up early, at 4 am, trying to figure out the best dress for the occasion. Should it be a black trouser with sky blue shirt and purple tie or should he wear something lighter and breezier? Was the occasion right for wearing a jacket or should he stick to a more summer attire? Should he address him as 'sir' or.... Going by his profile and picture, he seemed to be in his mid-fifties, making him almost as old as his *Daata*. There was no way he could address someone as old and as respected as him by his first name. Though Sandy had warned him that corporate culture was all about being on first-name basis. However, it was beyond his comprehension that why he should follow something, which was not in sync with his own culture and traditions.

He had studied all that he could find on CommTech and its marketing activities. Being a north zone topper and a product of Asia's best commerce college, were strong pointers to his above-average IQ. No wonder, within hours, he had figured out the entire marketing content.

Around 7 am he called up Sandy to seek more tips and clarifications. Sandy did not answer his call. Knowing him well, VVS assumed that he would still be sprawled on his bed, nursing his hangover. He was not feeling any better himself. The churn and growl in his stomach was growing which was a result of the eight large drinks consumed the previous night. The caretaker had got him some antacid, which he immediately gulped down and even sought the help of Shree Naathji in clearing his bowel. His prayer was answered as he did manage to expel last night's concoction of rum, coke, chicken *tikka, masala peanut, peeli daal tadka and tandoori roti.*

Murthi, the secretary to RC, informed that the interview would happen anytime before lunch. So he waited there, glued to his seat, with his eyeballs swinging between his Timex wristwatch, the small digital clock at the bottom, right hand corner of his laptop and the huge clock placed on the wall behind him. Each of them displayed the same time. Sandy had called him a couple of times, checking on the progress, if any. Every time he called, VVS would make sure that the conversation ended as soon as possible as he did not want to miss Murthi's call. After all, VVS knew that this was his last chance of keeping his dream alive and, therefore, wanted to take no chance whatsoever.

Manish was busy on one of his endless calls, trying to explain to the client that the maintenance contract stated that the three-year free AMC clause was only for 24 ports, whatever that meant. VVS thought of using the bonus time to revise the stuff. Using his GID and password, he logged on to the Intranet and straightaway went to the marketing link. The link had every chart, number, pictures, collaterals and campaign creative; year wise, which had anything to do with marketing. He started looking at the numbers for India marketing. The campaign spend, the ROI, creative for the various campaigns. His concentration was only to be disturbed by his quick glance at his watch, the computer clock and the wall clock.

He avoided Ashu, Aditya, Shubhankar and almost everyone who involuntarily tried to distract him. In his mind and heart, he knew that if he goofed up on this chance, the world would come crumbling down.

It was close to two o' clock when the phone rang. The display told him that the incoming call was from Jasmine—the conference room where he was supposed to meet RC.

"Yes," he tried his best to sound casual and confident.

"Mr Singh, RC sir has stepped out for lunch with a client. He won't be in for the next two hours. As soon as he gets back, I will let you know."

VVS looked at his watch. It was half-past-two. He calculated that another two hours would mean half-past-four. To be on the safer side, he set the cut-off point to half-past-three. So there he was, with a lot of things to do in the next hour or so. Grab a couple of coffees, munch on his staple diet—Monaco and Good Day biscuits, smoke at least three to four cigarettes, dial the property dealers and check his get-up once more. God, he had too much on his plate! Ever since he joined CommTech, for the first time he felt that he was leading a justified existence.

3.30

4.00

4.30

5.00

5.30

6.00

He was losing patience and justifiably so. Since 9 am he had been on the 'wait' mode. Tired and exhausted, also a little angry, he dialed 1620—the Jasmine Conference Room. No response and the call was transferred to the voice mail box. He dialed again. The same response. He dialed again and again.

Finally, he got up from his chair and took the stairs to the seventeenth floor, to the Jasmine Conference Room. There it was, all dark and deserted. When he enquired, the guard told him that RC had left around lunchtime.

His ears turned coal hot and his cheeks flushed—with anger, embarrassment and humiliation. He was panting and felt like hitting the big glass door hard. On his first day at CommTech, it was the same door, which had let him in. Suddenly, in his trouser pocket, his mobile vibrated. It was Sandy.

"Hey have you been to this place *Shayama Kulche Wala* in Gurgaon?"

VVS felt a strange disgust for Sandy. His casual tone shred his eardrums.

"No," he controlled his rage.

"I was speaking with RC and he told me that today he had gone to this place which serves the best *Cholle-Kulche* he has ever had. It is somewhere near the Sahara mall. Dude, the next time I am in town, you have to take me there."

VVS weighed his pros and cons; the consequences of abusing Sandy, then calling up RC and doing the same. The wait, the stress, the mortification had fogged his sense of reasoning and judgment. In a blind rage, he wanted to get over with all of this and then go back to Udaipur. He knew that Neeta Madam would hire him back. After all, he was her star performer who could multi-task like no one else. He saw no harm in being a part of Web Link, the *banas* and Akhepur again. That life was definitely better than this one—of utter shame and disgrace. A life where he was just a GID number on an excel sheet and where his whole existence, or lack of it, did not make a difference to anyone —neither the company he worked for nor the people he worked with.

"RC did not see me," VVS slurred.

"Oh shit. I forgot to tell you. Yes, he did tell me the same. Actually, he was neck deep in meetings. But he has promised to meet up with you the next time he is there."

Bruised and hurt, he stood there. He still could not believe that the meeting, which could have changed his life and career, did not happen because the interviewer—RC found something better to do—relish *cholle-kulche* in this case. A tear rolled down his eyes. After all these years of leading a wretched life, finally, when he was beginning to gain confidence, the incident with RC tore his confidence to shreds. He was missing Rajeshwari and Udaipur. Yes, he was also missing *banas*. At least, with them, he knew what to expect. Nothing!

***

After a long, ego-crushing day, it was just another evening at the guest house. VVS was having his favorite session with his best and long-time friend, Old Monk rum. Sitting in his room, flipping channels, he was unable to articulate his feelings. Should he feel happy or brood, or just walk away, out of sheer disgust? Was it his lack of understanding of the corporate functioning which made him miserable, or was he just overreacting? He took a drag and sipped the black drink, while nursing the minute cobweb pattern on the neck of the familiar bottle.

But he knew that irrespective of whatever transpired during the day, he had a reason to feel happy about and celebrate. After all, just before getting off the call, Sandy did mention that RC had approved of his candidature.

VVS had no clue if he was supposed to thank Sandy for the huge favor or hate him for his indifference and lack of empathy. With confusion about Sandy in his mind and heart, he lit a cigarette. As he inhaled the smoke, he was transported to another world, his college days, rather the first day of it...

...How could he ever forget the first day, rather the night, at the SRCC hostel. After topping the north zone, with 90.5 per cent, SRCC was the obvious choice. Since childhood, though he had seen *havelis*, horses, guns, portraits of his great grandfathers hung there on the wall, stories of hunting trips and the past glory, but for some reason, he could never identify with all of that. On the other hand, *Dadosa*, his elder brother, always loved every bit of it. No wonder, to preserve it or to rot with it; depending on the way one looked at it, his *Dadosa* took to politics. While VVS, unlike most *banas,* took to commerce.

The first night at the SRCC hostel was a terrifying one. The fear was multiplied by the fact that he was hundreds of miles away from *Rawla* Akhepur, in a metro called Delhi, where he knew no one.

The hot and humid July weather was overpowering and in the long corridor of the SRCC hostel's B block, the air was thick with fear, awkwardness and shame. All the *fachas*—the freshers—were lined up in the long corridor, like a train. They had been standing there for hours, sapped and tired. More than the physical exertion, it was the humiliation and embarrassment of standing there; naked, which was proving to be unbearable.

Seniors, who passed by the '*Facha* Express'—the name of the naked fresher's train, hit them anywhere they felt like—head, tummy, arms, some even on their private parts.

He remembered how petrified he was when he was dragged to the room of a super senior. His fault? Well, he had refused to hurl profanities on his batch mates.

It was black with some cracks. There were leftovers of the posters, which had been torn away in a great hurry. The sliding lock of the old Indian style was badly bruised and battered. It was the door of Room No. 26B. As one of his seniors pushed him in, he had almost choked on the smoke, which was an integral part of the room's persona. It took him a while to figure out the room and its owner. Sparsely furnished, it just had a cot with a dirty bedsheet, a writing table with a cheap table lamp on it. Beer and rum bottles dotted the floor, even the bookshelf. A huge, almost the size of a large bowl, circular ashtray made out of empty Navy Cut cigarette packets was lying in the middle of the room. The bowl-sized ashtray was swarming with ash and cigarette butts. The room had no living soul.

Then he walked in. Tall, strapping, debonair and nothing like a student. In shorts and a crumpled T-shirt, he would easily be well over six feet, a lean and mean-looking man. He walked like a tiger on the prowl—silent, agile and menacing. His thick moustache further accentuated his devilish charm. VVS had never seen any student like him. The senior, who had brought him to the room, jumped from the chair as if he had touched a live wire.

"Sandy sir, this *facha* is not taking orders from seniors. We asked him to abuse and he refused," the senior, Aakash, whose name he came to know, in due course, pleaded his case. The super senior, Sandy, looked at him, his eyes piercing.

"Is this true?" For some reason, his deep voice instilled fear in him and told him that this guy was the judge, the jury and the executioner.

"Sir, but... I cannot abuse...I mean, I come from a good family...."

Even before the word 'family' could be completed, something moved like a thunderbolt, fast and cruel, and landed on his cheek. The room echoed with the sound of the thunder and the impact sent him flying to the floor sobbing.

"Where do you think we come from? A whorehouse?," Sandy massaged his right palm, which had just delivered the impactful slap. He lit a cigarette and turned towards Aakash. Despite being a senior himself, Aakash trembled as if he did not know what to expect next.

"Ok sir, I shall take your leave now," Aakash stammered.

As he walked out of the room, Sandy called out Aakash, who froze and turned around. "And when you know you are not worth being a senior, never ever rag anyone. Being a senior is a huge responsibility. You have to essay the role of a friend, a mentor, a guide to your junior not only for three years but for the entire life. And God be with the juniors who have no option but to look up to seniors like you."

"I am sorry sir." Aakash felt small and disgraced, more so because all this happened before a *Facha*, a fresher—a first-year student. He was still lying on the floor. The tight and hard slap had hit his right cheek like a whip. He was sure that the impression of Sandy's large palm would stay there for long. But what he did not know was that the imprints were deeper, on his heart.

"And tell your batchmates to keep their hands off this kid. He is with me now."

Sandy closed the door and handed him a cigarette—his first and also the one which would turn him into a chain smoker.

Since that day, Sandy was a God to him. He wanted to be like Sandy sir—to talk, walk, act and impress people the way he did.

"Sandy sir, thank you for everything," he murmured. His face had the expression of a devotee and no devotee can ever mistrust his God.

***

Making Waves

"*Thakur*, for sure, you have long hands which do reach the right pair of balls," Aditya laughed. VVS felt a little embarrassed and smiled, which had no trace of joy. He did not like the idea of his hands stretched, holding Sandy's balls. The guilt inside him was now multiplying. He knew that earlier he took a salary for not doing the work, which he knew. But from now on, he was supposed to get salary for not doing the work which he had no clue about. His new, rather revised, offer letter had clearly mentioned his designation as Brand Manager, Enterprise Product and Services Portfolio.

In this new role, he was a part of Lawrence Kilam's marketing team with Sandy as his line manager. His KRA or 'Key Responsibilities Areas' included planning & implementing the marketing strategies, monitoring and analyzing the sales figures, launching products through ATL & BTL activities and interacting with the vendors. When he raised an alarm with Sandy, warning and pleading that he knew nothing about any of this, he was told to relax as being a Chapter 11 company, in any case, there would be no marketing activity. This meant that his entire KRA would never come into existence. It all sounded so brazen to him.

"*Thakur*, you are one hell of a lucky guy. I am so happy for you," Ashu patted his back. They were all seated in the smoking room, filling their lungs with nicotine—both, by way of active as well as passive smoking.

VVS blew a smoke ring and shot it with a dart of smoke. Aditya, Ashu and Shubhankar were impressed and clapped. VVS smiled and repeated the same feat. Aditya tried to emulate him but got his lungs filled with more smoke than he could handle and landed up in a coughing bout. They all laughed while they took turns patting his back to expel the smoke.

"Boss, tell me something, you are from web background, aren't you?," Shubhankar enquired.

"Well yes. Why do you ask?" VVS took another drag.

"Then how did you get the brand management portfolio?"

"Simple, cause there is no brand to manage. Buck has already screwed them all," Ashu's explanation sent them all reeling under an attack of guffaws, but for Shubhankar.

"This is the precise reason why we are in this situation," Shubhankar sounded grim.

"Shubhankar, stop this mind fuck riddle of yours. Get to the point," knowing Shubhankar's habit of taking the meandering course, Ashu warned him.

"Boss, you see the point is that it is appointment like these which have fucked us. I mean, how could a guy doing web designing get into brand management? I might be a techie by profession but I have done my MBA and surely know what brand management entails."

VVS got a little uncomfortable as Shubhankar's voice had a crusader's tone to it.

"Hey Shubhankar, just shut up and enjoy your smoke. Aren't you happy to see *Thakur* safe? After his boss Nick got sacked, and with strong rumors of the entire web division being axed, poor thing would have lost his job," Aditya sounded logical.

But there was no change in Shubhankar's expression. His face was determined and his eyes focused.

"Shubhankar, do you think hiring someone like me, a brand manager, will upset a company like CommTech?," VVS tried to soft play the whole thing.

Shubhankar looked VVS in the eyes. His eyes had something about them, clear and honest, and VVS was afraid to look into them. Shubhankar stubbed the butt in the stainless steel, CommTech branded ashtray and adjusted his specs.

"Look *Thakur*, I have an ailing father, who has been diagnosed with cancer. I know he won't live but I can't leave him to die. It takes a minimum of fifty thousand rupees per month to keep him going. I have two sons, aged eight and eleven. Their fees alone amounts to a lac per quarter. I am not even including the EMIs and the household expenses. VVS, I am sure that you know CommTech is full of real people like me. People with families, responsibilities, dreams and fears. And when CommTech goes down, it is these people who will suffer the most. The top guys have worked out their retainment bonuses and have their exits planned. It does not make any difference to them if CommTech sinks today or after two years. Irrespective of its fate, they will be afloat. But it is people like us who will drown and die. Where would a CommTech factory worker, who has worked here for twenty long years go when he is told that CommTech can't pay him his PF? Don't we know that in the West, elderly people depend on their pension, as they don't have sons like us to support them. How would this guy go about his life? Tell me VVS?"

Shubhankar's eyes were slicing through VVS. So much so that suddenly VVS felt that it was the extra burden of his salary, which was breaking CommTech's backbone. Nervously, he lit another cigarette and looked towards the ceiling.

"What are you trying to prove?," Ashu countered Shubhankar.

"That if we all acted like concerned employees right from the day one, no CEO or MD or anyone for that matter could have forced us to crawl towards the doomsday. It's not they who have failed us as much as we who have failed our own selves. We got complacent, too self-centered, too parochial and assumed that anything which does not concern us won't affect us. And see where we are."

"Shubhankar, stop this *gyaan* of yours. Let's go," Ashu got up.

"Ashu, you know what I am saying is right. But being the sales guy that you are, you will never accept it as you are in a habit of pleasing everyone but your own self."

Ashu stopped and turned towards him. "Shubhankar, let me ask you something, straight and simple. Now that he has been hired as the brand manager, what is it that you can do?" The confrontation was inevitable.

"I will do whatever is right. I will complain to the HR head, Zeenat, and on the mail, will mark RC, Lawrence, Buck and every single executive who should know about this. Boss, I have a family to take care of. This *Thakur* will go back to his *haveli* and make merry. But where would I go?"

Very unlike him, VVS called up his boss Sandy, to update him of the recent development.

***

"Dear Mr Singh,

Despite our constant reminders, it has been brought to our notice that you have not vacated Room no. 25, which you have been holding for more than three weeks now.

Owing to a clear mandate on cost cuts, the guest house won't be functional from this evening. It is advised that you remove all your belongings with immediate effect.

For the extended stay of 12 days at the guest house, kindly get an approval from your line manager on the prescribed form attached herewith and mail me a scanned copy of the same not later than tomorrow evening, failing which deductions will be made from your salary.

Andy Choo
HR Shared Resource
CommTech"

The ESN rang. It was Sandy. VVS knew that he would be upset.

"Are you a complete idiot?," he thundered. VVS did not respond, as he knew that it was his fault, to some extent. "Didn't I tell you to leave everything and concentrate on finding a house for yourself?"

"I am sorry," VVS mumbled.

"VVS, you need not be sorry about anything." Apologies always tend to work, and Sandy too mellowed his tone. "It was in your own interest. Now tell me with the guest house facility closing down, where will you go? Have you planned anything?" He sounded genuinely worried. It was confusing for VVS as he was still not over the humiliation of the RC episode.

Ever since college days, Sandy had always been a mystery to him. After getting under his wings, college life was like a dream party. Within his first week, he was ragging his batch mates and no one dared question his seniority. From his three-seater room, which was allotted to him like any other first-year student, he moved in with Sandy, in room no. 26B. With every passing day, he learnt a little more about him and it made him respect his 'God-like senior' even more. Every evening, it was not only students from SRCC, but also from the nearby colleges—Hansraj, St Stephen's, Ramjas and Hindu, came to room no. 26B to pay their respect to Sandy. Of course, with a bottle of rum or whisky. VVS wondered how he was so well connected and knew everyone whom one should know for a king-sized life.

The day began with a dose of nicotine, right there in the bed, to shake them out of their hangover. The next thing would be to call out Irfan, the boy who ran a small shack just outside the B block building. The entire hostel wing would echo with Sandy's voice ordering Irfan to serve him *nimboo-paani.* Unlike other hostlers, Sandy never went to the dining hall for breakfast, lunch or dinner. The reason was only one—conflict of timing. By the time he got up, which would be around 10 or 11 a m, it would be too late for breakfast. For lunch, which was served between noon to 2 p m, Sandy would be fighting his hangover with more nicotine and '*nimbu paani.*' For dinner, served between 7.30 and 9.30, Sandy would be busy drinking again. There were times when VVS would go to the mess and get bowls of mutton or chicken to compliment their sittings with Old Monk. Life was on a roll with nothing to worry about. During the weekly telephone calls from *Daata* and *Bai ji*, Sandy made it a point to speak with them, assuring them of VVS's well-being. For some odd reason, which VVS could not comprehend back then, *Bai ji* never liked Sandy.

Sandy never let VVS pay anywhere, at the booze shop, for cigarettes, at the canteen. VVS lived there for free, well almost, if one discounted the money which Sandy borrowed from him and never returned.

'Have you planned anything?," Sandy's voice shook him out of his thoughts.

"What? Sorry," VVS was lost.

"Dude, where are you gonna stay? Take that mail seriously. I have been copied along with Lawrence."

Damn! The mention of Lawrence's name made VVS sit up. Giving him a wrong impression was the last thing he wanted.

"Did Lawrence say anything?," VVS was getting nervous.

"Yes, he was very concerned and asked me to send you over to his place where you can sleep, eat and fart for as long as you like."

It took a while for VVS to get the sarcasm. Sandy laughed.

"Dude, people at his level have secys. And these secys are cold bitches who only forward mails from a certain level and designation to their bosses. CCs and BCCs never even reach them. So the other day, when you were petrified of that loser, what was his name?"

"Who?," VVS could not get the context.

"The guy who wants to play the whistleblower to your appointment," Sandy clarified.

"Shubhankar?"

"Yeah, Shubhankar. So when you told me that he has threatened you with sending mails to Lawrence, RC, Zeenat, Buck and to the entire world, I pitied him. Someone like RC, who is not even on a regional level, just on country level, gets around five hundred mails a day."

VVS's jaw dropped.

"Most of them CCs and BCCs are sent to the trash can immediately. The direct mails are scanned by his secy, Murthi. Any mail from anyone who is lower than the JCI 5 cadre gets trashed." VVS knew that CommTech had this grade system called JCI—Job Complexity Index. On the basis of the JCI, one was assigned a band. He was in JCI 3, which meant his job complexity index was lesser than the JCI 5 one, in which Sandy was.

"But don't you think that a few of the CCs could be important as even someone from a JCI 3 or JCI 2 band can have a valid viewpoint or a great idea?"

"Certainly! And for resolving, sharing and putting the same forward, he is supposed to go to his immediate senior, not rush directly to the CEO. Think of a situation where everyone is writing to everyone, with their grudges, suggestions, viewpoints. Won't there be a complete pandemonium, complete anarchy?," VVS could see Sandy's point. Sandy clarified further, "So when Shubhankar writes in to RC, Lawrence and Buck, firstly his mail would be trashed. On a very good day, if the charges are serious, for example, huge embezzlement of funds, sexual harassment, the respective secy would forward the mail to Shubhankar's line manager, who in this case is a guy named Mandy Dunabe, based out of Sydney. If Mandy Dunabe would find merit in the mail, he would send it to Feona Keely, who sits out of Hong Kong and heads the Services portfolio and is Shubhankar's big boss."

The complexity of the whole mail thing was inexplicable. Sandy continued with his explanation, "If Feona wants to pursue the case, she will write in to RC. Her mail will reach RC as it comes from a department head. However, the catch is that all the leaders, RC to Buck, Feona to Lawrence, understand the demands of managing an organization and the adjustments which are needed to maintain the equilibrium. Therefore, they will completely ignore the whole issue."

VVS felt so relieved. However, at the same time, he felt bad for Shubhankar. He remembered a time, when he used to be a replica of Shubhankar—honest, upright and fearless.

Sandy being a focused guy got back to the track. "You didn't answer me. Where are you going to stay?"

"I have no clue. Don't know why I can't find a place to stay."

"Ok note down an address."

"What for?"

"Please don't irritate me. I don't know if I have hired you or is it the other way round."

VVS was hurt again and Sandy knew it, yet again.

"And I am sorry. I did not mean it. It is just that I am little over worked. Hey come on dude, don't be a sissy and stop sulking over every little thing."

This time VVS did not make up by smiling. Though like a good junior he did write down the address, which was of a guest house, which belonged to Sandy's friend. Sandy assured VVS that he could stay there until he found a place. Probably, Sandy was trying to make up for his curtness.

***

Ding-dong.

He waited. It was almost seven.

Ding-dong.

No answer or any sign of movement inside the house. He went downstairs.

Ding-dong.

Silence.

It was almost 9 p m and any working woman should be home by now.

VVS scribbled a note, rolled it and stuck it between the circular loop of the big lock, on the iron door. As he looked around, pulling out his pack of Navy Cut, he could see two big suitcases, two bags, a laptop bag and a small suitcase surrounding him. For some reason, the moment he held the stick between his lips, he felt disgusted. He immediately crushed the stick and threw it down from the second floor. He needed to get back in shape and for that he needed to stop smoking.

***

"Ok smile, one, two and three." The camera clicked.

One more! Please hold your expressions, please smile a little more."

Click, click, click, the camera went again and again.

Daata was sitting on his high back, ancestral chair

with now-fading and cracked leather upholstery. He had taken extra effort in getting his *Jodhpuri jacket*; with golden *zari* work around the collar band, dry cleaned. To match the importance of the occasion, he had also put on his special gold and saffron *safa*. Attired in his favorite black hunter coat, khaki breeches and tan riding boots, *Dadosa* was standing to *Daata's* right. Being the youngest son, dressed in a smart blue bush coat and a polka dotted scarf, he was there, to *Daata's* left hand side.

The photo shoot for *Dadosa*'s upcoming, heritage hotel's website and brochure was over. "*Rawla* Akhepur will be the most sought-after heritage hotel in this part of Mewar," *Dadosa* was his exuberant self. "Here a *gora* can stay with a martial family, as their guest, go horse riding, visit the village and the fields and watch our dominion over others in all aspects of daily life. I bet the *goras* are going to lap it up."

He felt happy for *Dadosa*. After all, he deserved so much more from life. He felt good to see the family together, happy and united. *Dadosa* hugged him tight. His arms were strong and he could not breathe.

"Hey mister, get up. What are you doing here? Hello?"

He was running out of oxygen. He tried inhaling more air but couldn't.

"Are you alive, hello?" This time the words were followed by a nudge.

His eyes hurt as the July sun was right there, shining on his face. It took a while for his pupils to adjust to the real world, shifting from the surreal one. Within a fraction of a second, he was able to place himself correctly. Last evening he decided against going to the guest house suggested by Sandy. The only option left was the apartment, which he had rejected for having women as flat-mates. Out of options, he had decided to take a chance and see if it was still vacant. Due to lack of a place to keep his luggage, he got it with him. On finding the apartment locked, he had assumed that even if she were out partying, she would be back by midnight. He did not realize that the wait had turned into a nap—a very long and sound one.

"Aren't you the one who had come here looking for an apartment? The one with a long name?"

He nodded his head.

"But what are you doing here, at my door, so early? And is this your baggage?"

He nodded again.

"I hope you were not here all night, waiting for me, assuming that you can walk into my apartment any time you like?"

He nodded again.

"Gosh, you are impossible." She opened the iron mesh door first, using a long key and then the wooden door with a smaller key.

His second long look at her reaffirmed his first impression. She was beautiful by any standards—Udaipur or Delhi. 5'5" or 5'6", fair, long tresses, which looked well cared for, her long eyelashes, played the perfect shutters to the most beautiful pair of eyes he had seen. Eyes with a mystical aura around them, full of stories—some read, some unread, some told and some waiting to be told.

As she unlocked the door, VVS watched her rear. Ripe and full. It reminded him of Rajeshwari. Separated by miles and every other factor—socio and economic, both the women had something in common—Both were so ripe and full and both turned him on. He scoffed the size zero fad and watched her get inside the house. She was dressed in a khaki trousers and a sky blue *kurti*. Her tan bag was slung around her right shoulder. The door opened and she turned towards him.

"Look, I don't know what made you take this extreme step, of landing here with your luggage. But it surely indicates that you are in a mess. However, I won't be able to help you as we have already finalized an apartment mate. I am really sorry."

He just looked at her, too absorbed in her eyes to realize that he had no place even to take a shower.

"Hellooo, what are you thinking?"

He was blank, still lost in her.

"I know you had come here with hope. Would you like to have some tea?"

As he sat there, on the beige sofa with orange prints, waiting for her to get the tea, his eyes scanned the hall. It was a decent L-shaped hall. One portion of the 'L' was the sitting room, while the other, the dining area. The sitting area had a beige sofa set. The upholstery had turned to brown after all the years of neglect. The curtains hung limply, without adding to the décor. The glass-top side table was covered with stains of teacups, spilled curry and some wax. The dining area had a dark, glass top, dining table with four chairs. The table was placed close to the left wall, to save the precious carpet area and was loaded with books, newspapers, juice cans, some odd wrappers and what not. The glass shelf kept adjacent to it had some books and a TV sitting there. Not bad, he thought to himself. He wouldn't have felt out of place here.

She entered the hall, from a door adjacent to the dining table, holding two cups with Mickey and Mini mouse printed on them. He smiled. She reciprocated.

The tea was nice, light yet with strong flavors of basil, ginger and honey.

"Nice tea," he complimented her.

"Thanks," she accepted it gracefully.

"I am sorry for this," VVS pointed towards his luggage.

"No, that's perfectly fine by me. I know life in a metro could get stressful at times, especially if you come from a small town."

"And what makes you so sure that I come from a small town?," VVS enquired as he sipped on the comforting warmth.

"Well," she smiled naughtily. "Only a decent guy coming from a small town would have turned down the offer of staying with two single girls."

They both laughed, one due to her candid admission and the other due to the embarrassment.

On his way back to the office, with his entire luggage, which he had planned to dump in the mailroom, he was thinking about the girl. His mind kept replaying images of her big, beautiful eyes, her ripe rear, shiny tresses, her laughter, her kindness. He felt like a fool for not asking her name.

***

On the Plate

It was a day filled with anxiety and restlessness. In the humid and sticky July weather, surviving without a bath was a torture by itself. After reaching office early, rather very early, around 7 a m, in a WC cubicle of the office facilities, he did manage to change into a fresh pair of trousers and a shirt, brush his teeth and shave. But no amount of deodorant could replace the freshness of a nice cold shower. He was tempted to use the WC jet for a bath, but felt a little uncomfortable after considering the actual purpose of it.

Apart from the fact that he did not have a shower, his day was a normal one—a few rounds of coffee and cigarette break with a dozen pieces of Monaco and Good Day, some gossip about the top guys. During the first half of the day, he kept avoiding Sandy's call. He did not want to tell him that in spite of his instruction, he did not go to his friend's guest house. He knew that Sandy would be offended to learn that his orders were not followed, and more so, if he knew that his favor was turned down.

His mailbox had a couple of congratulatory mails, on his appointment as the brand manager. He felt a little embarrassed replying to them. What if they knew that he had no training, experience and exposure to brand management? What if they knew that his was just a case of disguised employment? Worse, what if they found out that he was the hidden flab, tucked smartly under the pleated waistband of the trouser? While he was sending out the 'thank you' notes, his inbox received yet another mail. It was from Sandy.

He got very uncomfortable for a moment. But he knew that he had to open it and also respond to it as now Sandy was his immediate superior—line manager in CommTech's parlance.

> " Know that you did not go to the guest house suggested by me. That's ok. Now you are a grown up man and don't need me or my help. Just want to tell you that there is a call with Lawrence at 2 sharp. Please log on to the bridge five minutes in advance, the logging details are provided below.
> **PS:** Congrats on your new appointment."

VVS got the sarcasm loud and clear. He wanted to call him instantly, but it was already 1.45 and there was hardly any time for settling personal scores. The wait on the bridge was a long one.

"Hi, welcome everyone."

Various ping sounds happened indicating that people who were waiting were allowed by Lawrence on his bridge. MCS was another tool that fascinated VVS. It was nothing but a soft-phone installed on the laptops of CommTech's employees. This meant that even while travelling, or from home or any other place, which had an access to the Internet, they could access the office desk phone—take calls and make calls. The interface of MCS was also an interesting one. It showed the number of people on a call and like any other messenger allowed the user to send messages, files, even videos. He knew if he would tell people back in Udaipur about MCS they would laugh at him, assuming he was trying to impress them.

Lawrence Kilam's voice sounded like a seasoned commentator's-cigar-abused vocal chords, perfect diction, throw and a great passion for speaking.

The MCS log list told VVS that there were sixteen people on the call.

"This call has a simple mandate," Lawrence went. "To introduce my new team member in India to you and then to discuss the Q4 agenda. So first things first, I welcome Virendra Vikram Singh on board, as a Brand Manager, Enterprise Division, India. Welcome on board Virendra and I am sure that with your experience you will be contributing a lot during these troubled times." It took about a minute to accept all the congratulatory messages from the fifteen other call participants, Sandy included.

"Virendra comes from web background and has got the expertise to leverage technology in increasing the reach and penetration of our messages. Also, his experience in running the backend and frontend for various B2B portals will be of immense use in extracting the best out of our system."

VVS was slightly confused, as he never knew if he had ever done whatever was being said. Suddenly a messenger box opened. It was from Sandy. He could see him typing something. "When Sandy makes your CV, see how good you look." The line ended with a wink, which confused VVS further. He was under the impression that Sandy would be offended and the tone of his mail pointed towards the same direction. But there he was, proving VVS wrong again.

"During his previous stint, with one of the leading web agencies of India, Virendra did use his comprehension of the web, to execute effective online campaigns for leading technology brands." Now, this was getting too much; VVS could not believe his ears. How blatantly had Sandy turned the six people, a small web shop into a leading web agency of India. What if they Googled? He got scared. The chat box was still open.

He typed, "What if they Google Web Link?"

"Lawrence already has," Sandy replied.

His guts churned, as he knew that Lawrence would have discovered the truth.

"Didn't he find out the truth?," VVS enquired.

"Are you a *Rajput?* I doubt it at times," Sandy hit back.

Lawrence was in no mood to stop. "He will be a part of Sandeep's team. So Virendra, I once again welcome you on board and I am sincerely looking forward to working with an adept professional. I am sure it will be a great exposure for all concerned."

"Say thank you, you idiot." The chat box flashed with Sandy's instruction.

"Why should I say thank you for something which is nothing but a lie?," VVS typed back.

"Idiot not me, on the call, to Lawrence," Sandy was infuriated.

VVS realized his mistake. "Er…thank you Lawrence for your kind words. I hope I live up to your expectations."

"Now moving on to the next part, the Q4 agenda."

"There would be a mute button on your headset, switch it on," Sandy's instruction popped on the messenger and VVS complied.

"How come being a *Rajput* you are always shit scared of everything and everyone. Aren't you guys supposed to be the epitome of valor and courage?"

"Yes we are, it is just that I can't lie," VVS typed in.

"And who told you that I lied?," the chat continued.

"Didn't you tell everyone that Web Link is one of the leading agencies of India and that I have worked on leading technology brands?"

"Open the site of Web Link right away. Open it," Sandy challenged.

He typed the url www.weblink.com

As the site loaded, he shifted his focus to what Lawrence was saying. "Q3 was good in terms of ROI. Allan did some smart work in the ASEAN region. Allan, would you like to share what you did?"

"Have you opened the page?," Sandy pinged him again.

"Yes." The page loaded and VVS could see the line "India's leading web communication agency" right there on the home page.

"Sorry," he apologized.

"And now about the leading technology clients, under the client link, if you bother to have a look, you will find names like Cisco, HP and Microsoft," Sandy clarified.

"But we did just some micro-site for the distributors in Jaipur," he bleated.

"Did I tell Lawrence the scope of work? No! I just wrote on your CV that you have worked on Cisco, HP, Microsoft etc. Neither did he ask me, nor did I tell him,"

Sandy's explanation flashed in the messenger box.

"I am sorry sir," VVS typed, though he hated doing so.

"Lol, you need not be. Just get one thing clear in your mind; I am your friend not a foe."

Allan was still describing how he participated in the CIO 100 exhibition and how deftly he arranged a CIO round table around the 'Green IT' topic to propound CommTech's green initiative. VVS felt terribly out of place. After Sandy told him that CIO meant 'Chief Information Officer' and how the CIOs were the key decision makers in all technology-related purchase, to VVS, whatever Allan was describing; as the marketing head of the ASEAN region sounded so elementary.

His phone vibrated again. It was from the same number. Instinctively he knew that it would be some property dealer, as no one else would call him so frantically. Since he was on mute mode, he decided to answer the call. However, before he could take, the caller hung up. As he kept the phone on the table, it vibrated again. This time it was a shorter vibrating tone, the one he had set for messages. Again the same number. He opened the SMS and could not believe his luck.

> *"apartmnt mate who ws sppsd to shft in, refused. Thot wud let u knw. Bt seems u r nt intrstd." – Ambica*

"Shree Naathji, please please, please. I want this

house. One more day without a shower and I will be stinking like a pig. I don't want to take any more obligations from Sandy sir. Poor thing, he has already done enough for me." VVS dialed the number while muttering his prayer. "Pick it up, please," he prayed desperately. No one answered the call.

He dialed again...no one answered.

Again...same response.

Again...same response.

Maybe she just got into a meeting, he consoled himself.

His phone vibrated again. He grabbed it without wasting even a single second as he assumed that it would be Ambica, returning his call.

"Guess who?" It was a male voice. VVS was not in a mood to talk to anyone but her, as she was the only one who had the key to his temporary happiness.

"Come on, take a guess." The voice insisted. It sounded familiar but amidst all the mental chaos, he found it hard to place.

"Well, for sure you are not Shah Rukh Khan."

"How right," the voice chuckled.

"Emmm... well I am sorry. Can we get over with this 'guess who' game?" He said with a bit of irritability in his voice.

"What's wrong with you *bana*. I am Harsh from Udaipur."

Shree Naathji not now, please, he pleaded. Harsh *bana* was the last person he wanted to talk to right now. But then apart from granting his each and every wish, Shree Naathji also had other work. No wonder, this time, his wish was turned down.

"What a surprise. How are you?" He tried his best to sound happy but had no clue how far he succeeded.

"You are a strange man *bana*. You left Udaipur without even telling me and then changed your number too. I am sure there was nothing wrong between us, which should make you act in this strange way." Harsh's grudge was genuine.

Harsh owned one of the largest travel agencies in Udaipur, Welcome Travels, and was one of the *banas* with whom VVS used to drink. A typical *bana*, he was too fond of his past and tried his best to stick to whatever leftover he had with him. His house, though a modern one, had all the paraphernalia of a falsely glamorized feudal system. The huge iron-gate had a coat of arms with a brass sun, two flags and spears on each side. The living room resembled a mini museum. With *Kota stone* tiles on the wall, the right side had a huge sun made up of some fifty-odd guns, arranged in a circular pattern. The other wall sported three hunting trophies—the head of a reindeer with huge horns, wild buffalo and an innocent-faced deer. Just below the trophies, a stuffed panther balanced itself precariously on a wooden trunk.

The room had heavy and vintage-style furniture with intricate carving. Generous splash of golden color, ornate curves and heavy silk dotted the room. Near the stairs, which led to the dining area, a man-sized Roman armor stood, holding an English-looking Claymore sword. How did the two fit, aesthetically or historically, was something no one dared to question. Maybe the online auction store, which sold them as a pair, would have the answer. A chariot wheel as the base of the centre table, barrel of cannons as lamp holders, the place reeked of the incurable '*bana*' syndrome.

"*Hukum*, it is nothing like that. It so happened that I had to leave immediately. In fact, I was planning to call you."

"*Bana*, at least be honest. How would you have called me? You have not even saved my number."

"*Hukum*, it is not so. This is a new phone, a Blackberry. Your number is on the old Nokia one. I was planning to sit one day and transfer all the Udaipur numbers. It's just that I could not find the time. Life has been hectic."

Harsh laughed, like an evil medieval ruler. "Good that you have a Blackberry. Someone had gifted me one long back, but I could never get used to the damn thing. I prefer my simple Nokia; press to talk, press to disconnect."

VVS was well acquainted with the one-upmanship genes of the *banas*. He knew that Harsh would never let him prove that he was ahead of him in any way—phone model included.

"Listen, what are you doing right now?" Harsh enquired.

In his wildest dream, a *bana* could never tell another that he was desperately waiting for a woman to call him so that he could figure out the exact location of his next shower stall.

"Well! Nothing much. You are asking as if you are going to invite me over for *laal maans* and *daroo*," VVS laughed.

"Yes, I am. That's what my forefathers have been doing. I have to continue the tradition. Room No 324, Hotel Claridges, Delhi. Be there. And I will not take no for an answer."

***

The cab ride from Gurgaon to Hotel Claridges was a long one. At peak hour, the traffic was maddening. As the radio taxi snaked through the traffic, VVS cursed himself for getting back in the *bana* cesspool again. But considering the present situation, he knew that it was the only way to get bed-breakfast-shower for a day or two. Knowing Harsh, he was sure that he would insist on spending a day or two with him, as he was fond of people around him. In Udaipur it was easy, but in Delhi, getting even one soul to listen to his stories was difficult. So smartly, before leaving to see him, he had packed another set of fresh clothes from his luggage, which was stashed away in the mailroom. As hope is a potent source of life, therefore, just a little of it had put the smile back on VVS's face and a song on his lips.

The Claridges had managed to retain its old-world charm and grace. The virginal white building stood there gracefully. The huge spiral staircase took VVS to the third floor. Unlike most of the five-star hotels, this one had no carpeting in its already warm, inviting and broad corridor.

Ding-dong.

The door was answered by Harsh. A man in his mid-forties, he looked like a Bollywood *Thakur*. With thick twirled moustache, he was wearing a black silk shirt, a red cravat, khaki breeches and tan brogues. A golden Rolex sat on his hairy wrist, and a few heavy gold rings on his spatula shaped thick fingers. Regular and heavy drinking had gifted him a permanent potbelly and a puffed face. His fast receding hairline made him look a lot older than his actual years. A warm hug and a few drinks later, with a loosened tongue and a slight slur, the old-time camaraderie was back.

"*Bana*, I miss your company. No one in the entire city of Udaipur can match your intellect and IQ," Harsh was getting sentimental.

"*Hukum*, this brother of yours is just a phone call away. The truth is that I was missing Udaipur too. These big cities are not the place for guys like us. We are too naïve, too straight and honest."

"You are right brother. We have been passed on the genetic code of loyalty, sacrifice and courage. And none of these things cut any ice in today's world, not even amongst *banas*."

"*Hukum*, all well? Why are you sounding dejected? We all respect you." VVS was genuinely concerned at the statement of acceptance coming from Harsh. Harsh Singh Ranawat *aka* Harsh *bana* was the epitome of what Rajputana had been—all the good things, plus pride and ego.

Harsh laughed and downed his drink in one gulp.

"You know *bana*, I claim that my lineage can be traced to *Suryavansh*. My *Daata*, Late Hukum RanVijay Singh Ranawat, the great *Suryavanshi*, *thikana* Dadraula, had a prostrate issue. He could not control his pee and wore diaper under his breeches. Can you believe, the great descendant of *Suryavansh* wearing diaper?" His voice trembled, "and I can never say or share this in Udaipur as I know, if any of the *banas* even get a whiff of this, like a pack of dogs, they will tear into my family reputation. Pulling me down will give them so much pleasure. But you are my brother. I love you. I really do." Liquor was the undisputed lubricant of the moment.

"*Hukum*, I still look up to you."

"Fuck you *bana*. Please don't. I am a loser. I was so happy that you left Udaipur and took a wise step to make your life worthwhile. Or else, you would have… either become a tourist guide, living off the commission from the handicraft stores, or got into the travel trade like me. Though every evening I miss your company, but I am so glad that you could leave that shit hole."

"*Hukum*, I am so indebted to you for your support. I really mean it. I really wish I could do anything for you, anything at all."

"Come on, I know that you can, but you are my younger brother. I can never ask you for a favor. Can I?," Harsh had a question in his eyes.

"*Hukum,* you can. It will only make your younger brother feel good." VVS was down by eight drinks.

"Ok, just to please my younger brother."

VVS, who was all set to sip his ninth one, stopped midway. He knew that his generous statement was going to cost him dearly. How much was the question.

"You know our industry, the travel industry, is a cut-throat business. The margins are wafer thin and the new players, who are hungry for business to keep afloat, are further eating into it."

VVS now knew that this was not a free drinks session and did a bottoms-up. Also, he lit a cigarette.

"The travel and tour business thrives mainly on

foreign group travel. Travel agents like us get good deals from the local hotels and then depending on the group, we decide to pass on a fixed percentage to them. So if a hotel's card rate is five thousand, we get it for twenty-five hundred; depending on our terms. If the group is large, we sell the same room for thirty-five and if it is small, for forty-five. In either case, the group is getting a better deal than dealing with the hotel directly. The hotel is happy, as we buy in bulk; the tourist is happy as he is getting cheaper rates; and so are we."

VVS knew that the monologue would be long and, therefore, he poured himself another one of the single malt that started it all.

"Have you heard of Om Travels and Mewar Travels?"

VVS nodded.

"Then, I am sure that you would also know that both of them are being run by two *Baniya* brothers, Rajan and Deepak."

VVS nodded again. He was well aware that despite being *Baniyas*—hailing from trader community—they tried their best to emulate the local *banas* by wearing bush coats, scarves and ear studs. The in-charge of Ranibagh police station, who was known to him, had told that they had applied for a gun license.

"For some reasons, during the last tourist season, I lost every big group to either one of them. I assumed that their rates would be better. This season, one of my agents called me and accused me of sending him some obnoxious rates, which I had never sent. When I requested him, he forwarded me the mail. To my surprise, though the mail was sent from my mailbox, I had never sent it. I did not know how it could have happened. Then it hit me that maybe my account was being hacked. I had no proof as to who could be behind this. Though, going by Om and Mewar Travels' last year's windfall income, it was simple to figure out."

Even nine drinks down, it was simple for VVS to anticipate the favor which was about to be sought.

"*Hukum*, you want me to hack their account?"

"Well, not exactly, but I want to get back at them," Harsh tried his best at being an honest netizen.

Liquor and emotional speeches always work, right from elections to hacking.

***

Even Dead Cats Bounce

The nice cold shower gave VVS a new life. Fresh set of clothes, Harsh's expensive perfume, polished shoes and after a hearty buffet breakfast of boiled eggs, milk, muesli, toast, butter and some sausage, he was eager to face the day. Today was an important day, his first major call as Brand Manager. He had been preparing for this call for the last three days.

Since morning, Harsh had been after his life to hack the account as soon as possible. Little did he know that VVS was just a web designer, who knew a little bit of programming and next to nothing about hacking. In addition, Harsh had no clue that hacking into something as robust as a Gmail or a Hotmail account was next to impossible. But for reasons beyond all this, Harsh knew that if VVS had said a 'yes' he would do it.

On his way back to office, VVS was wondering about the strange ways of life. Till last evening he had no place to stay and then Shree Naathji was kind enough to bless him with a five-star suite, best of single malt, some exotic prawn curry, not to forget a nice shower and hearty breakfast. In return, hacking a couple of inboxes, which belonged to unscrupulous *Baniyas* was no sin.

Ever since he had moved into the brand management role, there was a huge influx of work. Well, yes, at least that's what ninety per cent of CommTech referred to as work—playing call-call. It was Manish who educated VVS that 'call-call' was a syndrome, which had bitten the entire IT industry. For some reason, maybe to justify the cost of setting up the mammoth communication infrastructure, the organizational structure across the IT spectrum was weird, to say the least. Manish explained that he was responsible to RC, as his salary came from India's P&L, but he was accountable to some jerk sitting out of Sydney, whom he had not even seen. Now with the functional head sitting out of Sydney, there was a huge need to communicate with him. Having his entire team spread over the geography, further complicated the issue. This warranted calls, to communicate between the teams, taking stock of the situation, trouble shooting and more.

VVS could never understand why the IT industry followed such complex reporting. He could also not figure out how someone like a Lawrence Kilam, who would not be able to differentiate between Gurgaon and Goregaon, could comment on the marketing strategy made for such a diverse geographic region. No wonder, his line managers, everyone of them, were taking him for a ride.

VVS put on his headset and sat on the executive chair for a marathon call with Lawrence and his team. They were supposed to discuss the brand campaign for a new range of switches—the PRS series.

"Good morning everybody!" Lawrence was as chirpy as ever.

After the customary good mornings, they quickly moved to the main agenda.

"I am pleased to share a heartening piece of news. We have been asked to launch a new series of switches, the PRS 5600. Before we proceed, I would appreciate your views on the same."

VVS had his mind in an overdrive, but then, something pulled him back—maybe lack of confidence or just plain shyness. He was in the habit of not speaking up until asked in person. Probably, Lawrence read his mind.

"Virendra, I am sure being the youngest member on my team, your ideas would be refreshingly different from what we have heard in the past. What do you think of this launch?"

Immediately, a chat box popped up on his screen. It was Sandy.

"If you don't have any ideas, tell him the same," the safe suggestion.

"What if I have some?" An aggressive query.

"Then go ahead." The 'go at your risk' nod.

"Well sir, I would beg to think a little differently."

"That's a new one. And till the time the Queen decides to knight me, I could manage without a sir," Lawrence quipped.

Everyone laughed and VVS was embarrassed.

"So go on young man, let your new ideas show us some light," he coaxed him.

The message box blinked again.

"Be careful of what you speak. Honesty is not always the best policy" was the piece of advice.

But it was too late. VVS was already elaborating his point of view.

"Sir, I mean Lawrence, to me it sounds like the wrong timing. If the company has gone bust…."

"How can we use such terms even on internal calls?" Allan reacted vehemently. "We have only filed for bankruptcy protection. And this is the message which we intend to broadcast to the external audience too. At the CIO table, I had a tough time convincing the CIOs, but I managed."

Sandy stepped in to save VVS. "Allan, please don't get worked up. At least let us hear Virendra first. We can save the semantics for the latter part of the discussion."

"Sandeep is right. Virendra, please continue," Lawrence sounded unperturbed.

"Well, when I got the request for the call, I did try to

do a little research on the product. Being a new product, not much was available on the website. However, going purely by its technical specification, which I managed to get from our Product Marketing team, it seems that PRS 5600 is a set of premium, high-performance, highly-efficient, stackable switches. It will have a comprehensive layer 3 routing, advanced security and unified communications features. As a flexible, multi-role platform, it will be suitable for wring closet, data center aggregation and network core applications. A key aspect of this range will be that these models will be 100 per cent stack-compatible with the original PRS 4000 series products. Any combination of PRS 4000 series units—4200 or 4600 models—can be stacked up to eight units high, or to a maximum of 400 ports," VVS continued, "the PRS series will deliver highly scalable and flexible power overethernet, with high-density and ultra-density models available to simplify deployment in high-intensity convergence centric network. And its closest competitor would be the HS series switch from Sailnet."

There was silence. No one spoke as no one knew anything about the product, which they all wanted to launch.

"Mr Virendra, could you please stop reading out the tech specs. What points are you trying to make?" Allan again wanted to prove his superiority.

"Well, whatever I have mentioned about the PRS

series makes it a mid-cycle product, with its service requirement for up to five years."

"So?" Allan was being his obstinate self.

"Why would any enterprise buy this from us when they are not even sure of our existence?" VVS proved his point.

"But with an aggressive campaign, some CIO roundtables and some plugged PR, we can surely deliver the numbers." Allan suggested a way out.

"Well young man, what do you have to say?," Lawrence challenged VVS.

"Well, my point is simple. One of the largest American auto brands, GM, faced the same situation. The end buyer did not get into the legality of the term, whether it implied going bust or bankruptcy protection alone, and just stopped buying GM cars altogether. No wonder, they had to shut down a couple of plants."

"But that was a B2C scenario." By this time, Allan was crying blue murder.

"Allan, I am a very junior person. I think that I do not deserve to be a part of this call, which has senior and seasoned marketing brains like you. But with all due respect to everyone, buyers are buyers. We look at customers from a Business to Business or Business to Consumer, what we term as B2B or B2C perspective. Tell me honestly, when you go to buy at a supermarket do you buy thinking that you are a B2C customer? When you buy a printer or a fax or even a laptop for your office, does it occur to you even for a moment that now you are a B2B buyer? No! The buying consideration sets are the same—brand, value, offer, service and value for money. Believe me, and please correct me if I am wrong, not a single buyer categorizes himself as B2B buyer or a B2C. He buys as a buyer and wants to be treated like one— with honesty, dignity and care. Period! Therefore, I think his buying rational will be the same, during buying a new switch from CommTech."

Again, there was a silence.

"So Virendra, if buyers won't buy our switches, what are we here for? Don't you think we all should just put in our papers or get axed?" Lawrence posed a tricky one.

"Well…," VVS had no explanation.

The message box glowed again.

"Didn't I tell you to keep shut?" It was Sandy.

Then, it was as if Shree Naathji showered VVS with his healing and guiding white light and he knew that he had the perfect answer to Lawrence's 'nail in the coffin' question.

"I said that new buyers might not buy us but never said the same about the existing ones."

"For God's sake, please stop driving us around in circles," Allan was getting irritated.

"Allan, may I request your attention please," Lawrence's tone was soft yet firm.

"Virendra, I know what you have in mind, but could you elaborate on this." Lawrence gave the permission to proceed.

"I mean, let us do a campaign, but not for a new audience. We do it for our existing one. They are already using our switches and have an AMC tie-up in place. So, irrespective of CommTech going bust or not, they will be serviced, as a large part of their technology infrastructure is riding on our technology. So why don't we give them an upgrade? They will be too happy to get a new product, the latest in its class, and we will be happy to achieve our targets. What do you say Allan?"

"Sandeep, I like your knack for identifying sharp people. Keep it up," was Lawrence's parting remark.

***

On Boarding

"*Arre*, even if I was in a meeting, you could have SMSed me that you were still keen," Ambica smiled at him as she opened the wooden door of her second-floor apartment.

"Welcome to your new apartment," she swung the door and stepped aside, to let him enter the hall.

VVS placed his luggage on the floor and looked around. Seeing a house had never made him so happy. Finally, he had a house to himself. Thank you Shree Naathji, thanks a ton. He did his ritual of folding hands and closing his eyes.

"Oh so are you the religious types?," she remarked.

He was a little embarrassed, as he never expected her to catch him doing his ritual.

"Well, not really."

"And why are you ashamed of being religious? Does it hurt your macho image?"

Her blunt statement embarrassed him further.

"Come, I will show you the apartment."

The guided tour started from the hall, which looked like a typical male bachelor's apartment. On to the right hand side was the kitchen, which was in a mess. Unwashed dishes, packets, wrappers, an uneaten pizza slice in a trademark blue and white carton, a couple of beer cans. "Well, sorry about that. Actually the maid is on leave," she apologized. On to the left, there were two doors.

"This room belongs to me and this one is Chaitali's," she smiled. "Chaitali is a journalist and I am with a PR agency."

Interesting apartment mates, he thought. "You are with Manish at CommTech, right?"

"Yes."

"You don't look like a geek. I mean…," she laughed. VVS noticed that her laughter had a bell-like sound, soothing and almost child-like.

"I am on the brand management side," he smiled. For the first time he noticed that 'brand management' definitely sounded better than announcing his arrival as 'Senior Web Designer'. She opened the door at the end of the small passage, barely four or five steps from the door to her room. It was a twelve-by-twelve room, completely square. The first thing VVS noticed was the fuchsia pink on the walls. Well, he knew he could not do much about it.

"Your room," she announced. He smiled. The front wall had a white-colored wall-to-wall wardrobe. There was a double bed, which looked sturdy and was placed opposite the wardrobe. Towards the wall, which was on the right hand side of the bed, there was a functional writing table. An LG air-conditioner was mounted to the left side of the bed. Adjacent to the writing table, there was a white-colored door, which he assumed would lead to the washroom. As he stepped in, he noticed that it was clean, with a clearly demarcated wet and dry area. It also had a huge window, which let in enough light. Not bad, he thought.

"The rent will be eight thousand. Electricity will be separate and divided equally. We have a house cleaner for dusting, cleaning and cooking. One thousand per head. Groceries cost around three-four thousand a month, which gets divided equally."

Damn cheap, VVS calculated. For twelve thousand, he would get home-cooked food, a room and not to forget two women as apartment mates, out of which one was good looking too. Thank you Shree Naathji.

The latter part of the day was spent unpacking and arranging the room. Within three hours, he had his room in order. Clothes were in the wardrobe, toiletries and towels in the washroom, shoes in the shoe rack. He thought of placing the framed picture of Shree Naathji on the writing table, but then, for some reason he kept it in the wardrobe. Ambica was kind enough to make some tea for him.

He was supposed to go and meet Harsh and hack the mail IDs. He dearly wanted to be at home, sleep a little; maybe spend some time getting to know Ambica better. Something pulled him towards her, maybe his libido. It had been quite some time since he got a chance to get closer to the opposite sex. While he was thinking all this, his phone vibrated. It was Rajeshwari. Amidst all the hype and commotion, he had completely forgotten that he was a married man.

"I knew that you just wanted to go to Gurgaon to get away from me." The volley of complaints started.

"Raj, you know you are not being fair." For known reason, he did not want Ambica to hear the conversation as he wanted to keep his marital status under wraps, at least for now. "Where are you?" The favorite question of every wife was fired at him.

"What do you mean? It is Sunday and I am at the guest house."

"I don't know, something tells me that things are not right. Who is there with you?" The second question was not far behind. "I am alone." It took him some courage and effort to utter the words. "Who do you think will be here with me at the guest house?" He sounded defensive.

"Why don't you look for a house? I want to come there and stay with you. I can't handle your parents any more. Their taunts are getting worse. By the way, *Dadosa* is going to Delhi. He will come to meet you."

"*Arre*, why would he take all the pain? There is no need. I am perfectly fine here." VVS knew that if his elder brother came, he would insist on seeing his guest house, or the place where he was staying, and there was no way he could get him here.

"I am telling you what I was told. The rest is between you and him."

"Can I ask you something?" Rajeshwari quipped.

His heart pounded, as he knew that something unexpected was coming his way.

"Sure."

"Hope you are not asking 'how was it' there too?"

"You know Raj, you are just an over protective woman and a nagging wife. Don't know why I got married to you in the first place."

"I know you are doing it there. Aren't you?" The sobs started.

During the next few minutes, between tears, forced smiles, explanations and vows of temporary celibacy, VVS almost forgot that on her way to the kitchen, his angry and muted whispers had made Ambica decipher what he was hiding away—his marital status.

***

"*Hukum*, I have hacked the accounts and downloaded the emails. You can have a look and see if they are up to something." Using the hotel Internet, he did what was required. Hacking the accounts! He used the simplest trick of logging on with the wrong password and then requesting for a change of password. When the answer to the secret question was asked, guessing was easy.

Harsh hugged him. "I knew that I could trust you. Thank you brother. Thanks a ton."

Harsh offered him a cigarette, a Marlboro.

"Thank you *hukum*, but I smoke Navy Cut."

Harsh smiled. "Navy Cut was for the Udaipur boy. This brand suits the corporate guy more." He bent down and pulled two cartons of Marlboro from the bottom shelf of the center table. "I got this for you," he handed over the cartons fondly to VVS.

"*Hukum*, you are being formal." VVS felt shy accepting them, as he knew that Harsh was trying to pay for his small help.

"Shut up and take it." He chided him affectionately and walked towards the side table, which was beside the huge bed. He opened the carved drawer, pulled out a small handmade paper bag, and handed it over to him.

"What is this?" VVS was surprised.

"See for yourself," Harsh smiled.

VVS pulled out the contents of the envelope. His eyes lit up and then flickered with embarrassment. It was a beautiful, transparent bottle of Aqua by CK. Flummoxed, he looked at Harsh. Harsh was still holding the smile on his face as he knew the reaction that was coming. "It's for you."

"*Hukum*, but…?," he protested meekly.

"Yesterday when you had come over, I noticed that you really liked my perfume. I was at Khan Market, killing time, saw this one and bought it for you. Now calm down, wear it and pour me a drink."

VVS mumbled a sheepish 'thank you'.

He handed over the laptop to Harsh. "I've saved all the incoming and outgoing mails on the desktop, in a folder named 'mails'. You can see if there is anything that would interest you."

Harsh put on his specs. "I've got a bottle of Glenlivit stashed somewhere there." He pointed towards the side drawer again.

With drinks, the gossip around the dirty world of travel and tours, Udaipur and the unscrupulous *Baniya* brothers got juicier. When VVS enquired about the content of the hacked emails, he told him that his doubts were not misplaced and the emails had some proof that both the travel companies were poaching his clients.

"*Bana*, tell me something, how did you do this?, Harsh looked at him with admiration. "You are a genius."

"*Hukum* it requires just some common sense, nothing else."

"You are being modest. I spoke with Bharat Jaiswal

regarding the same job and he told me that even someone like him, an IT expert, could not hack into a Gmail or Yahoo. But look here, you did it."

At the mention of Bharat's name, VVS was shocked. He placed his drink on the thick glass top table. He was frightened, since he had a premonition of trouble.

"*Hukum*, does Bharat know of your intention to hack into these accounts?," his voice trembled.

"Yeah, I told him that I wanted to take them out," Harsh was his boisterous self.

"*Hukum*, the thumb rule of hacking or any other guerrilla warfare is the surprise element—catching your enemy off-guard. What makes you think that Bharat would not have told them?"

"Why would he?" Harsh was adamant.

"Because Bharat is the only IT expert in Udaipur. When Jain received kidnapping threats over email, Bharat was summoned to trace the mail trail; when the police wanted to investigate the money trial in the famous Shakir Banno case, he was called; when Central Bank's website was hacked, he was the man who plugged the loopholes. IT threat and solving cyber crime is his bread and butter. And to ensure the same, he would go to any extent."

"What do you mean?"

"Like going to your competition and telling them that so and so is planning to hack their account."

"VVS, you are sounding like a chicken and that too

a confused one. What would he gain out of this?" Harsh poured himself another one, a large one.

"Firstly, he would get a tip for the advance warning. Secondly, he could get an offer to set a trap and implicate you."

"But what would Bharat gain?" Harsh was getting irritated.

"Directly he won't, but your competition would. With you involved in a police case, they will walk away with all your clients. Are you getting me?" VVS was getting angry and frustrated.

"Are you threatening Harsh…."

"*Hukum*, please don't give me this. Please, not now." VVS was upset beyond words.

"VVS, how dare you speak to me like this?" Either it was the scotch or his false pride or his idiocy, but something provoked him in a big way.

"*Hukum*, trust me, if you have told Bharat about this plan, he would have set a trap for you. And when the cops come knocking at your door, you will have a tough time explaining your lineage to the Sun God."

Harsh laughed loudly. Like the evil, medieval Baron, straight out of a blockbuster. VVS was confused as he had no clue how a man could laugh in such a situation.

"Brother, firstly you are overreacting, secondly even if you are right, I will strangle that Bharat with my own hands and thirdly…." Suddenly his face assumed a comic expression as he shrugged his shoulders and whistled a tune. VVS could feel a chill descend on him and a lump build in his throat. Harsh lifted his weight from the plush upholstered chair and leaned towards VVS. "...it was not me but you who hacked the account."

His sinister laughter kept on ringing in VVS's ears, evoking a sense of fear, as he walked down towards Khan Market. He felt like a lamb—fed and taken care of, before being slaughtered. He bought a bottle of Old Monk, hailed an auto rickshaw, and asked the man to take him to the AIIMS, from where he wanted to get on to the much talked about Metro.

***

Up, Close and Personal

It was Tuesday afternoon. It had rained all morning. Heavy and dark clouds threatened to drown the city. VVS was fine tuning a PPT sent by Lawrence. Ever since the PRS call, Lawrence had become a big admirer of his out-of-the box and practical thinking. This scared VVS as he knew he had no clue about brand management or marketing and only relied on commo sense. Whatever he spoke or wrote was touted by Lawrence as a great piece of strategy or insight, much to the annoyance of Allan. Lawrence had entrusted VVS with the responsibility of planning the entire PRS campaign.

He also instructed him to report in to him directly. VVS was afraid that it would not go down well with Sandy's radar mechanism—of monitoring and controlling thoughts, action, promotion, work and even life. Contrary to his apprehension, Sandy was more than happy to see him shine.

Now, VVS had only two reasons to live—living

up to Lawrence's expectation and living with his new-found fantasy, Ambica. To him, Ambica was every man's dream and desire rolled into one. Fair, tall, dark brown eyes, full lips, a taut frame with just the extra pounds on the desired spots. She had the looks to pierce any man's armor and VVS was no exception. She worked for a multinational PR agency but was nothing short of a fashion diva. *Chanel, Prada, Gucci, Nini Ricci* were her most favored brands. She drove a black Scorpio—the beast of an SUV suited the gem of a beauty. Apart from all this, she had something else, which few women could boast of—a simple heart and a compassionate approach towards everything and everyone. The purity of her soul reflected in her voice—almost temple-bell like, soothing and confidence evoking.

Ever since his first meeting, VVS was drawn to her. Now, as her apartment mate, he tried spending more and more time with her. Helping her with the morning tea, grocery shopping, he would tag along everywhere. For VVS, her company had three benefits. One, he would get up on time, rather before time and go out for a jog; secondly, he would eat a healthy breakfast—milk, porridge, fruits and eggs as she had the same and most importantly, his cigarette and booze consumption reduced considerably as he never smoked inside the house nor did he invite Old Monk over.

She seemed to be fond of him too and took him to

events which her company sponsored or where her clients participated. Fashion shows, product launches, etc. VVS was good company, as he was full of stories; incidences from his college and hostel life, stories of the valour and courage of his ancestors, interesting cases of the crazy *banas* and more. To her, all this was a figment of his imagination, as she could never imagine such plots actually taking place anywhere on the face of this earth.

The apartment was shared by another girl, Chaitali. She was a petite, fair girl, 5'2" or 3", pretty and dainty, with her hair always tied back. Her kohl-lined eyes and a small *bindi* on her forehead gave her a very distinct and arty look. Also, she sported a silver nose ring. VVS thought it made her look very attractive. A tight shirt paired with blue *Levis'* and *Lotto* sneakers was her all-time favorite attire. Hailing from Jharkhand, she was a journalist with a leading news channel. As she handled the political beat, she was well-connected—from cabinet ministers to the local SHO. She drove a red Alto. Because of the exacting nature of her job, she would hardly be home. Megadeath, Judas Priest, Iron Maiden and loads of other metal bands creating a pandemonium in her room would be the only proof of her being home. Ambica had told him that Chaitali's father was a minister in the Jharkhand government. But she gave up everything to find her own identity.

***

The phone kept on the dashboard vibrated. VVS picked it up and saw the number. Ambica, who was driving, watched him from the corner of her eyes. Casually, he kept the phone in the cubbyhole of the Scorpio, which was meant for coffee sipper or glass.

Sunday traffic was manageable. They were going to the nearby mall to shop for groceries. Back in Udaipur, VVS hated this but here, with Ambica, he looked excitedly forward to this part of the weekly chore.

The phone vibrated again. VVS picked it up from the cubbyhole and disconnected it. Ambica just moved her eyes and looked at his face. This time, he did not put the phone down and held it in his hand.

She steered left, towards the basement parking entry and the phone vibrated again.

"Veer, why are you avoiding your wife? Answer her call," her tone was stern. His face blanched.

"Come on Veer, I know you are married right from the day one. Now answer her call." He cursed himself for not being extra careful. Now, with no other choice, he did as he was told.

"Why have you been avoiding my calls? If you have found someone there, at least tell me. I know you well. You can't stay without asking 'how was it' for long!" VVS's ears turned red, as he was sure that Ambica would have heard the conversation, if not in totality, surely in bits and pieces.

Rajeshwari's outburst was justified. For the past few days, he had been avoiding her calls. But he could not help it as whenever she called, for some reason or the other, he was with Ambica.

"I am in the middle of something. Can I call you back?" He used his standard corporate excuse, as he needed time to recollect his senses, analyze the situation, the extent of damage and then take the next step. While he spoke, Ambica rolled down her window at the parking ticket booth and handed the booth guy a five hundred note.

"Madam, please see if you can give me the exact change," the booth guy hollered.

VVS knew that Rajeshwari would have heard the booth guy's voice and he was bang on.

"I can see that you are trying to get into some madam right now. Best of luck." He was too shocked to react and the call was disconnected.

"What happened? All well?," Ambica enquired, as she rolled up the window and guided the Scorpio into the basement parking.

"Yes, nothing to worry about" was the only thing which he could mutter. While pushing the trolley around the huge departmental store, picking up knick-knacks—butter, eggs, sauce, fresh vegetables, cold cuts, his mind was trying to reconstruct the whole scene, trying to recall the exact words of Rajeshwari, the background sounds, just about everything. He wanted to use the existing data in phrasing his exact response. Was he afraid that Rajeshwari knew that he was with a woman? Well, both yes and no.

He did not know why he should be afraid of anyone, Rajeshwari included, if he liked someone else! Rajeshwari was his wife, but there was nothing common between them—dreams, aspirations, likes, hobbies, just about anything. They both were married, as their parents wanted them to get married. The whole concept of getting into a marriage and being forced by the society to live with each other until eternity seemed so impractical. He always asked himself if a man could never dream of driving the same car, wearing the same pair of shoes or jeans, eating the same food, then how and why he was supposed to live and mount the same woman. Why wasn't he allowed to seek a new partner? Most of his friends in Udaipur were married and all of them cursed the man-made institution of marriage and wished there was a way out. Simultaneously, most of them also sought pleasure outside their marriage and had no guilt or qualms about the same. After all, men were not supposed to be monogamous creatures. Nature wanted them to spread their seed everywhere. Yes, he wanted it too and being a *bana* was entitled to it. His ancestors did the same. Was sex dirty? Could love be a sin? Can one really manage to stop feeling love and liking outside marriage? Wasn't it against nature? Ever since Ambica did walk into his life, his entire value system or lack of it had come under heavy fire.

His trolley was almost full. Ambica was silent. She was engrossed in reading the list and putting things in the trolley. VVS looked at her a couple of times, but either she was too absorbed or was purposely ignoring him. He cursed himself for the Rajeshwari fiasco and wanted to talk about it.

"You care for some coffee? There is a Café Coffee Day here." Ambica's offer made him smile.

They sipped the steaming cappuccino and waited for an ice-breaker. Finally, Ambica took the initiative.

"You know Veer, the day you shifted in, I overheard you talking to someone in whispers and I knew you were married."

"Ambi...." He tried explaining to her but she raised her hand and smiled, seeking permission to complete.

"I am not seeking any explanation. You do not owe me one. She is your wife. Why should I get upset about it?" He watched as she sipped coffee. Her face was so beautiful, so radiant, her eyes so deep and inviting.

"In fact, I owe you an explanation. You are such a nice man. You never bothered me with any question on my marital status. I know you would have wanted to, but you were too scared that it might upset me. I do not know what made you fear this, but you were right. My marital status is kind of complex. I am married, yet single. This is because I am not divorced yet."

Though somehow he had guessed that something

was not right with Ambica's life, but not even in his wildest of dreams, did he imagine that any man would let go off someone as precious and as beautiful as her.

"Veer, I know you are surprised. But then, everyone does not think me to be as special as you do." Ambica's statement took him by surprise, as he had no clue that she knew exactly what he felt about her. Being caught with your real emotion was as discomforting as being caught with your pants down.

"I was married at a very young age, at sixteen, could not cope with the demands of marriage, both physically and mentally, and by the time I was twenty, I had no option but to get out of it. I went back to college and simultaneously started working and here I am, single yet married. My husband wants to make me suffer by not divorcing me. Earlier, it bothered me but now, I am ok with it."

He was confused.

"You know Veer, all this has scarred my soul and has made me very cynical about this whole institution called marriage."

VVS echoed her sentiments and now with a common ground, he knew that the long journey to her heart now had a new short cut.

***

Brain Storming

Within a span of twenty days, it was the fourteenth conference call. Devoid of any clarity, both in the terms of direction and deliverables, no wonder things were not moving ahead. With more than a dozen views floating around, as the Brand Manager, VVS had no choice but to take all of them into consideration. Right at the start, Sandy had cautioned him to identify the power center, in this case, Lawrence, and to align all his conversation, strategy, creative and deliverables around his thoughts. But being the simpleton that VVS was, he was trying to deliver a perfect campaign, if there was anything like one.

To VVS, PRS was a switch, which delivered better speed, scalability and was being offered at a very attractive price. He had worked out a positioning statement, 'path-breaking technology without back-breaking price,' which was quite liked by Sandy. However, Marketing Head of the different regions wanted a different positioning. For the ASEAN region, which included Indonesia, Malaysia, Vietnam and Thailand, Allan wanted the communication to talk of speed. Jane Lui, the marketing prime of Greater China, which included People's Republic of China, Taiwan and Hong Kong, wanted to offer scalability to meet the demand of the booming Chinese economy. Amy Slater, the Marcom Head, had no clue about anything yet wanted to see options. Lawrence wanted all of it and more.

Considering the lower purchasing power of the Indian rupee, the Delhi branch of Panache—the worldwide advertising agency for CommTech—was entrusted with the job of creating a campaign. After their first round of presentation to Sandy and VVS, there had been some two dozen alterations, all in the opposite direction. Rajesh Aggarwal, the head for Panache, India, who was based out of their Delhi office, had flatly refused to make any further changes. Rajesh was the typical advertising guy—flamboyant, with long hair, accented English, wore expensive suits and shoes and was always getting into or out of meetings. VVS had requested him, rather begged him, to be on time for this all-important call, which was scheduled for Wednesday, 10.30 am, IST.

Rajesh, his sidekick Deepankar, and VVS were sitting in the phone booth number three to join the call, which was all set to define the course of advertising and communication for PRS. VVS logged on using the login ID and the password. He was a minute or two early. Groovy music greeted him. He put the phone on speakerphone mode.

"That rocks; never expected such groove at CommTech." Rajesh smiled.

"Well yeah, I guess they would have been very particular in choosing this track as it has to set the minds in the right frame to digest all the junk that comes during the call," VVS's comment evoked smiles.

"Good afternoon everyone and good morning to the team from India," Lawrence was back in the role, which he played so beautifully—that of a commentator.

Many beeps followed, which meant that some latecomers were also there on the call.

"So is everyone here? I can see, VVS, Sandy, Allan… no I don't see him. Where is Allan?" Before anyone could respond, Lawrence himself answered his question, "Ah, there he is." The messenger window on VVS's laptop came to life.

"This bastard Allan submits every single bill for reimbursement; lunch with girlfriend, shopping. Every bill under the pretext of business expense. Too bad can't claim his condom bill," it was Sandy.

"Lol," VVS typed.

"Hey, we were supposed to have Rajesh also. Virendra, is he there with you?" Lawrence enquired.

Before VVS could speak, Rajesh did the needful. "Hi Lawrence, Rajesh here. Good to hear you after so long."

"Hi Rajesh, it's good to have you on this call. And sorry for the inconvenience."

"Not a problem Lawrence. Till the time you are paying me by the hour rate, I am good."

They all laughed.

Sandy took the lead to divert the meandering minds and tongues towards the main agenda. "Well, the agenda of this call was already mailed to everyone by my team member Virendra. Considering the schedule, we are running way behind and therefore it is imperative that we close this today."

"Yes Sandeep, you are right. We are getting nowhere. I think between us, we should be able to freeze this today" Rajesh supported Sandy.

Amy Slater, the Marketing Communication Head for APAC, who was responsible for driving all the communication in the region, was feeling left out. In her typical squeaky and irritating accent, she always made sure that people knew that she was the boss when it came to communication. "Rajesh, without getting too much into the specifics of the strategy or the creative, just on the basis the rendition presented to me, I am forced to say that the work is below acceptable standards."

"Hold on Amy." Rajesh was not the one to be bullied; at least his grey hair suggested the same. "Please be more specific when you say that my work is below acceptable standards?"

VVS wondered how, in no time, the work, which he was supposed to do and has been doing for the past month or so, assumed a new proportion—'her work' and 'his work'. But he chose to be silent.

The messenger blinked again.

"I swear this bitch needs a good lay. During my last Singapore trip I did try but then at the last moment, like a tease, she told me that she was engaged." The message from Sandy evoked a 'lol' from VVS.

"Rajesh, there were two typos in the layouts."

"Amy, I know you have worked with an advertising agency and, therefore, I would assume that you know what a layout is?"

"During my tenure, none of the layouts had any typos," she countered.

"I am also sure that during you tenure none of your clients asked for a million alterations which made no sense whatsoever." Rajesh took her head on.

"Rajesh, please don't teach me advertising." Amy said condescendingly.

"I wish I could, 'cause if I did', I would have taught you that layouts are mere idea representations and are nowhere close to the final thing. They are just concept card, to seek approval on the route and then take the same forward."

During his term at CommTech, VVS had understood terms like layout, dummy, artwork, etc., which were various stages of presenting and releasing a creative for an advertising campaign. After the advertising agency was briefed, they went back and worked on various creative routes. These routes were presented in form of layouts. Once the layouts were approved, a dummy was made. This was in actual size, with the final text, which was called 'the copy'. After client's approval, they went for shooting the pictures, if required, or else used stock images from their worldwide library of pictures. All the big IT companies pressed upon the fact that only pictures from their existing picture bank should be used, to give the campaign a universal look and feel. So a campaign released in the USA looked exactly the same as the one released in the Philippines. However, it was beyond VVS's comprehension how someone in the Philippines could relate to a picture of an American.

When he asked Sandy, he was told that this was how big corporate worked. To verify, when he Googled, he was surprised to find that the ads for Coca-Cola and Pepsi were different in every part of the world, but for their logo. When he went back to Sandy again, with his observation and query, Sandy told him that the FMCG companies could work differently but this was not the way IT companies worked. Period! So, after using the stock and before releasing the ad, the advertising agency sent the final thing, the artwork, for the client's final signature and approval.

"Rajesh, have you forgotten that I am the client?"

"Then be a reasonable one and learn to appreciate the

fact that it's we, the agency guys, who do all the thinking and hard work to cover up for your incompetence."

"Rajesh, that's enough. And Amy please, Rajesh is on our side, he has always been." Lawrence intervened, with a pleasing yet no-nonsense tone. "You know, Rajesh, I really appreciate all the work which you have done for CommTech. In fact, I always count you as a part of my extended team."

The message box blinked on VVS's screen.

"Look how he is sucking up to Rajesh. He knows that he talks directly with his momma, Sue."

Sue Flaherty was the Chief Marketing Officer, CommTech and was based out of the HQ. Within CommTech, she was a very powerful woman. Being in the cabinet of Buck, the CEO, she was very close to him and exercised considerable influence on his policies.

"I think we all are here to discuss the pre-approved agenda and, therefore, we should concentrate on the same." It was Sandy. He continued, "From the Indian perspective, with this peculiar situation of Chapter 11, mounting a campaign based on a great offer and never before pricing is the only way to go. I also believe that China or Singapore, or for that matter Bangladesh and Pakistan, should not be any different."

"Sandy, sitting there in India, how can you assume things for China, Singapore or Hong Kong?" Allan was back claiming his turf.

"Well, no offense, but going by our past campaign history, APAC always had one campaign, as the basic buying patterns and behaviors across the region are the same. Didn't we run the same campaign for 'Green World, Green CommTech' and 'Super-connectivity?'" Sandy put up a strong defense.

"Well, yes and no. Yes to the fact that we did have the same campaign and no to the fact that now things are different." As usual, Allan was being adamant.

"And could you please tell me how things are any different there than in India?" Sandy took him straight on.

"Well, for starters, I have a more developed market to cater to."

"And does that developed market of yours translate into greater volumes too?" Sandy teased. "I doubt."

Lawrence had to intervene again. "Sandeep, as I sit out of the Hong Kong office, therefore I know for sure that what Allan is saying holds some ground."

"With all due respect to his point of view, if that market is so developed, as Allan claims it to be, then why does he take twice the budget to generate one-fourth the volumes that I do?" Sandy was getting in a confrontational mode.

"Sandy, I decide the budget and the volumes as it's my discretion," Lawrence's tone was stern.

"Then give me whatever you think will work in

India, as per your discretion, and I am good with it." Sandy sulked.

"Well Lawrence, I buy Sandy's point. Right now, nothing but a price route will work, not alone in India, but across the globe. I am saying this going by my experience of handling global clients. The price route is the safest and the most hard-hitting one. It has seldom gone wrong. That is the reason why we had presented this route to you during our initial presentation," Rajesh spoke up, ostensibly as the unbiased party.

"We are not here selling a soap bar or a shampoo. And, therefore, a twenty per cent cut would not swing the buying in our favor. We are selling technology; premium technology, and whatever is premium comes with a price tag." Amy was confident that her argument would put the discussion to a rest.

"Lawrence, I'm not here to have a debate which holds no merit. Having said that, I would like you to know I was in Singapore for four years, selling premium technology for a top brand. Then I moved to advertising. This took me to London, Sydney, Brussels, New York, Jakarta, Colombo and then to India. I am fifty-six and I can bet that I have more experience in brand management and communication than your entire team put together. However, if your team cannot value my experience or viewpoint, I see no use of sharing the same. Just to make things official, so that I am not made the fall guy when this campaign bombs, I will drop a line to Sue, sharing my views. I think she should know of this."

"Rajesh, maybe it's a bad day for all of us. To put things in the right perspective, we all value your experience and judgment. That is why you are here. I am sure being a marketing professional yourself; you would agree how possessive we are about our territories. But with this deadlock, I don't see a way out."

"Hi Lawrence, this is Virendra, can I say something?"

"Sure Virendra."

"Why can't we have the same template but different messaging for each region?"

"You bastard. You are a quick learner." The message box gleamed again. It was Sandy.

"I didn't get you," Lawrence sounded a little surprised.

"Well I mean, in any case we have to use the picture from our picture bank. It means that it will be a picture of an American smiling, or shaking hands, or looking up or…"

"Cut the crap," Lawrence was losing his patience.

"Sorry, I mean that with such a picture, whether the headline talks of price cut, or great technology or scalability, it does not make any difference. So let us just put the stock shot of a happy guy's face. He could be happy due to anything—the awesome discount, the unbelievable offer, the unmatched scalability or even great technology. The copy in any case will take care of all these points. So while the visual, the copy and the logo remains the same, for every region, we just change the headline to suit the specific requirements."

There was silence. VVS got scared.

He opened the message box and typed, "Did I say something wrong?"

"No, you nailed these dick heads again," Sandy was exuberant.

"Lawrence, why don't you make this guy your CEO? I am sure he could still save whatever little is left of CommTech," Rajesh laughed. "I will ask my team to send you the layouts by tomorrow. Good work Virendra," Rajesh patted his back.

***

Dialogue Marketing

It was an October evening: pleasant and enjoyable. Perfect month for some chilled beer with *chicken tikka* and fish fingers. On his way back from office, VVS had picked up two cartons of beer. Ambica had got *tikkas* and fish fingers packed from the food court, which was next to her office. Chaitali was covering the PM's Russia tour and so she was off for good four days. Sitting on the cane chairs, in their balcony, they were down a can each. The *tikkas* were getting more attention than the beer.

After moving in with Ambica and Chaitali, VVS had stopped drinking at home. With his increasing proximity to Ambica, he did not feel like wasting his time, sitting alone, drinking or smoking. He preferred spending the same time with her—watching TV, helping her in the kitchen, playing scrabble or just chatting up with her, trying to know her. She too found his stories hilarious and unbelievable. Seeing her laugh and smile made VVS feel good. To him, it seemed that keeping her happy was his life's only mission and objective. No wonder, within no time, she was the focal point of all his activity. Getting up early to wish her good morning, getting ready in no time to have breakfast with her, skipping lunch with his office colleagues to catch up with her over the phone and coming home as early as possible to be with her. Outings with Aditya, Ashu or anyone else became a thing of the past. Evenings would mean some green tea with her, then dinner, which spiced up with her giggles, laughter and sweet little nothings.

"Veer, at times I think that I am still dreaming."

"As long as it is not a nightmare, keep it going," he laughed.

"Very funny," Ambica displayed her anger, which actually was overflowing with love and affection. She continued, "No, I seriously mean it. You know, after my marriage, while going through my living hell, I assumed that life for me would cease to exist. But look, here I am with you, sitting over a beer."

"Lucky beer," he sighed.

"What do you mean?"

"Wish I was the beer. At least you would have sat over me." The horny rascal in him surfaced.

"You scoundrel, don't you have a one-track mind? I pity your wife." She blushed and pretended to hit him with a paper napkin, which he had very stylishly placed in a napkin holder.

"And why do you pity my wife?" He was looking at her, his cheeks fiery with the beer, need, lust and longing.

"Well, with a horny husband like you, any woman would need all sympathy and pity," she giggled.

VVS held her hand and pulled her on to his lap. She obliged, though after a little resistance.

"Mr Virendra Vikram Singh, you are a married man." Her eyes had the red threads of love and passion. Her cheeks were amber red.

"Ms Ambica, you too are a married woman." His eyes bulged and his entire body strained. Her warm breath caressed his face and, with every caress, he could feel his temples throb harder.

"But I am separated." Her lips quivered and he could see her sparkling teeth and her pink tongue.

"Ms Ambica, at the moment even I am."

She kissed his cheek, her loose hair suddenly exploding on his face and as the quaintest of murmurs began to quiver at the base of his throat, she jumped off his lap and stood there, in front of him, with one foot resting on his thigh.

"Remember, what I told you?"

"What?" He was too horny to get into any conversation.

"I am a bubble, admire me, fantasize about me, but the moment you touch me, I will be gone," she teased.

The fear of losing her curbed his testosterone instantly and his system replaced it with something more tender and lasting love. Their conversation progressed over beer.

"Career wise I am doing fine, but I can never trust men again. To me, all of them are bastards."

"What?" VVS displayed his shock and offense at her over generalization.

She laughed and corrected herself. "I mean, till the time I met you. You know Veer, even at my workplace or the client's office; men are men, just dying to get into my pants. I can read their dirty glances, groping every body part of mine, salivating. Earlier, I felt repulsed by it, but now, with time, I have got used to it."

"But men are not to be blamed. You are so beautiful." He assumed that flattery would lead her back, on to the carnal track, from where he was derailed a few seconds ago.

She smiled, "Aren't you a charmer? Ok, tell me something, you were such a good student, then why didn't you go for your MBA, rule the corporate world? You are cut out for it. In such a short time at CommTech, you are doing wonders. I mean as a Brand Manager on PRS, whatever you have done is remarkable." VVS blushed.

He opened another can and handed it to her.

"You didn't answer me?," she probed further.

"Well I was a good student but then I could not keep up."

"But why Veer? Someone like you who is so clear in his head about what he wants, IIM could have been a cakewalk for you. Did you take your CAT?"

A question which he thought was better left unanswered.

Many beers later, when finally she retired for the day, leaving him high and dry, he sat there, smoking the Marlboro, gifted by Harsh, recalling his days at SRCC.

Life was a party, until one day, while sipping *nimbu paani*, well past noon, he overheard some students talk about timetable, which was put up on the notice board. Suddenly, it hit him then that he was in a college and college had exams too. His mind went numb; with fear and realization, as he knew that *Daata* was used to ninety per cent plus, and any slip would mean disaster.

With the examination schedule on the notice board, he had run to his God—Sandy. Like a true chieftain, a great warrior, charmer and also his college senior, Sandy had smiled and handed him a Navy Cut. For the first time, he felt like throwing the cigarette back at his face. But even then, he was too meek to do it. He stood there holding the cigarette. The God smiled—a smile which had all the answers. "I have arranged everything. You will get the question paper a night in advance." He could not believe his ears. But after being with him for almost eight months, he had seen how well connected Sandy was.

Somehow God, the real one, Shree Naathji, was kind enough to bless him with some sense and, irrespective of the assurance of getting the question paper, he started studying –exactly two days before the papers. The first page of the micro-economics book made him realize that with all the alcohol and nicotine in his system, his brain had lost its sheen. It was just a defunct organ, as it was not put to use even once during his college stint.

No wonder, the question papers which were supposed to leak a night in advance never happened. Courtesy whatever little he did manage to study or copy during the exams, he sailed out with forty-one per cent.

"Damn neat. I am so proud of you. Two days and you have scored forty! This year, we will study for three days and will top the university." Sandy's laughter echoed in the college corridors and long after in his ears also.

***

Feeling the Heat

It was early morning when his Blackberry vibrated. With sleep-infested eyes, he looked at the phone screen. It was Sandy. He thought of avoiding the call as the soothing morning chills, with amorous thoughts were making him ache for Ambica. The vibration of Blackberry persisted, forcing him out of his pink zone.

The next five minutes on the phone left him in a state of panic, shock and utter disbelief. Sandy told him that their largest competitor, Sailnet, had launched their version of PRS, the HS series of switches, with almost the same communication route—the pricing one, and almost the same campaign. He instructed VVS to rush to the office, as Lawrence had scheduled an emergency call at 7 am.

"I am absolutely aghast I mean how could you let this happen?" Lawrence was seething with rage.

"But Lawrence...," VVS protested.

"Virendra, no explanation please. You were the

brand custodian. It was your moral duty to protect it," Lawrence blamed VVS.

"Lawrence, to be only fair to him, we should give him a chance to explain," Sandy underplayed his past connections, as he knew that a single wrong word could blow up the whole thing.

"Sandeep, I need not remind you that a lot of our field targets and other professional obligations were based on the successful launch of this wonderful piece of technology called the PRS. Sue has been calling me up daily, letting me know that the board is keenly watching this campaign. A hit launch would have projected us in a favorable light before the bidders. And here we are.... Everything is over. Gosh, I can't believe it."

"Lawrence, how serious is the damage?" For a change, Allan was lying low.

"Allan, for how long have you been in technology marketing?"

"Well...," Allan was flabbergasted at Lawrence's eruption.

Lawrence continued, "I am sure long enough to know that it is a first mover's market. IT products never flourish under the 'me too' policy. iPod was just a hard drive on which you could plug in a pair of earphones and listen to music. But it played on the 'first mover's' advantage. Every single company—Sony, Philips, Samsung launched a portable MP3 player later, but none of them could match the success of an iPod. Why? Because in technology marketing, there is no second chance. Either the first mover is a hit, which leaves no place for any other player, or it is a flop, which kills the entire product market and category. To answer your question, we are all doomed."

"Lawrence, but it is not that Sailnet developed the technology overnight and launched it. While we were doing a competitive analysis, we always knew that they had an identical range of switch. As a matter of fact, a couple of more companies. Fastnet, Jaico and Horte also have a similar product." Sandy tried to lessen Lawrence's reaction and steam.

"Sandeep, I would really appreciate it if you stop treating me as one of your cronies and also if you stop presenting yourself as the naïve one."

"But Lawrence..."

"Sandeep, please. Since my first day on this PRS project I had told everyone how important and critical it was for all of us. Your future, mine, as well as that of my boss, Sue, depended on the success of this launch. We have been working on this for months, streamlining communication, making white papers, getting reviews from analysts, ascertaining its power efficiency and getting the same certified and here, this morning, as I open my morning paper, I see a full-page advertisement from Sailnet, with the same proposition and the same layout. The only change is that instead of PRS, it was HS Switch. Do you think this could have been a coincidence?" Lawrence continued, "I log on to the website of Sailnet and right there, on their home page, what do I see? A beautiful shot of the switch with the headline saying 'Path breaking technology, less the back breaking price.' Virendra does that ring a bell?" Lawrence was panting. All his composure was lost.

"Well yes, that was our positioning. I mean the PRS positioning." Virendra couldn't believe his ears.

The messenger box popped up.

"Be very careful with your words. I am sure this call is being recorded. Anything that you say could be used against you." Sandy warned him.

VVS got petrified.

"Precisely! That's what I want to know. How did our brand promise reach our competition. Who leaked it?" Lawrence had assumed the role of a cop.

"Lawrence, do you mean it's a case of sabotage?" Jane sounded worried.

"Yes Jane, it is. Someone has intentionally leaked our plans to our competitors to jeopardize the future of this company, our product and us."

"But who would do this? I mean we have worked together for so long and never has anything like this happened." Allan posed a not-so-innocent question. VVS knew what Allan meant. His ears turned red and his blood pressure shot up. He could feel his veins throb. Never did he imagine that someone would accuse him of treachery and sabotage. Before he could react, the messenger box flashed again.

"Don't react. It's a ploy. Just answer when and what you are asked," Sandy cautioned. Though the *Rajput* blood in him felt like crushing Allan's skull, but he knew that it was best for him to listen to his college-time senior.

"Guys, we have to get to the bottom of this. The leak happened either at Panache or at our end. It is highly unlikely that it happened at their end, as they are in no way connected to our competition and have been with us for very long. Also, this launch was in their interest too as they would have made some money out of this. I have spoken to Sue about it and she will schedule a call regarding the same. Till then, I request you not to speak to anyone regarding this. Maintain a status quo and pretend that nothing has happened. I shall get back to you soon."

***

Sporadically, Sandy evoked many emotions in VVS—of love, fear, respect and hatred. But there was one emotion which he managed to whip up consistently—that of confusion. If VVS was asked to describe Sandy in one line, he would never be able to do so. Why? Firstly, describing someone like Sandy—larger than life in a line would be an injustice to his persona. Secondly, he could never get to know the real man in Sandy. After all these years, he had no clear-cut demarcation about his beliefs, ethos, likes or dislikes. Owing to this confusion, VVS kept going back to him.

"Dude, Lawrence is playing up. Somewhere down the line, he would have realized that owing to our Chapter 11 status, the launch of PRS in APAC would have been a dud. This would have exposed him and his non-existent marketing acumen. Therefore, he is trying to blame it on the rain. That son of a bitch could have leaked the entire thing himself." Sandy was as candid as ever.

"But I don't think…" VVS's mind had stopped working.

"You don't think of anything. Just stay put and pretend that nothing has happened. Never get into any argument or mail duel. Only speak when asked to. Do you get me?," Sandy was clear in his instructions and wanted an affirmative answer to be sure that VVS had no ambiguity about the same.

"Yes sir, I do."

"Before we put this conversation to rest, I want to ask you something as an office senior, not as your friend or your college senior."

VVS knew that something uncomfortable was coming his way.

"Sure sir," he put on a brave face.

"On your joining day, you would have got a file with various papers on salary break-up, appointment letter, terms and conditions, etc., etc. In the same bunch, there would have been a document titled 'non-disclosure agreement'. You would have signed it too."

"Yes sir."

"Under the same, if you are proven guilty of leaking information to an outside party, vendor or competitors, severe action can be taken against you."

His heart sank and he had to gulp down imaginary saliva to wet his throat.

"I know you have not done anything, still; I would like to ask you if ever, unknowingly, maybe to flaunt to your friends or some ex-colleagues, did you share the PRS plan with anyone outside the office. When I say anyone, I mean anyone."

VVS scanned his memory and the answer was no.

"No."

"Did you ever use your personal mail ID; Gmail, Yahoo or Hotmail to mail the PRS plan or the creative to anyone outside? Maybe to your brother or cousin." Sandy grilled further.

He again scanned his mind.

"No." VVS was getting a little irritated as why would he send out the PRS plan, or even the creative for that matter, to his friends? Why would an outsider be interested in the plan at all, when apart from the key stakeholders, no one within the company had any interest in it.

"So can I assume that you have not breached the non-disclosure agreement?"

"Yes sir."

"Good, will catch you later."

***

Every day, the mailboxes were flooded with goodbye mails, telling the same story—how fortunate he or she was being a part of CommTech and how he or she would miss CommTech and the team. But the recipients of these emails knew that it was just another way of slapping them, telling them 'losers', "I am on my way out. See if someone hires you too."

The morning had been a long and hectic one. It was nearly eleven when VVS got up for his first break. The cafeteria was packed with people. It seemed that no one had any work but to sit there, testing the coffee machine's patience. There were small clusters of people; standing there. The discussion point was the same—'the list'. While VVS filled his mug, he could make out that some sort of list had been compiled and it had the names of the people who were being sacked from the APAC region. Everyone, every group was busy estimating the number of people who would get sacked from the India team. VVS spotted Abhishek Saxena, the Prime Payroll for APAC. He was a cute-looking man, who was always too smartly dressed, considering that at the end of the day, he was just an accountant. Standing there with his team, he was enjoying his coffee.

"Hi Abhishek, long time?" VVS greeted him.

"With no money, the accounts department and the accountants just do their favorite disappearing act," he guffawed.

"So what is the news?" VVS enquired.

"Nothing. From India, courtesy the high number of resignations, the head count has already gone down by twenty per cent. And twenty per cent was the number they wanted to trim. So, as per me, India is safe," Abhishek was confident of his calculation.

"Any gossip?"

"Nothing much." He was in no mood to share but his smile said that if probed, he might reconsider his decision. Taking the cue, VVS scratched the surface to get out some juice and he got lucky.

"Well, last week, someone from the sales team had submitted his expense voucher."

"Who?" VVS was curious.

"Well, I can't tell you his name but I can tell you that though it was signed and approved by his line manager, I did not pass it and there was a huge hue and cry."

"And if I may ask what was this all about?" VVS was getting curious.

"The voucher had a sum of thirty-five thousand and the details column of the voucher said 'tea with client at Hyatt, Mumbai'."

"What?" VVS was horrified.

"And when I did not approve it and sent the voucher to RC, he called the sales guy to Bangalore, to seek clarification. I don't know if the same was sought, but I got the same bill again. Only this time with an additional amount of thirty-five thousand—to and fro air ticket to Bangalore and a day's stay at the Leela. This was followed by a mail from RC instructing me to clear the bill without any further delay."

Anurag, Abhishek's team member quipped, "Sir, why don't you tell him the descriptor, which you have coined for RC and his cabinet?"

"Anurag shut up. You will get me sacked for this."

The entire team laughed. Anurag pressed him again, "Sir, *Thakur* is a nice guy. He is one of our own. Tell him please."

Abhishek pressed his lips, looked around and whispered, "Pirates of the Carebian."

They all burst into a laughter. The Blackberry vibrated in VVS's hand. He was surprised to see *Dadosa* on the line. He excused himself, as he knew that *Dadosa's* call meant trouble.

"*Khamaghani.*" VVS's greeting had an element of fear.

"Sukhram Meena, the Circle Officer at Ranibagh, had called. He told me that some case of Internet forgery has been registered against Harsh *bana* and it has also got your name as his accomplice." Everything melted around VVS as he could see his worst fear come true. He knew the severity of cyber crime and also how easy it was to trace one.

"*Dadosa* ...," he did not know how to frame his reply.

"I had a word with Harsh *bana* and he told me that you did help him. The whole thing has taken the shape of *Baniya* vs *Rajput*, therefore the *Baniya* lobby is pressurizing the police to take action. Sukhram is my friend and he has told me to inform you that a team might also go there to investigate. VVS, let me warn you, if this stupidity of yours, gets in the way of my assembly ticket, I will surely kill you."

VVS knew that *Dadosa* was one of the coldest people he had ever seen. When it came to his prestige, or his own interest, nothing mattered to him—relations, emotions, care or love, just about nothing. The fear of losing everything, which he was clinging on to so hard—the job, the sheen, the Blackberry, the laptop, and of course the love of his life, Ambica, suddenly started to dissolve. He did not know what to do. But what he knew was that after the PRS fiasco, if anyone, Sandy included, knew of his involvement in a hacking case, without an iota of doubt, they would assume that the leak happened at his end. He felt lonely and afraid. An incident like this would have meant nothing to him back in Udaipur, but out here, in this unknown land, where he knew no one, had no friends, he felt helpless and desperate.

Should he speak with Manish? He was nice and kind. But he knew that involving any office colleague could spell more disaster. In a company like CommTech, the grapevine was very active and people like Shubhankar waited for an opportunity to pull others down.

He tried reconstructing the hacking episode. He could see how Bharat Jaiswal would have approached Deepak and Rajan—the *Baniya* brothers, and would have tipped them off. To prove it, he would have offered his services and then would have got to his task of generating and tracking log reports. In no time, he would have traced the hacker's footprint, which finally would have been the supporting document with the complaint.

VVS shuddered. He knew for sure that his days were numbered. *Shree Naathji, please help me this last time.* His scared heart said a little prayer.

Whom should he call? He scanned his mind again.

Shree Naathji, please show me a way, please.

***

The office was deserted—silent and dark. The big hall, which never ended, was lined with cubicles, and more cubicles, on both the sides. Because of some loose electrical connection, the bulbs and the lights flickered irritatingly. Strangely, the coffee vending machine was humming and spewing freshly-brewed beverage on its own.

"Manish," VVS whispered, as he was scared to disturb the eerie silence.

He tiptoed towards his workstation. The floor was littered with paper, broken glass, coffee mugs and pieces of plaster and debris.

"Manish?," he whispered again, this time a little louder. No response.

He pushed the debris with his feet and inched forward, in the long passage, walking towards B-9, his workstation.

Trinnnnnnnnnnnnnnnnnnnn.

His heart almost jumped out of the rib cage as the shrill telephone ring sliced through the thick air of stillness, making it creepier. His forehead was covered with beads of perspiration and his pulse was racing. On a workstation, he saw a CommTech phone, with its illuminated screen, ringing. He hurried towards the phone. As he moved, his feet got tangled in a mesh of wires and he triped. The volume of the ring kept increasing, assuming a deafening proportion.

He supported his body frame, on his hands, and crawled towards the ringing phone. The shrill ring tone was hurting his head. He could see the workstation up ahead, where lied the source of this cacophony and disruption. The workstation was high as he was on all fours. He held the edge of the workstation and pulled himself up.

There it was! The source of his irritation.

"Hello."

"Your train leaves now," a metallic, bone-chilling voice announced and hung up.

He was standing there, lifeless yet scared, his pulse still racing and his blue shirt soaked in sweat. He dropped the receiver and turned back. A visual onslaught hit him. He pinched himself but the visual failed to disappear. It was still there. A train with a giant steam engine hissing and puffing, right there in the passage. As if under some spell, he started walking towards the train. It seemed as if the train was just waiting for him to move as it hissed and started moving too, towards the exit. Something in him told him that the train was his only hope to escape. He marshalled all his strength and tried running towards it. Out of nowhere, the cables lying on the ground came to life and wrapped themselves around his ankle. Using all his strength, he tried to set himself free. The train gathered momentum, as the piston of the engine pumped more horse-power. "Please, wait for me, please," he shouted but could not find his voice. His vocal chords were paralyzed. He gave it all that he had to set his feet free. But the grip was almost like an iron clasp, not letting him budge even an inch. More steam passed between the pistons, powering the engine more, giving it more speed. The train chugged along the passage. "Please, don't leave me here, please," he howled in silence. The train started chugging along the passage faster. He gave it one final try, pulling his feet free.

He could see the tail light of the train disappear as he stood there, trapped by the wires, letting out a silent howl.

"Veer," the voice seemed like a far-off cry.

"Veer," it was a bell-like voice, sweet and filled with care.

"Veer, are you ok?," a pair of hands shook him.

Sweating profusely, he got up, with his pillow wet and his face looking dehydrated. As he looked around, he realized that he was lying in his fuchsia pink bedroom, with Ambica's pretty face, bent over him. She was clearly upset and worried. Thankfully for him, the nightmare was over. He hugged Ambica and pulled her closer. For a change, she did not resist and let him embrace her. Lovingly, she placed her head on his chest. The world stopped for him. With her in his arms, there was nothing he cared for—job, cops, Udaipur, Akhepur, even Rajeshwari. Ambica swung her legs to get on the bed and lay beside him, with her head on his chest and her thighs on his legs. His hands stroked her head feeling her soft hair. A wave of Elizabeth Arden filled his senses, soaking every pore, covering every single strand of his being.

"Ambi, with just a hug, you have driven away all my worries. Why can't we always be like this?"

She freed herself from his embrace and sat on the bed beside him. "Because you are married and I don't want to have anything to do with a married man."

He sulked, "Don't you like me?" His eyes told her a negative reply would break his heart.

"Yes, I do but…"

"…You needn't put a rider to that, please. I am happy with the fact that you like me," he smiled.

"Were you having a nightmare? You were shouting as if someone was leaving you."

"Yes, I saw that you were leaving me," he smiled and laced his fingers into her tresses and tried pulling her close again. She ducked and jumped off the bed laughing.

"You are not as fast as you should be," she teased him. He gave out a feeble smile.

She looked at him intently. "Veer, is everything alright?" It did not take her much time and effort, as she used the age-old trick of making men speak the truth by placing his hand on her head, looking into his eyes, "tell me the truth."

***

It took good seventy-eighty minutes to reach Chaitali's office. For VVS, it was the first time that he had entered any news channel office. The floor was bursting with activity. Employees wearing doc ties were moving briskly around the place. The workstations were all done up in red and yellow laminate and imparted a happy aura to the place. The average employee age would be mid to late twenties. There were various open shoot floors, where everything was ready—the news reader's chair and table, the lights, the camera, everything. VVS was mesmerized. He knew that he would love to be part of this entire hustle bustle.

Chaitali walked in, sporting her routine outfit—shirt, jeans and sneakers.

"Busy?" Ambica enquired.

"Some last-minute fight *yaar*. A senior Congress Party leader has issued a statement, which has not gone down well with the party members. Everyone wants to give his or her reaction. I have been covering this since morning. Just when I thought it was over, got a flash that the PM would also like to issue his statement. Bloody hell! Why can't he beg his mama-mia to relieve him of his miseries? He is such a gentle person, but then, politics isn't about being the Mr Nice. What says you Veer?"

"Well...," the sudden question caught him off-guard. In any case, he had no idea about the country's political system or the ongoing politics. It was during his hostel days that he completely got off newspapers or even news. After all, when headlines changed every fifteen minutes, it did not make any sense for him to scan the newspapers around noon, the time he usually got up and ordered a *nimbu-paani*.

"And what have you got yourself into?," Chaitali asked him again, with slight irritation on her face. VVS was embarrassed. He had told Ambica that he was not comfortable seeking help from a woman and that too his flat-mate with whom he hardly had any conversation. Not paying any attention to his MCP stuff, she had gone ahead and dialed Chaitali's number.

"Come, let us move to the canteen," Chaitali said and walked down the hall. Ambica and VVS followed her. The canteen was done up in yellow and red and was bursting with people. VVS was taken years back, to his college days, when a canteen used to be such a pulsating joint, the hub of activity. Looking at the canteen again, made him long to be a part of that culture. A place where it was normal to wear anything, act normal, and be yourself. Maybe, somewhere deep down, he was not too happy with the switch to formals, laptop and Blackberry.

Over cups of tea and coffee, like a true journalist Chaitali grilled him, covering every aspect of the hacking bit. For the first time he realized that being a journalist was not only about holding the mike and asking inane questions. On the contrary, it required immense alertness and articulation.

"See Veer, as I understand it, you have been part of a hacking operation. As a foolish hacker, you used the network of the hotel where your friend was staying. Now, with the aggrieved party, Om and Mewar Travels going ahead and filing a complaint and with proof on their side, a police enquiry is bound to happen. And that too, the preliminary enquiry will happen in Udaipur, where I can't do much." His face faded, as she was his last hope.

"But maybe, I can ask my Udaipur correspondent, Yudhveer, to speak to the cops and figure out if something could be done. Maybe, he can manage to pull a few strings so that in the case of an FIR, the charges against you are kept lenient. If the police team comes to Gurgaon, I will handle it here. So, to cut a long story short, you won't have to spend your life in jail." As Chaitali completed her statement, color returned to his face.

"Chaitali, are you sure the cops won't come to my office?," he wanted to clarify further.

"You know that I am doing this as a favor to Ambica, not you. So stop being demanding. And no, I cannot promise you anything." Chaitali was curt. Ambica knew that being the gentle soul that he was; he would be hurt. She intervened to salvage the situation. "That's ok Chaitali. I know that you will do whatever you can as you fully understand that, for someone like us, career is very important. Yes, he has been stupid in indulging in all this but I can vouch for the fact that his motives were never malicious. He did it for a friend. The same way you would do it for me."

***

As they walked out of Chaitali's office, VVS switched on his mobile and the 'missed call alert' service came into play. One after another, there were missed call messages. Manish, Ashu, Sandy, Sukhram Meena, Rajeshwari and twenty two missed calls from Harsh. Going by the way things were placed, but for Rajeshwari, all the missed calls were important.

"*Khamaghani,*" VVS was extra polite to Sukhram.

"*Bana*, how have you been?," Sukhram Meena, the SHO of Ranibagh police station, who was handling the hacking case in Udaipur, was on the other side.

"Fine sir. I wanted to speak with you…," VVS was interrupted.

"Deepak and Rajan have filed a complaint against Harsh *bana* and you. As the complaint had your name, I avoided it for a few days. I even spoke with your *Dadosa*, as I wanted him to know. But he did not show much interest. Also, the *Baniya* lobby is pressurizing me to take some action. So I will do a *dabish* on Harsh and will bring him to the police station. It will be a routine enquiry."

"Sir, do you think I need to come there?"

"No, no. You need not worry. Let us see what Harsh has to say. *Bana*, why did you have to get involved in something like this?"

VVS felt ashamed.

"The investigation of cyber crime is not done by us. It is done by our forensic lab. Knowing you, I assume that you would have not done anything illegal. But God forbid, if they find any trace leading to you, then let me warn you that even I won't be able to help you." VVS got the message loud and clear that doomsday was just around the corner.

Ambica's Scorpio was at the Gurgaon Toll Bridge. As the Scorpio took the exit 7, towards Signature Tower, VVS lit a cigarette. Though Ambica was aversive to smoking or smokers, VVS got away with a promise of quitting soon.

"Ambi, if you don't mind, can I make another call?," he inhaled deeply.

"Sure."

"It might take a while to wrap this one," he cautioned her.

She smiled and patted his cheek. He felt nice and loved and dialed Harsh.

"*Khamaghani.*"

"VVS *bana*, I have called you a million times. Where have you been? The Ranibagh SHO had called. They are coming to get me. Please speak with him. I will give you anything that you ask for. Help me *bana*."

VVS felt a little awkward. Being a *Rajput* himself, seeing another beg; who always took great pride in his *Suryavansh* lineage, did not make him feel good. He knew that even now there were loads of people in Rajasthan who looked down upon everyone who was not a *Rajput*. Especially in some of the bigger *thikanas*, people from backward tribe or caste were not allowed to cross the street or ride a horse if a *bana* was anywhere in sight. Though post-Independence, everything had changed—the princely states, the royal titles, the sheen and glory of the Rajputana. Like him, there were many who were left only with dilapidated *havelis*, faded pictures and rusted swords. Few of the *banas*, who claimed to be a descendant of the some fancy lineage, Harsh *Hukum* included, turned into chronic diabetic due to their sedentary lifestyles and love for *laal maans* and booze. VVS wished if it were possible to do a DNA test on the Sun God himself, it would have put an end to the decades of misery of these fanciful clans –at least they would not have to live up to the pressure of justifying their existence as per their delusive origin.

"VVS, are you there?," Harsh shook him out of his sepia thoughts.

"*Hukum*, you do not worry. We will do whatever can be done." With a truck load of worry on his own head, he tried comforting Harsh.

"I swear I am not going to leave Bharat, Rajan and Deepak. I will put all the bullets that I have in their head." His threat sounded more like a protest, trying hard to live up to his macho image.

"*Hukum*, let us get out of this mess and we shall see what needs to be done with them. Did Sukhram mention anything about me or my name in the complaint?" VVS popped up the litmus test.

"Oh, I forgot to tell you. Yes he did. I am sorry."

Harsh failed the test. The man, who was so full of stories of loyalty and friendship, under the first signs of stress, even forgot to tell his friend-cum-brother, VVS, that he was also under the same cloud, which was making him so scared.

Before he hung up on Harsh, VVS was clear that Harsh did not deserve '*Khamaghani*' any more.

***

Change of Guard

"Lawrence has been removed."

"What? But why?" Sandy's opening line shocked VVS.

"It seems that Sue was very unhappy with the PRS fiasco. She had to take some corrective action and removing him was the most logical thing."

"You mean that he has been sacked?" VVS was still shocked.

"No, he has been shifted to his home country, Australia, to take care of the Channel Marketing."

"But then who will replace him?"

"Amanda Wither."

"Who?"

"Well, the grapevine says that in a hush-hush manner she has been hired from a leading bank where she was heading the consumer branding division. She joins the board soon, maybe in the coming week or so."

"But isn't Sue being unfair to Lawrence?"

"No, she is just trying to save herself. Lawrence was not performing in any case and I guess she was waiting for a reason to pluck him out."

"But if he is not performing, then why have him in the system at all?"

"Cause, going by your logic, not even one of us should be seen here." Sandy was being honest and the prospect of losing his job scared VVS.

"But at this point, I mean under the Chapter 11 situation, shouldn't they have hired someone from the same industry, as it would have made life easier for everyone. This new lady coming from a different industry, a different function, would surely need some time to understand her role and the market." VVS was trying to think rationally.

"And we have everything but time?" Sandy completed his thought. "See dude, there is no point in racking our brains over things which are well beyond our control. Please ask Rajesh to stop the campaign and compile all the creative, the final ones, and send you the CD."

"Are we dropping the PRS campaign?"

"There is no point in running it either."

"Hmmm, guess you are right."

"And tomorrow, I am going to Amby Valley for an offsite cabinet meeting. Mobile signal would be weak there. Send me an SMS if anything important comes up."

***

Offsite

Amby Valley—some ten thousand undulating acres of verdant expanse—snugly nestled amidst picturesque Shayadari mountain range. Promoted by a private developer, it was touted as the five top destination cities of the world. No wonder, executives who wanted to get away from the maddening rush of the city life and take a break, flocked to this serene retreat under the garb of something called 'an offsite'.

The entire cabinet of RC checked into Timber Chalets—the plush and swank wooden cottages, which were built on the lines of Swiss cottages. CommTech team had taken seven cottages. But for RC, everyone shared the chalet with one more cabinet member. All the cottages overlooked the beautiful valley and the green hills, which were so far yet seemed so close.

"Sandy, I think you know why I chose to be your roommate," Neel quizzed him while unpacking and putting his stuff in the beautifully-carved wooden wardrobe. The whole chalet was nothing but wood. From flooring to ceiling, to the walls, cabinet, bed, drawer, everything was in wood. "And could you please elucidate?" Sandy smiled back.

"Because with you, I will get to choose the best of the babes and maybe more than one," he laughed as he winked.

The casual and derogatory remark offended Sandy. "So you perceive me to be the in-house pimp?"

Maybe, the offsite atmosphere prompted the ever-boisterous sales guy in Neel to go a little overboard. "Of course, Mr Marketing Man. We are no FMCG company and, therefore, don't rely on smart marketing campaigns and the number crunchers responsible for them. We are a B2B, IT company, which is all about frontline sales guys like us. We get the precious dollars. No offense, but you people just blow it away on running some frivolous marketing schemes and campaigns, just trying to justify your existence. So playing a pimp to please the bread-earners will not do you any harm. Would it?"

Sandy knew that he was underqualified and overpaid for the job as no one but RC would hire him, a PR guy, to head the marketing function. Also, that Neel was an all-powerful guy at CommTech India. Therefore, any sort of face-to-face confrontation with him could put a full stop to his career. Sandy stood by the window, smoking and feeling terrible about himself and his whole existence.

His climb to this chair had been a long one. From a one-room PR agency to heading a function with a budget of some five million USD, he did whatever it took to climb. Now there was no way he could lose it all, even if that meant playing pimp to the VP, Enterprise.

He dialed a number. Everything was just a phone call away—young girls included.

***

The conference room at the Amby Valley had the cabinet around the table—Rohit Dhawan, Amit Kukreja, Shailainder Bajwa *aka* Shelly, Sanjay Singh, Edgar Augustine, Sameer Roko, Prashant Kulsherstha, Keshav Khurana, Animesh Mishra, Digvijay Bhamri, Neelesh Dang *aka* Neel and Sandeep Khandelwal *aka* Sandy.

RC scanned their faces closely. All of them were blank. He adjusted his purple turban, which was perfectly matched with his purple tie and shifted his attention towards Neel.

"Neel, the sales funnel for India is almost dry. I fail to understand what you guys were doing all this while? I mean, on my monthly calls, I was always shown prospects and leads. Where are they now? Why aren't they converting into sales?" He punched in a few keys on his laptop. "Every month, the reports have more than a dozen 'A' category prospects. Why aren't they converting into sales?" In any organization, for a close monitoring of the sales process, the marketing team is supposed to generate leads and feed the same into a central system, the sales funnel. The owner of the sales funnel consolidates the same and passes on the leads for further categorization. After a few rounds of tele-calling, sending out mailers, etc., basis the response, if any, they get passed on to the sales team. All the leads, which go to the sales team are categorized as 'A' category prospects as the chances of them converting into sales are fairly high.

"Well, we have been trying. And we have been trying hard." Neel adjusted his specs.

"But I don't see it translating into numbers. Guys, sales function is a number game and numbers translate into profit. If we don't achieve our targets, we lose up to forty per cent of our salary, forget the bonus bit. With forty per cent gone, what are we going to take home this quarter? Have you ever thought of it?" RC looked at Sandy. "Sandeep, I am very disappointed with your efforts. None of your campaigns is giving any ROI. To top it all, you hoodwinked me into hiring one more team member."

"Sir, you know what you are saying is not correct. We have been doing some aggressive marketing. My campaigns have generated some good leads. But for some reason, the sales team is not able to close them. As you rightly said, sales is all about numbers and so is marketing. Let me pull up the stats." Sandy looked at his laptop screen.

"Sandeep, could you please stop this act? I have the numbers. What I don't have is the reason for them not materializing." RC meant business.

"Sir, we know the situation we are into..." Sandy pleaded.

"My boss, Crompton, sitting in Singapore, is not ready to listen to this anymore." RC shouted as he lost his cool. "He is breathing down my neck. He wants numbers as Buck has told him to perform or perish," he threw up his hands in exasperation, "and he has told me the same."

"RC, aren't we all panicking maybe a little too much?" Neel curled his white lock of hair, with his finger, playfully.

"I wish I had pushed the panic button long ago. We all know the takeover is just around the corner. There is a huge urgency for us to show numbers. Whosoever buys us will be closely watching Asia. For CommTech or any other company, it has to be Asia. Therefore, it is crucial to show the buyers some hope with figures. You get my point?," RC adjusted his purple turban again.

"If the angels play their harps and if the devil rests for a while, in this quarter, my region would be able to cover up for the Q3 and Q4." Shelly looked positive.

"Can I be honest with you Shelly?" RC was still

worked up. "I have been listening to this mumbo jumbo of yours for the past five years. There are no takers for your Omnipresence conferencing solution and Unified Communication as well. I know they are great products, but somehow we have not been able to position them. And that's where I blame Sandeep. After spending a fortune what do we get? Some obscure leads, which get knocked off in the first round of tele-calling? Don't they Sandeep?"

Sandy was silent.

"Guys, I want some answers, some solution. Let me warn you, the party is over and heads will roll."

"Rohit, Amit, Edgar, I mean come on guys, you are the star performers. Show me a way."

Neel smiled a wicked one. "Buck and Crompton want numbers. Right?"

"Neel, don't you give me that Holmes grin of yours. Tell me if you have anything concrete in mind." RC was clearly agitated. "Let us give them what they want. After all, running a household with sixty per cent of salary, less any bonus is an impossible proposition."

"And how do we propose to do this magical feat?" Edgar was curious.

"Simple. Ask our existing clients to let us install our new range of products, say the PRS series or a couple of UC solutions on a trial basis."

"But that would be a trial basis. How will it reflect in the sales funnel?" Edgar shored his apprehension.

"Because we will tell the client that we are willing to install a shining piece of technology at no cost and obligation, trial basis, only if they give us a Purchase Order. No client would mind issuing a conditional PO. Put the PO in the system, it will automatically reflect in the funnel. Simple!"

"Neel, and what are we supposed to do when the clients return it back?" RC was seriously considering his idea. "We will take it. Only by that time CommTech would have been history and we all would be gone for good." Neel patted his white lock and gave a greasy smile.

Rohit Dhawan, the Sales Head for the west zone, was not too comfortable.

"But that is a straight case of unfair practice."

"You have any better way out?" Neel challenged him. "I am sure we can do something about it. In the past too, we have been achieving our targets. With Chapter 11, it requires some more effort. My team is ready to put in their every bit." Rohit's face had an air of honesty. "Rohit, let the cabinet vote and decide" Neel wanted to make it fair.

Within the next few seconds, the consensus was out. "As we don't have any better plan, I guess we can raise a toast to Neel's plan." RC was back to normal, the complacent self.

"Cheers!"

***

Invent, Innovate and Synergise

What would you call a place where trains stopped? A railway station! And where a tram, tube or metro stopped? Well, a tram station, a tube station and a metro station. And a place where work stopped? Mmmm....

The entire two floors of CommTech were a big workstation. Nothing happened on the five hundred-odd workstations. Well, almost nothing. On every monitor, one could only see planting of crop, harvesting and selling them at Farmville, scrapping at Orkut and Facebook, managing numerous chat windows—Yahoo, MSN, G-chat and a few others of dubious distinction or updating resumes for the millionth time.

VVS was also a proud owner of a workstation. With the PRS campaign dying a premature death, Lawrence on his way out and the new boss still on her way, there was nothing to be done. Trying to keep himself gainfully employed and following Sandy's instruction, he always had a couple of PPTs opened on his screen. With the PRS fiasco over, he was a proud owner of a few PPTs, which belonged exclusively to him. Tired of them, and the Rubik Cube, he started to focus on increasing his general knowledge. And what better way than Google. He started to Google almost every word—cyber hacking, PRS, CommTech, Sailnet, what women want, top lingerie brand, Victoria Secret, Victoria Secret-India, Online bra size, Elizabeth Arden, Elizabeth Arden-India, Tag watches, Tag-India-prices, Ambica, Amanda Wither, how to stop smoking, ten signs to know she likes you, gain inches right there, six pack in six days, the art of seduction, Marwari horses, stop drinking in two weeks and just about everything under the sun.

One day, while on a call, he stumbled upon a great way to keep himself gainfully employed. It was another long boring call. By this time, he had learnt the art of taking a conference call. Logging on at the specified time, exchanging the pleasantries and when the main speaker started his speech; which during most of the calls made no sense to almost ninety per cent of the people, to put the microphone on mute and heading towards the coffee machine, only to return five minutes before the end time to say 'have a good day'.

One such day, he was sitting with his headset on. Some obscure product marketing guy with a more obscure name was giving a product update. He was three cups down and was seriously contemplating on cutting down on caffeine as it had started giving him acidity. He was looking at the three paper cups lying on his table; small, white-colored cups. With nothing better to do, he picked one of the empty cups and started scribbling on it—the building in which CommTech office was located—a tall, imposing building, with black glistening glass façade. He was happy with his drawing skills. He continued with his new-found hobby. Within a week, he had an enviable collection. Cups with buildings, faces, cartoons, pictures of Gods, voluptuous women—anything that caught his fancy. People started to stop by his workstation to have a look at his mini art gallery, which was now gaining popularity as 'Coffee Art'.

The project manager in Manish suggested making the optimal utilization of the available resources and talent. Using the Blackberry, pictures were clicked—of individual cups, in groups and in various combinations. In no time, a special page, named 'CommTech Coffee Art', was created on Facebook. With Manish and VVS as admins all the pictures were posted on it. Using their combined friend list, within two hours, the page had fifty-six 'likes'. VVS could not believe his eyes and Manish smiled as if he knew that this was coming. Manish quickly logged on to BlogSpot and created a blog for the same.

The creator of CommTech Coffee Art, VVS, basked in the glory of appreciation and positive comments.

People in Gurgaon, Mumbai, Chennai and Bangalore started making and posting their own rendition of Coffee Art pieces. The number of pictures in the album swelled and so did the number of 'likes'.

***

Updates

"*Thakur*, there is some good news."

Sitting amidst people, who were either waiting for an offer or a sack letter, happiness had lost its meaning. Therefore, when Ashu came in with some good news, VVS was genuinely excited.

"Well, the first one is that I have got my offer letter from Sailnet!"

"Congrats," VVS hugged him. His unabated enthusiasm and excitement made a few heads turn—out of curiosity, disdain and indifference. The turning heads made him realize that even right intentions ought to be displayed in a right manner. He controlled himself and signaled Ashu to follow him— to their favorite joint, the coffee-vending machine. As they poured cups of caffeine, the glow on Ashu's face made him a little envious.

"Have you told your boss, Shelly?"

"Yes, he was the first person. Bastard could not believe that despite his bad mentoring, constant bickering and harassing, I still did manage to get through at Sailnet." Ashu laughed. "He was giving me *gyaan* as to how this is not the apt time to leave CommTech as it needs me blah blah. Mother fucker, he himself is busy floating his CV around. Just because he can't get another job, he wants to pull me back in this shithole."

His phone rang and Ashu stopped to answer a call.

"Thank you sir. No I will just wrap up my things here, in a day or two, and move. As I am joining the competition, Sailnet, even you guys won't be too comfortable having me around. Sure sir. Thanks again sir."

He got back to their conversation. "Rohit Dhawan". He shared the caller's name. "Pretty decent chap. It is just that he has been caught in the coterie of Pirates of the Caribbean."

"Who told you of this pirate thing?" VVS could not help but smile.

"*Arre*, everyone knows it. Why do you ask?"

"Nothing. Just curious."

"Did I tell you what did Capt Jack Sparrow's most useless pirate, Shelly, said while I was coming out of his cabin?"

Naturally VVS had no clue.

"He had this expression of disbelief on his face and then he asked me how could they have hired me without doing a ref check with him."

VVS knew that within large organizations, ref check

or 'Reference Check' was an integral part of the hiring process. The remarks of your present boss or line manager did make a lot of difference. Adverse comments from your existing boss always proved fatal. Therefore, everyone tried real hard to keep their bosses in good spirits. Knowing the same, the bosses used it to their advantage.

"I told him that during the HR round, the first round itself, I had mentioned a bad line manager being the reason for my looking out." Ashu laughed again.

"I am so happy for you. Now tell me what's the other piece of good news?" VVS was inquisitive.

"Well Shubhankar has been sacked."

"What? Is the list out?" VVS was hit by a bolt of lightening.

"No, the list is not out, but this jack ass got himself out by biting more than he could chew." Ashu casually sipped his coffee.

"But wasn't he just promoted?," Ashu's revelation was not making any sense to VVS.

Ashu ignored the comment made by VVS and went ahead with his own explanation. "Well, we know that he was upset with your appointment as a Brand Manager. So to set it right, he wrote a number of emails and sent them to various people."

"And then?"

"Nothing, his childish behavior annoyed some high-placed executives as he was pointing direct fingers at RC and Lawrence, who are a part of the leadership team. As you know, more than our Parliament, it is the corporate cabinet that believes in collective responsibility."

"I didn't get you?"

"Le us assume for a moment, that you are not the right guy for the post."

VVS's face turned red, which was well noticed by Ashu.

"I am just taking a hypothetical situation," he clarified and carried on with his explanation. "Now you were hired out of RC's budget and your candidature was forwarded by Sandy and approved by Lawrence. So, if you are not the right guy and still managed to get hired, it means that all the three—RC, Sandy and Lawrence—did not discharge their duty properly. Therefore, for intentional dereliction of their duty and gross negligence they should be placed under the scanner. This, in turn, would place the APAC leadership under scanner who had hired such incompetent people and assigned them leadership positions. This would go on and the buck would stop nowhere." VVS could see the long chain of action and reaction.

"But on what ground was he fired?" He knew that despite the collective responsibility of whatever, they could never fire anyone without any valid reason.

"You know, these leaders are *haramis* of the first order. When they want you out, they plan it so beautifully and when they want you in, they do it so effortlessly." He winked at VVS, which embarrassed him, as the point of reference was his own candidature.

"Ashu, what could be beautiful about sacking someone? Don't we know he has an ailing father, a family to take care of?" VVS was losing the whole charm of being a corporate soldier.

"If he knew that he had responsibilities then he should have realized it and stuck to his role without being the Don Quixote."

"But he was just being honest," VVS countered.

"So you mean that you are not a worthwhile candidate for the role of the Brand Manager?" This direct question was far too close for comfort and sent VVS on the back foot.

"It is not that. But then, we all know people react differently to the same stimuli. Maybe Shubhankar did overreact." If VVS had his way, he would have just swept the entire issue under a carpet.

"*Thakur*, this is corporate world. And the only way to act and react is to mind your own business, suck up to your boss and keep out of the way of the high and mighty. Hope you get this in your head too." Ashu was clear in his articulation.

"But how and why did they sack him?" VVS wanted to get Ashu back to the point of correlation.

"He was made Prime-Business Intelligence, APAC and was to be based out of Singapore. For this new role, he was sent to Bangalore for a two months' training."

"Yes, the other day we had gone drinking to celebrate his promotion," VVS could still remember how happy Shubhankar was. He had planned everything. With his increased salary, how much more he would save, how he would prepay his home loan and then the car loan.

"Correct," Ashu continued, "Before taking up his new role, he had to resign from his present position. The moment he did, someone else was hired in his place. The headcount was complete. While he was in Bangalore, the position for which he was hired, got axed. So naturally, he was also axed. When he went to his line manager, she simply expressed her inability to do anything. So now it seems that the management, knew of this role getting axed, and therefore, lured Shubhankar by offering him an out-of-turn promotion."

VVS was shivering with rage. The genetic violence and anger curled inside him. "You alright?," Ashu patted his shoulder. VVS just chose to walk away from the scene dialing Shubhankar's number.

***

"How are things between you and Rajeshwari?," *Bai ji's* tone was unsympathetic.

"*Bai ji*, what a surprise. It is so good to hear your voice." VVS was quick to use his corporate way of handling callers, who dropped out of the blue and then upset you with their straight questions. He was in office, his swivel chair reclined at precarious angle, laptop on his lap, updating his Coffee Art page on Facebook.

"Stop lying. Since you were kid, you have been a terrible liar and would always get caught. Just answer my question, I am your mother, don't hide things from me."

"Who told you this?"

"The neighbors," she sounded irritated. "Why are you asking all this? Can't I sense that something is wrong?"

"Did Rajeshwari tell you anything?" VVS felt the anger raise its ugly hood.

"You should have known her better than this."

"Then how can you assume things?," his city dweller tone and patience was fading fast.

"Because she has gone to her father's place and is not ready to come back. Her father came over and requested us to look into things and rectify them."

Never during his married life had he assumed that someone like Rajeshwari—docile, and submissive, with no idea of the world or its working, could ever take such a definitive step. In a Metro, married women walking out of their marriages was normal. But back in Akhepur, it was something unheard of. He knew that to avoid serious social repercussions, he would have to do something right away.

"I will call her and will ask her to get back immediately," the man in him took charge.

"No, you are not going to do this. Your *Daata* and *Dadosa* are coming to Delhi, after three-four days, to attend a marriage. They will come to see you and have a word with you."

"*Bai ji*, but..."

"Can't your father and brother come to see you?" The conversation ended.

***

Many hours later, sitting with Ambica, at Rockman's Beer Island, he looked exhausted. The place brewed fresh beer and both of them experimented with a few samples before settling for wheat beer accompanied by Ceaser salad. She was silent and was observing various shades play hide and seek on his expressive face. Both sipped on silently.

"All well?," she enquired.

"Yeah... almost!"

"What's bothering you?"

"Nothing in particular."

"Ok, let me rephrase my question. What is bothering you generally?"

"Nothing as such. I am good." He replied with a forced smile, the vacant look in his eyes, now, very pronounced. "Ok, I won't ask if you don't want to share." Her last line worked.

"What should I tell you? Ever since I have landed in this city, there has not been a single day when I have felt totally happy. The day I landed, the company went bankrupt, then my job was on the line, the tension of shifting within the organization itself, the PRS campaign fiasco, Rajeshwari being after my life, the hacking episode and now the news that *Daata* and *Dadosa* are coming to meet me."

"Who?" She did not get the colloquial salutation.

"I mean, my father and elder brother."

"But you should be happy about it. Shouldn't you?"

"Under normal circumstances, yes. But not right now."

"And why is that?"

"Cause they would insist on visiting my place."

"But what is the problem?" She could not see his Achilles heel.

"Ambi, how would a father feel when he comes to know that his married son is staying with two women, in the same apartment?"

"Hmmm", she could see the reason for his discomfort.

"So what have you thought?"

"I can't think of anything."

"But I can," she smiled.

"Can you? What is it? Tell me," he got excited.

"Not until you buy me another beer."

It took many rounds of beer and starters to finalize the detail.

The plan was simple. VVS would meet them at his office, giving them the story of too much work. If they insisted on coming over, he would bring them to the apartment. It would be absolutely safe to do so as Chaitali would be out of town, covering the PM's visit to SAARC nations. The rest was a breeze. To lock the two rooms and tell his family that they belonged to his apartment mates. If at all, they insisted on staying over, Ambica would spend the night at her friend's place.

Jai Shree Naathji, VVS thanked his deity. To thank the other God, rather Goddess in his life—Ambica, he was only too happy to offer her what she wanted—another day out with beer and chicken *tikka.*

***

The Bitch

It was a big call, an important one and in all probability to have far-reaching consequences on the APAC marketing team. It was a call to welcome Amanda Wither, the new Marketing Leader, APAC. Sue was also joining the call. Everyone who was anyone in the marketing function was on the call. Sandy's other team members, Kaustav, Payal and Shubha, were also present along with VVS.

The entire APAC marketing team had logged on a few minutes in advance. Burying their differences of the past, the team got together to face the stranger on board. A group chat box was initiated by Allan to have the entire marketing team on it, less Lawrence.

The chat started.

"So, the King has stepped down and we are here to welcome our new Queen." It was Allan.

"Queen my foot. I have done a little background check on her. She is a mean bitch who is known to be a control freak." Amy was offensive.

"From where did you get this info?" Allan enquired.

"Linkedin, check out her lame recommendations and I also happen to know a few people who had a chance to work with her in her previous org. Going by the feedback, we are in for trouble." Amy explained.

"There is nothing much she would be able to do any which ways. The sales funnel is almost dry and we are not getting any new leads to replenish it." Jane sounded sarcastic as she was hoping to replace Lawrence. After all, she was managing the largest of the territory and had been with CommTech for over eleven years.

"Sandy, what is keeping you silent?" Allan probed.

"Nothing," he replied.

"Scared for your team?" Jane enticed him.

"Do I have a reason?" Sandy was the cool one.

"Going by what Lawrence said to me, you ought to be." Jane was known for her proximity to Lawrence.

"And why is that?" Amy jumped in.

"It seems that Amanda has been sent here to do a clean-up act. The leadership found Lawrence to be too soft. Before the acquisition, the leadership wants to streamline the APAC marketing as whosoever acquires CommTech, will have to focus on Asia for the numbers," Jane explained.

"Hey Virendra, you there?" Allan prompted.

"Sure Allan."

"Any headway on the leak of the PRS campaign?" Before VVS could type anything, Sandy took the question.

"How is he supposed to clarify anything Allan? The leak did not happen out of India. If it ever happened, it happened at your end."

"Do you mean, I leaked the thing?" Allan was quick to jump into the aggressive boots.

Another message box popped on VVS's screen. It was from Sandy. "Don't respond to Allan. Let me handle him."

VVS knew it well that it was not just one chat box, which was happening between Sandy and him but there would be numerous chat boxes, active between numerous people—Jane and Allan, Allan and Amy, Sandy and Kaustav, Kaustav and Shubha, Shubha and Payal, Payal and Kaustav, Kaustav and Sandy. No one was a permanent friend or a foe. Relationships were based on mutual convenience or depending on the need and call of the hour.

The MCS interface on his screen showed everyone that the chairman of the call, Lawrence, had joined in. Within a few seconds, the green light against Sue also blinked, announcing her presence. With his boss, Sue, on the call, Lawrence got straight to the point.

"Good morning friends. Thank you all for making it here at such a short notice. As you must be aware, I have been asked by the global leadership to take up something more critical within the CommTech system. Today is my last day as VP, Marketing and Communication, APAC."

"Hey Jane, do you know what role he is moving into?" Allan asked Jane in the main chat box.

"Chicken roll. Lol. He has been asked to pack his bags and leave asap. He will be based out of Sydney. Role will be decided later," Jane replied in the private chat box going on between her and Allan.

"I am very proud to leave APAC marketing in a healthy shape, achieving its numbers, quarter after quarter, and I am sure that this trend will continue. It was great working with you guys and surely we will be in touch. Now I would like to hand over to Sue. Sue, please." Everyone on the call noticed that the flamboyance in Lawrence's speech was missing.

"Morning guys. It's good to be here with you again." VVS was hearing Sue for the first time. She had the voice of a charmer—silky smooth yet powerful, deep and in control.

"Hey Jane, I have been hearing a lot of good things about you and your work, especially the grand success of the last three CIO events."

"Thank you Sue. I guess it is all in a day's work."

"Your spirit is appreciated and I must congratulate you on the number of leads you have managed to generate from those events. I hope that your counterparts do something similar. Replenishing the sales pipeline and the funnel with good leads is the only focus action area right now."

"Sue, I have briefed the entire marketing team on the criticality of generating good leads. With a solid strategy in place, Amanda will have no problem." Lawrence patted his own back. "I hope so Lawrence. Though at times, hope becomes a lethal drug." Sue had a warning tone in her last line. "Ok team; let me introduce to you Amanda Wither, your new team leader. She comes with ample experience in lead generation and has a proven track record in handling the c-suite target audience." Sue elaborated further.

The rest of the call was more of a resume reading and a formal introduction with the team members. Nothing much really except an overdose of smart and spicy comments whizzing across countries via message boxes on each screen!

***

"Afternoon team, well this is my first direct call with you. I know it has been two weeks since I took over this new assignment and I am sure you guys would be wondering about my prolonged silence. But I decided to take stock of the situation before speaking with you."

Messenger boxes were blinking constantly.

"Boss, something tells me that we are in for trouble." Kaustav to VVS.

"Boss, hope we don't get sacked on her day one." Kaustav to Sandy.

"Nice opening line." Amy to Jane.

"Working with a woman boss could be a real pain." Payal to Shubha.

"I swear." Shubha to Payal.

"Welcome to the jungle where we are led by a lioness, not a lion. Lol." Allan to Sandy.

"Just hope that she is a man eater. Lol." Sandy to Allan.

"Gosh, she is so full of herself. Lawrence gimme a break." Jane to Allan.

"Welcome to the jungle with a lioness ruling it." Allan to Jane.

"I am feeling so nauseated by her accent." Amy to Jane and Allan.

"Kangaroos are well known for their accent Lol." Allan to Amy.

"Chk out her LinkedIn pic. She looks like two parallel lines Lol." Jane to Amy.

"I don't know how this place was run earlier, but the results and the sales funnel show that things were just not right. I am not here to change things arbitrarily, but I will demolish anything and everything, which is not efficient. I dream, sleep, eat and drink numbers.

Numbers are my motivators, my inspiration, I live for numbers and I would advise you to start doing the same if you were not already doing it. After all, marketing is a number game. Isn't it?"

Amanda had a direct, business like voice. It was bereft of any emotions and the tone was just intended to get the work done. The voice of a master.

"Amanda, you are right. Marketing has always meant the same to me." Allan, who by this time was feeling too scared and insecure, jumped in.

"I hate sycophancy and sycophants, so anyone who intends to waste his or my time should please excuse. If you really want to prove a point, get your numbers right." Her whip-like tone hit everyone hard and made it clear that she meant business. "Allan, don't you think that your region has been sucking up funds without showing any numbers? Eh?"

Allan was caught off-guard, after being dressed down in full forum. "Amanda, with the 300k spent, if you look at the leads which I have generated, it works out to around 12.6 per cent, which is 4.6 per cent higher than CommTech's performance matrix." Allan tried to fight it out.

"Going by the same performance matrix, when this 12.6 per cent of your moves to the last step, the buying stage, this percentage turns into a zilch. I mean ZERO." She had her facts right and this forced Allan on the back foot again. "But in this Chapter 11 situation, we are trying to do our best. I mean how can you expect anyone to buy from us?," Allan whined.

VVS was surprised at Allan's change of tone. For the brat that he was, today, on this call, he was singing a different tune.

"Team, I believe that within every roadblock there is a great hidden opportunity. All it takes is a man with conviction and faith to explore it. If anyone in my team, I repeat anyone, thinks this to be a hopeless situation, I guess he or she should start looking for a job right away."

VVS was in for a huge perception shift. To him, Amanda came across as one of the smartest leaders with whom he had managed to interact. Straight talking, no-nonsense and focused. He knew that CommTech needed more of her type, but then, maybe it was a bit too late.

"From now on, every strategy, every plan, every creative shall be approved by me. Every sanction exceeding 10k will need my approval. I want you all to put your heads together and submit a consolidated marketing vendor list by Monday morning, 10 am, my time.

"Amanda, that won't be necessary. I have the list with me. I shall forward the same to you." Amy ventured, but maybe on the wrong foot.

"Amy, if you have the list sitting with you, would you mind explaining how almost all the marketing primes are not working exclusively with our authorized vendors?

Why the invoices have a new vendor name on them every time? As the Marcom Head for the region, did it ever cross your eyes and mind? If it didn't, don't you think it should have?" Amy was silent and so were the marketing primes. The messenger boxes stopped blinking, as if they slipped into a state of shock.

"Now that you have told me about your role Amy, please ensure that the list of vendor hits my mailbox, Monday morning at 10 am." Amanda reminded her just in case there was any ambiguity left. "Also, Amy, please ensure that you send me a detailed report of all the campaigns which were run in APAC. Your report should have the 'dollar spend', along with the 'conversions' and 'business generation'." But for Amanda, every other caller was silent. After seeing Allan and Amy being masticated, others had realized that silence indeed was golden.

"I have to share two more things. One, the PRS campaign and the reason for the way it got derailed and, secondly, the new campaign which we will be launching shortly." Some people never learn and Allan was one of them. "Amanda, that's great. If you don't think I am jumping my guns, would you mind discussing the campaign details with us?"

"Allan, please get your facts right on two grounds. The first one being that I share only on a need to know basis, and the second, yes, as of now I would surely mind sharing it with you or anybody for that matter."

"I am sorry." Allan retreated.

"Sandeep, please set up my call with your team for tomorrow 8 am, my time. I don't think there should be any problem with that. Right?"

"Sure Amanda," Sandy had no choice.

The call left every one shaken. The junior guys got on to portals like naukri.com and monster.com and the senior ones started looking for the number of headhunters.

***

Talking Turkey

"I am sick and tired of this life." He slurred big time and lit a Navy Cut.

"Now what happened? With the hacking episode lying low for the moment, I thought your life was getting back on track." Ambica sounded concerned.

"I know, I should not be bothering you with all this, but I have no one else to share it with."

"It is ok Veer. You can count on me."

It was mid-November—Delhi's most pleasant season. The mornings and evenings were cold and the days were comfortable. It was the perfect time to flaunt the pure cashmere pullovers and cotton jackets. Also the ideal season to make a transition from beer to something warmer— rum, vodka or scotch, which Ambica and VVS just made; from beer to Black Label.

They were sitting in their balcony, which overlooked the vast expanse of the Aravali range. On a small center table, they had their routine chicken *tikka*, fish finger and paper napkins. This time, instead of beer bottles, there were two glasses, some soda and water. The half-empty bottle of Black Label suggested that they were loaded enough to feel more than tipsy.

"The bitch is after my life and happiness."

"Bitch? I thought I am the only one in your life?" she giggled and her slapstick humor made him smile.

"You are not a bitch. You are the bright spot, my only bright spot. And never ever call yourself a bitch," he sounded a little offended.

"I am sorry cutie pie. I really am. But then who is this bitch?"

"The same old hag, Amanda Wither," he mimicked the name in an Australian accent.

She laughed aloud.

"No, really, when I watched Baywatch and other serials on Star, I always assumed Aussie babes to be hot. Never knew the land had its share of ugly and cold bitches too."

"Veer, you are such a nice man. So considerate, compassionate, sensitive and just so nice. Adjectives like the one you just used for Amanda do not suit you. So please, could you refrain from using them, at least when I am around?." He had the look of a pup just caught gnawing on a pair of socks. She smiled and patted his cheek. He smiled back, once he was reassured of her never-ending affection.

"But initially you were so impressed by her. I remember you telling me that CommTech needed more like her kinds. To you, she was a true leader and blah blah blah. Then what went wrong." Ambica probed.

"I don't know. I still stick to what I said about her. But for some reason she hates me to the core and eyes me with suspicion."

"And what is she suspicious of? That you are seeing some woman, other than her?," she giggled.

VVS wasn't amused. "She thinks that I am the one who leaked the PRS campaign. I mean, I only wish I were so well connected." He threw his hands up in despair. "I don't belong to this place, this industry, even this screwed-up corporate world. How on this earth can she expect me to know someone at Sailnet and sell the campaign?"

"Did you tell her all this?"

"Not in so many words, but yes, I did my best to convince her," he poured a large one.

"But going by what you are saying, it seems your best isn't good enough for her." She looked into his eyes and at his face intently. "Come here my pup." She put her right arm around his neck, pulled him close and kissed his cheek. VVS smiled.

"You know, every time she calls me, under some pretext or the other, she rubs in the fact that CommTech APAC suffered a huge blow due to the PRS leak."

"But Veer, are you sure you did not mention anything about the campaign to anyone?"

He looked at her with the lover boy still in his eyes. "No, I didn't."

"So, you mean to say that you never shared the plan or anything with any outsider."

The lover boy in his eyes was getting irritated. Ambica continued, "I mean, if she suspects you, I am sure, she would have some information or some theory to support her notion. Why does she not suspect anyone else? Why isn't she suspecting your boss, Sandy? He is very well connected, the smart mover. I mean why single you out."

"Ambi, please don't start this interrogation again. I have been through this many a time. Now not you, please." The lover boy in his eyes was gone.

"Veer, I am just trying to help you find the reason for her not trusting you. Once we can identify the reason, we can solve it." She was being reasonable, but a drunk, irritated and worked-up man, that too a *bana,* never takes kindly to reason or logic.

"Ok, my Lord, I swear on the *Geeta* that I didn't leak any information. Ok?" His voice was curt and he banged the glass on the table and got up from his chair. His long sitting posture, three to four hours at a stretch, topped with five large shots of whisky had slowed the intake of oxygen to his body. As he moved, to cope up with the sudden activity, his body asked for more oxygen. To get the same, it pumped more blood and oxygen to his heart and brain, and the sudden influx made his world swirl. His head spun and he immediately sat down holding the armrest of the chair.

"Are you ok?," she jumped out of the chair and rushed to him. She got on her knees and held his hand.

"Yes, I am." Being a *bana*, he could never accept that he was hit by alcohol, or for that matter even a tank.

"Veer, please don't get offended. I care for you and I am just trying to help you. Don't take it otherwise, but in good faith you did share the plan with me. Didn't you?," she smiled.

"Yes, and you went ahead and sold the plan to Sailnet. Ambi, please stop sounding ridiculous." Spinning head and the woman whom he loved, casting aspersions, was proving to be a heady mix for him.

"What makes you think that I am not capable of doing so? Just because I am a woman?," she countered.

"Please don't bug me."

"No Veer, please answer me. What makes you think that I couldn't have leaked the plan?," she insisted and her tone was a sure give away of being hurt.

"Baby, it's not a press release which you go around distributing to journalists. It is strategy, numbers, data. Now, could you please get me some more *tikkas*." His voice had equal portions of sarcasm and pity for Ambica.

"Veer, I expect you to show some respect towards me and my work. And stop treating me like your *gaaon wali biwi. Tikkas* are on the table. Heat them and shove them up your..." She stomped away.

VVS knew that he had exceeded his brief by every stretch of imagination. He got up and followed her.

"Ambi, I am sorry. Ambi, listen to me. Please."

Bang! The door closed on his face.

***

Ding-dong.

Ding-dong.

Ding-dong.

The doorbell went for the third time. VVS could only hear the bell but was in no position to answer it. His eyelids felt lead heavy and temples throbbed with a dull ache. Maybe, his switch to Black Label did not go well with his system. Fortunately for him, the disharmony of the doorbell stopped. He assumed that someone would have got the door and he tried slipping back into a recovery sleep.

Knock knock.

Knock knock.

"Yes", he could barely speak as his throat and lips were parched.

Knock knock.

Knock knock.

The intensity of the knocks increased. He dragged himself out of the bed and opened the door. It was Ambica. Even with a bad hangover, he was happy to see her. He assumed, maybe she had come to say sorry about the last night.

"There is a gentleman sitting in the living room who claims to be your *Daata*."

The word, *Daata*, hit him like a train. His hangover vanished immediately. He panicked and his mind went numb—with fear. He did not know whether to run away or just hide somewhere, or maybe go out there, hold *Daata's* feet and beg for forgiveness.

"Veer," Ambica whispered, "what am I supposed to do?"

He realized that she was standing right there in front of him. He was in no position to suggest anything, but he tried.

"Could you get some tea?"

As she turned towards the kitchen, he got into his track-pant and sweat shirt and hurried towards the living room.

"*Khamaghani Daata.*" He bent to touch his feet.

Daata inspected him minutely. His face was bereft of any expression.

"I thought that today being Sunday, you will be at home. I tried your number but it was switched off." He cursed himself for keeping his phone switched off. If only he had answered his call, he could have thought of some excuse to stop him from coming over.

"Your mother has sent this bag for you," he pointed towards a big bag.

Ambica came holding a tray with two cups on it. She had changed from her robe into a long skirt and shirt. *Daata* looked at her as she placed the cups on the table. "Tea," she murmured.

Daata took a sip or two and then got up. "I am getting late."

VVS did not know if he should ask him to stay or should see him off. He chose the latter. "I will come downstairs with you. How have you come?"

"No, no, you carry on. Satyaveer was kind enough to lend me his car and driver."

Downstairs, near the car, they both stood silent. *Daata* looked at him. VVS moved his eyes down, as if trying to search for something on the road.

"Today, for the first time you have proved that you are my son, a true *Thakur*."

VVS was confused and he looked up.

"Just ensure that you can maintain the balance between the two. You sure have good taste in women."

He got into the car and closed the door. VVS stood there, baffled yet happy that the storm had passed.

***

Neel was playing with his white lock of hair. His face had an air of restlessness as his eyes scanned the room casually. It was a big glass-walled office, which was furnished with just a large oak table, a high-back leather chair for RC, two leather upholstered visitor chairs, a small sofa with a set of two small center tables. Three huge planters with potted ferns acted as a curtain from the outside world.

He resumed his playful tryst with his white locks.

The door swung open and RC entered. A black suit with mustard yellow turban and matching tie made him stand out. Neel smiled as RC's combination reminded him of the famous black and yellow taxi.

RC removed his jacket and carefully placed it on the sofa's arm. He walked towards the large oak table and went over to the other side taking up his position. Neel looked at him.

"Anything serious?"

"HR has lodged complaint against you." RC probed his face, trying to decipher the changing hues and contours. Neel was calm. "They claim to have a case of sexual harassment against you." RC elaborated.

"They cannot be serious." Neel tried to smile.

"Neel, didn't I tell you to stop fucking your payroll? Tell me, didn't I?"

In a common man's term 'fucking payroll' translated into having sex with a co-worker. "RC, but I am not. Trust me," his confidence was waning.

"Look Neel, you are a senior executive, the number two here. The day I move up or move out, you will head this company in India. The whole office knows that you are sleeping with that girl, Payal, from the marketing department. Even someone like me can notice it. You guys have lunch together, sit there openly in the canteen for hours, gossip together, even when you are travelling she is on leave. Your calendars are almost synced."

"RC, you are not being fair. She is just a friend."

"And the same friend of yours has filed a complaint that you have been forcing her to sleep with you in lieu of a promotion. I mean, it sounds outright disgusting. You know that this charge probably is the gravest of all. If proved, no one, I mean not even Buck will be able to do anything for you."

"I will kill that bitch." Scorn and revenge was all over Neel's face. His knuckles were taut on the armrest, as he could clearly see his career sinking.

"And Neel, please stop this rhetoric of yours, I will kill that bitch," RC mimicked Neel. "Are we gangsters? Now tell me what transpired between you two. Before you start, let me warn you that this is your last chance to be truthful and to save yourself. If this goes beyond me, then God be with you." RC made his stand clear.

Neel fidgeted. "Ever since our B-school days, you and I have been friends. If you know what the real problem is, as a friend, why can't you solve it? Why do you have to prove it to me that you have superseded me to become my line manager?"

"Neel, you are mixing a cocktail which you know you would not be able to handle." RC was curt.

"Very well I can, RC. Yes, I have been humping that whore. I have been humping her for two years now. The entire CommTech knows it."

"Only then she was not talking." RC clarified. "Could you tell me what was it that you promised her and didn't deliver that she is going hysterical?"

Neel was silent.

"Neel, I am being your friend, not your boss. I am trying to help you out. If we don't nip this thing right here, you know it is going to blow out of proportion. We cannot afford any sort of bad PR at this stage. Tell me what went wrong."

"That bitch wanted an out-of-turn promotion. One night, I promised her that I will speak with Sandy regarding the same. I would have done it too, but then this Chapter 11 happened. I know that she can't be promoted in this scenario." There was not an iota of guilt on Neel's face. All he looked was a little irritated.

RC picked up the receiver. "Sandy, what action do you propose to take on the sexual harassment mail from the HR?" Certainly, RC wanted clear action points. He was listening to him. "No, he is here with me and is apologetic about it. You speak with her and please keep me posted. Also, the resolution of the same should be treated on priority."

RC looked at Neel. "Neel, you have to promise me that you are going to keep away from her. Look at me and assure me." Neel smiled and took a deep breath and excused himself.

Power corrupts, and absolute power corrupts absolutely.

***

Cards on the Table

Amidst a roller coaster ride—the demon of Chapter 11 looming large, employees getting sacked, cross-function switch, the PRS leak, the hacking episode, VVS completed his five months at CommTech. Torn between Amanda's growing demands—in terms of instant replies, regular calls, updated time sheets and datelines, and the other two women in his life, Ambica and Rajeshwari—he was trying his every bit to strike an equilibrium.

Rajeshwari had come back to Akhepur. But she had stopped calling VVS after a night of intense argument where she wanted to speak with his apartment mates. Of course, he had to turn down her demand. The refusal on his part strengthened her hunch that he was engaged in asking 'how was it' with some other woman. Her intuition was confirmed when VVS refused to swear on Shree Naathji, telling her that it was not right to drag God into such petty matters.

On the other hand, Ambica had moved quite close

to him. Except for her minor mood swings, she was the only constant source of joy in his life. From hand holding to necking and petting, everyday promised and delivered something new and more.

On the 27th of every month, without fail, his salary got credited to his corporate salary account. On the Intranet, with his GID, he could print his salary slip and see the entire salary structure, the deductions made, etc.

The Lead Generation and End Customer events, and the CIO round table conferences, held in Delhi, Mumbai, Kolkata and Chennai, gave him a chance to travel and stay at the best of the hotels. Like a smart corporate dude, he would always plan these events on Fridays so that he could mix business with pleasure. Of course, Ambica travelled with him every now and then.

Even after getting a chance to lead his dream life—working with an MNC, flouting his laptop and Blackberry, staying with the woman he loved, miles away from the *banas*—something was amiss. Something or the other kept bothering him, both on personal and professional front. The realization that his so-called dream life was just a big bubble and the day his name would appear in the dreaded layoff list it would burst, scared him. Also, the face-off experience with the corporate world had left him disenchanted. He tried being like other CommTech employees, who were scared but loved the whole rigmarole about their existence—playing call-call, sipping coffee, idling and doing nothing. However, restlessness always haunted him. He realised that his problem was neither Udaipur nor Gurgaon, nor did it have anything to do with Web Link or Comm Tech, but the root cause was somewhere deep within him. More than anyone or anything, he was the reason for his permanent state of quandary. After all, life was all about adjustments, compromises, alignments and acceptance as there was no world or life, which was perfect.

Failing to accept and imbibe this fundamental did not let him live the moments fully and he wanted some divine intervention, some guidance, some help.

***

They sat there, in the waiting area.

"Ambi, are you sure this is the place?"

"Yes and please be patient," she whispered.

Suddenly the door on their left opened and a couple walked out, discussing something.

"Please send them in," a strong, female voice instructed the servant.

They removed their shoes and sandals and entered the room. It was sparsely furnished. A large mattress with white bedsheet occupied one-third of the room. A few cushions were placed against the walls. On the mattress, towards the far end, sat a woman. Dressed in an obnoxious floral, green and red gown, she was in her late forties, more than plump; with a round face and a pleasant smile.

"Please be seated," her sweet voice greeted them. "Tell me what would you like to know?"

"Usha *ji*, I have been facing certain glitches in my life and would like to find out the reason and cure for the situation," VVS briefed her.

Usha smiled and adjusted herself on the cushion. "What is your name?," her question was directed to VVS.

"Virendra Vikram Singh."

"I see that you do not belong to Delhi. Do you?," she looked at his face.

"No, I am from Udaipur, Rajasthan."

"Ah, I have been there. Beautiful place, quiet and serene. But coming from such a peaceful city why are you so confused in life?"

"I guess we all are. Aren't we?," he smiled.

Usha closed her eyes and her head bobbed, slightly, and her eyelids twitched, as if she was trying to read something in the air around her. She opened her eyes and looked at him. "But your confusion is deeper, to seek or to let go, to exist or to perish. Good that you are here. First, we will do a simple spread for you."

She opened a small wooden box, with an ivory inlay, and pulled out a small pack wrapped in a piece of red velvet. She opened the folds of the velvet carefully and took out the pack of Tarot cards. As she started to shuffle the deck, she looked at VVS. "Virendra, you will have to close your eyes and call upon your guardian angels and guides. When I spread the deck before you, you will have to pick three cards, using your left hand, one by one. You shall place the same card, without looking at it, before me. Are you clear?"

VVS nodded his head. He closed his eyes and invoked Shree Naathji to come down and guide him through the cards. Usha spread the deck in front of him. "Keeping your eyes closed, and using your left hand, run it over the spread, without touching it, tap the card you would like to pull." He stretched his hand and let his instincts guide his hand over the purple card spread. He tapped a card, which he felt like pulling out.

"This is your past card." Usha placed the card in front of her, still upside down.

He started again, moving his fingers over the spread and seeking divine guidance until he felt like picking another one. "This will indicate your present. Now, give me your future also," she smiled. With his eyes closed, he prayed to Shree Naathji and pulled out the last one.

"Now you can open your eyes."

Ambica placed her right hand on his hand for support and comfort. VVS looked at her and smiled. Usha picked the first card and showed it to them. It had the picture of a skeleton, wearing armor, riding a horse and carrying a flag. There were dead bodies all around. Few people were down on their knees seeking forgiveness. The visual was quite discomforting. Ambica pressed his hand, softly yet firmly. VVS licked his lip and removed the imaginary spec of dust from his chin. Usha smiled.

"Good. Don't worry, It's a major arcana card. It says that in the recent past, something has come to an end and is replaced by something better and new. Have you walked out of a stagnant relationship, job or a situation?"

"Yes, I did move to a new job, from Udaipur to Gurgaon," VVS avoided the relationship part.

She picked up the next one.

"If you don't mind telling us, we would like to know about arcana?" Ambica requested in her bell-like voice.

Usha smiled and pressed her lips as if thinking. "Ok, arcana means hidden. Secret known only to a select few. There are two arcanas—major and minor. The major arcana, has twenty-two separate cards, each of which holds a powerful image. It denotes a broader spectrum. The minor arcana cards are far more specific and talk about things like love, career, wealth, domestic life and so forth."

As she saw the second card, her brows moved. She placed the card on the white bedsheet. It had the image of a castle, perched atop a hill. The castle was hit by a bolt of lightening and was up in flames, with the king falling down, his crown floating in the air. The emotions it evoked were not comforting, to say the least.

"Something quite upsetting has occurred in your present. This would have come unexpectedly. Court case, bankruptcy, marital tension, family tension..."

"But how would you rate my present?" VVS could see that she was right with her next card also. It made him more keen to know about his future.

"A period of chaos and muddle." She looked in his eyes and then shifted her focus to Ambica. "You are his wife?" The question was unexpected, direct and almost fatal and caught both of them off-guard. "Well no, she is my friend, my colleague," VVS jumped to her defense. Usha nodded her head as she picked up the last, the third card. She let out a sigh and kept the card, open before them.

Against the white bedsheet, the blue-colored card with a picture of a red heart with three daggers pierced through it needed not much of an explanation.

On their way back, as the talkative RJ raved and ranted about something which made no sense to either one of them, VVS's mind was trying to decipher Usha's last words, 'Expect Worry and Tears.'

***

Bridge Over Troubled Water

The Tarot reader was quite precise in reading his past and present. Yes, he had moved out of a dying situation—job, city and relationship and moved into a better one. Working for a Chapter 11 company was surely not one of the best things and the hacking incident along with the PRS leak were surely unexpected events. However, what VVS feared the most was the third part, her prophecy—'expect worries and tears'. The line was registered so strongly in his subconscious mind that it had changed him as a person. Every small thing started to play on his mind, every incident made his already taut nerves scream with tension, every time the phone vibrated, he would fear some bad news and would get upset. Living in a state of paranoia, insecurity and fear was eating him up.

It was another normal day when his phone vibrated. It was a call from Sukhram, the SHO of Ranibagh, Udaipur. He asked him to come over to Udaipur for a routine enquiry. Though he assured him that it would be just a routine one, but something told VVS that there was more to it. He told Ambica about it, who in turn called up Chaitali so that she could activate her contact in Udaipur.

VVS took the morning flight and reached Udaipur around 8.30 am. Before he reached the police station, he called up Chaitali's journalist friend, Yudhveer.

"You don't worry *bana*. I have spoken directly with the DIG. He is a close friend of mine. I have told him that you are innocent and Harsh is behind all this. The same has been conveyed down the line. Just sign the paper at the police station and, if you want, you can take the evening flight back to Delhi," Yudhveer sounded cool about the whole thing. For sure, in a small town like Udaipur, if one was working for India's leading news channel, he surely had the contacts to tackle and handle anything—police, mafia, politicians and the system. Thank you Shree Naathji, VVS bowed down his head in reverence.

"And what about Harsh *bana*?" Despite what Harsh had done to him, he still cared for him.

"Nothing. Once the routine enquiry with you gets over, an FIR will be filed naming Harsh as the conspirator and the perpetrator, and then he will be arrested."

VVS got a shock. He never assumed that things would really turn this ugly. "But don't you think... well... can't you do anything?," he felt embarrassed.

"See, this issue has political shades to it and police have to take some action. Chaitali *ji* asked me to see to it that you should go scot free, which I did. And why are you bothering about him? Let him have a taste of lock-up food. Trust me it isn't that bad," Yudhveer laughed.

"Sir, if it's ok with you, can I meet you?" VVS pleaded, as he knew that the journalist was the only key to unlock the door for Harsh.

"Sure thing! And stop calling me sir. The name is Yudhveer."

When VVS reached the police station, as promised, Sukhram was there, ready with his set of standard questions. In the employer's detail, VVS mentioned Web Link as he knew connecting the enquiry to CommTech would mean the end of everything. Sukhram was kind enough to offer him tea and some biscuits. Everything was smooth and VVS knew that Yudhveer had done his bit.

"I was very surprised when I heard your recommendation coming from none other than the SP *saheb*," Sukhram confided. "He is a very upright officer. He told me to exclude your name from this case." In his heart, VVS thanked Chaitali. Sukhram was in no mood to let go of him, he continued, "I knew that you must have used your Delhi connection. Good that you went there. This place has nothing to offer. When SP *saheb* told me your name, I told him that we both belong to Akhepur and that we have known each other for years." VVS smiled.

"Sukhram *ji*, could you please share with me what will happen now?," VVS had saved the most important question for the last.

"*Bana*, there is too much pressure. We will have to take Harsh *bana* in PC." VVS knew that PC meant police custody. Harmless though it might sound, but for a normal man, just a night in PC was enough to haunt him throughout his life. "Do you think anything could be done for Harsh *bana*?"

Sukhram nodded his head in the negative. "You see, if we have to save you, then he will have to be taken in. In the proof submitted by Deepak and Rajan, they have clearly mentioned that the hacking was done from such and such IP, which belonged to a hotel in Delhi. The hotel register showed that Harsh *bana* was there. His bill has got four hours of Internet usage. His laptop has the mails, which he had downloaded from Om and Mewar Travel email IDs. He can't go scot-free."

VVS knew that instead of Sukhram, he should be investing his energies on Yudhveer.

"So, am I free to go?"

"*Arre bana*, when SP *saheb* is with you, who am I to stop you." They both laughed.

***

The rendezvous point was Hotel Swaroop Vilas. It was a mid–sized, fifty-room hotel, which catered mostly to foreign clientele. Located opposite the Swaroop Sagar Lake, during the monsoon, the rooms offered a breathtaking view of the same. VVS was surprised to see that a journalist could not only pull strings within the cops-politicians-bureaucrats nexus but also with hoteliers. On the hotel terrace, under a big *chatari*—a dome structure, central to Rajasthan architecture; a table was laid with four chairs, Glenfiddich and some salad. Two waiters stood there with folded hands. The whole setting was very exclusive and spelt grandeur.

"Yudhveer *bana*, I belong to this place, but this treatment makes me feel like an outsider. I mean, no one has ever treated me like this." VVS laughed.

"The owner of this place, Kumar *bana*, is my friend. He is kind enough to let me use his hospitality once in a while." Yudhveer was a man in his early thirties and was built like a bull. Despite being a journalist with a leading news channel, he still sported earrings. He had a thick moustache and a voice to match his overall persona.

VVS was accompanied by Harsh. However, Yudhveer had pre-warned VVS that under no circumstance should Harsh know that any influence was used to clear VVS's name from the case.

"*Hukum,* as I told you, Yudhveer *bana* is from Bikaner and has been here for the past three years. Being a journalist, he says he can find out ways and means to help us." VVS proposed.

"Help us? No, it's help me," Harsh was sarcastic.

"Harsh *bana*, see, I don't know what this case is all about, therefore, I won't be able to comment on it. But what little VVS *bana* has told me, if the complainants have the proof..."

"They had a cyber expert to do the entire legwork. With the complaint, they have submitted around a hundred pages of log report as evidence." Harsh could not help but share his frustration. After sharing his frustration, now he was ready to share his intellect. "You know, Yudhveer *bana*, I am a law graduate. And being one, I know that the moment my lawyer tells the judge that the *Baniya* brothers had engaged an expert, even before the crime happened, in anticipation of the crime, the judge will rip apart the whole premise of their case."

"Harsh *bana*, unlike you, I did not go to a law school so I wouldn't comment on the intricacies of the case. Going by my experience, what I do know is, that after interrogating VVS, and collating all the proofs provided by the cyber expert, in all probability they will arrest you." He did a bottoms-up and looked towards the waiter for another refill.

"Yudhveer *bana*, why don't you suggest a way out? Is there any?" The glint in Harsh's heart reflected in his eyes too.

The waiter refilled their glasses.

"Harsh *bana*, have you tried the *laal maans* here?"

"No."

"Then trust me, you have not had the best *laal maans* of this entire region."

He looked towards the waiter, who got the hint and ran downstairs to order the same.

"See *bana*, there is only one way out, and that's to grease the system."

In no time, the journalist had transformed into a broker—a power broker, a fixer.

"I know a couple of guys, who can fix this for you."

"But my lawyer says that on the basis of the complaint and the proofs, which are so inconclusive, they can never arrest me," Harsh wanted to negotiate.

"Suit yourself," Yudhveer did another bottoms-up.

***

"VVS *bana*, they have arrested me."

"What?" VVS was shocked.

"That *harami* Sukhram bluffed me. He kept me under the impression that the investigation was under control, as there was no conclusive proof. But a few hours back he arrested me."

"Have you called up your lawyer?"

"He has gone to Jaipur to attend some marriage. These bastards knew that he won't be in town and, therefore, chose a Friday to arrest me so that Saturday and Sunday being court holidays, there could be no bail. I will kill them all. You wait and see, they will have to pay for this," Harsh was howling. VVS pitied Harsh, who had still not woken up to the change of guard and the wind.

"*Hukum,* where are you?"

"At the Ranibagh police station," Harsh bemoaned.

"Ok, you don't worry. I will be there in another hour or so. I am starting right away."

Last night at Akhepur was a tense one. *Bai ji* and *Daata* both avoided VVS. *Dadosa* completely ignored him. His involvement in the hacking case did not go well with them. Khudabaksh and Khudanoor, his two horses, were the only ones who were happy to have him back. Rajeshwari, like a dutiful wife, served him dinner and then took a bedsheet and a pillow from the bed and made the floor her bed for the night. VVS sat there, on the bed, trying to control his guilt.

"Yudhveer *bana*, police has arrested Harsh *bana*," VVS called up the journalist, seeking his help.

"If that idiot could not see it coming, can anyone do anything about it?," Yudhveer was cold and curt. "Let him rot there. Maybe he will learn a thing or two."

"You have a reason to be annoyed with him. But he is my friend. I can't leave him. I have to do something."

"VVS *bana*, you are a nice guy, a reasonable guy. We

come from similar backgrounds, went to decent schools and colleges and chose to carve a niche for ourselves in the professional world, unlike the other morons of this place. I like you, and as a friend, would advise you to stay away from Harsh. He is not a stable man and will surely get you into trouble."

"Yudhveer *bana*, I completely understand what you are trying to tell me. As we have a lot in common, therefore, I would request you to do whatever you would have done in my situation."

After a couple of hours, VVS was sitting outside the office of SP, Udaipur City. Just a few hours behind the bars had taken the sting out of Harsh. His wine-colored silk shirt, twirled-up moustache and even the gold Rolex failed to impart him any aura or charm. As soon as he saw VVS, he burst into tears. VVS could not believe that the cruel, medieval baron was crying, that too like a child.

Harsh's entire conversation just revolved around the fact that he wanted to get out at whatever cost. Maybe, God heard him. Yudhveer called VVS and gave him a deal. The offer was simple—to pay the SP City a sum of five lakh. In return, he would get Harsh shifted to a constable's quarter, where he would get a bed, home-cooked meal and then the next morning would be presented before a magistrate. There his lawyer could get bail for him. The offer also included filing a weak *challan* within ninety days, enabling him to go scot-free.

The transaction was swift. He handed over the money to the SP City and called up Yudhveer to inform him. Everything was planned for Harsh's smooth exit. He was shifted out of the lock-up to a constable's quarters. His driver got food and a set of fresh clothes. On Monday, he was supposed to be presented before the magistrate.

VVS called up Sandy and informed him that he would need to extend his leave. Sandy did not bother much and asked him to take it easy.

The police team was supposed to present Harsh before the magistrate at 10 am. As his lawyer was still not in town, he was given a government lawyer to argue the bail. However, the lawyer goofed up and the magistrate had no hesitation in granting the cops 'Judicial Custody' for four days. As the magistrate passed the verdict, Harsh lost whatever little sanity he had left. While the cops took him away, the hall reverberated with his yells, "You can't do this to me. I have paid five lakh. How can you put me in jail?" VVS stood there in the courtroom surprised, shocked and clueless, looking at Harsh, who had come dressed in black silk shirt, and red scarf, all decked up to celebrate his bail . He could see Harsh's eyes on him, burning a hole through him.

Outside the courtroom, Harsh was huddled up in the police gypsy and was driven off to Udaipur jail. VVS stood there, outside the court, watching the crowd, feeling lost. He dialled Yudhveer to update him on the development. Yudhveer was a little surprised and asked VVS to get in touch with him after lunch. There was nothing more VVS could do. He got into his car and drove off to his place, Akhepur. He knew that spending a few hours with Khudabaksh and Khudanoor would make him feel good and alive. It had been quite some time since he went riding.

***

Just a night in the prison had changed Harsh completely. He looked miserable. "*Hukum* let me tell you something for once and for all. You got me into all this. I hacked the accounts, just because I respect you. I warned you, didn't I? They were tracking you for a very long time. Even before I hacked into their account, they were waiting for you, as they knew that you would do it. Even after I did it, I warned you about not getting into their account again. You did not listen. And see where you are today."

"VVS please, I know it is my fault. I could not see two outsiders, two *Baniyas*, walk into my city, the city of my ancestors and take away business from me. I am sorry for misguiding you. Maybe, that is why I am here. But, please get me out of here."

"*Hukum*, don't get emotional. I had a word with Yudhveer and it seems that Deepak and Rajan bribed your lawyer and also the public prosecutor, just to put up a weak case. No wonder your bail was rejected." Unlike his earlier self, where he would have threatened to kill everyone, Harsh just nodded his head.

"I have spoken to another lawyer who will argue for your bail in the High Court and by the grace of Shree Naathji, every-thing will be fine."

Nevertheless, there are times when nothing seems to go smoothly. Maybe, Harsh was going through a similar period. The lawyers of the High Court went on an indefinite strike. The law and order machinery of the entire state came to a standstill. VVS could do nothing but drop in to see him every day, with a fresh set of clothes and consolation. The greased palms were still lubricated, so Harsh did not face any major inconvenience in jail.

On the other hand, Ambica was getting anxious and paranoid. She called up VVS at least twenty times a day, enquiring about everything—his breakfast, his schedule, his conversation with Harsh, Yudhveer and the lawyer, the latest development, even about his office work. She transferred twenty thousand rupees to VVS, as he needed some money. Being in love was such a good feeling and when your loved one cared for you, it was even better. Amongst all the confusion, alienation, chaos, accusation and muck around him, it was only Ambica and her thoughts that gave him all the support he needed. He felt blessed to have someone like her in his life.

VVS had informed Sandy about the actual situation. Being a person, who always stood by his friends, Sandy understood the state of affairs and had no issues with his leave. But then, considering the change of guard at the APAC level and Amanda's whimsical ways, he suggested VVS to buy a USB modem as it would let him connect to the Intranet, enabling him to take the calls on the new campaign. In any case, he was getting his official mails on his Blackberry.

Rajeshwari acted like a stranger. She served VVS food and looked after his basic needs, but chose to sleep on the floor. VVS did not like it one bit as he did not want his stay to cause her such an inordinate amount of inconvenience. He did try to communicate with her, but she was in no mood even to initiate a dialogue. *Daata* and *Dadosa* just remained obscure shadows. Maybe even *Bai ji* was instructed by *Daata* or *Dadosa* to boycott him. For a change, VVS loved staying at the *haveli*. He would get up early and go for long walks. The razor crisp, fresh winter air gave his lungs the much-needed break. Coming from a concrete jungle like Gurgaon, the sight of the yellow mustard fields and corn plantations were extremely soothing. After the walk, instead of green tea, he would have *raab*—crushed and boiled corn mixed with curd. Then he would saddle up either Khudabaksh or Khudanoor and go riding, for an hour or two. He was happy to see that his riding skills were still intact. He would also ensure that he gave the horses a good scrub and massage. This was followed by bath and breakfast and then he would leave for Udaipur jail to meet Harsh.

If there would be an important call, he would search for a quite place, boot his laptop, hook up his modem and join the call. In any case, with Amanda on the call, no one else was supposed to do any talking. Life was under control. The only thing he missed was Ambica.

***

"Hi, how are you doing?" The bell-like voice was always so nice to hear.

"Missing you!" The lover boy replied.

"You liar, when I call you start to miss me otherwise you don't even bother to call me."

"You know it's not true. Apart from you, who else do I have to miss?"

"Well how about Amanda?" They both giggled.

"Ok listen, one of my colleagues is going to Udaipur. I have sent something for you."

"What is it?"

"You impatient man, didn't your Mom teach you that patience is the biggest virtue of all?" She chided playfully. "Tell me what it is?"

"You know that I won't?" She was playing the perfect tease.

"Ok, I don't want to know."

"Is my baby sulking? Is he?"

"No, he is not."

"Oh my baby, Mama misses u soooooo much."

"Baby misses Mama too," VVS could not resist her charm, even over the phone.

"Listen, he will be putting up at Lalit Laxmi Vilas, room number 2116. Be there at six, he will be waiting for you. His name is Sameer. After collecting the package, let me know."

***

Overlooking the Fateh Sagar Lake, the Lalit Laxmi Vilas Palace had the majestic Aravalli Hills in its backdrop. It radiated the charm of an era characterized by the grandeur of royalty. Built by His Highness Maharana Fateh Singh in 1911, this heritage hotel was on a hilltop.

VVS entered the lobby and straight away took the stairs. Ever since he had come to Udaipur, which was just six days ago, despite all the tension, he felt fit and bursting with energy. His meeting with the lawyer had taken longer than expected. He was late and hurried towards room number 2116.

He briskly walked through the carpeted corridor checking out the room numbers. There it was. Etched on a gleaming brass plate, screwed to the shining oak door, the numerals—2116. He adjusted his hunter coat as he wanted to make a good impression on Ambica's colleague.

As he knocked the door, he could hear some commotion inside the room, and then someone walk to the door. The door opened just about few inches. It was dark inside so he couldn't see the man behind the door.

"Hi, I'm Veer. Ambica has sent me…"

A hand darted and grabbed his collar and pulled him in. He was too unprepared for this assault and could not put up any resistance. By the time his senses adjusted to the new environ, he was inside the darkened room, engulfed by fear. He strained his eyes, to see anything around, but it was too dark. Beads of perspiration were on his forehead. Fear had almost paralyzed him. Something moved beside him and he felt his face warming up. He did not move out of sheer panic. The warmth moved closer to his ear. His heart was beating violently, hitting at his rib cage. He raised his hands involuntarily, ready to counter any assault. The warmth became more intense, now with a sound that of a hissing snake. He was drenched in sweat, waiting for whatever was coming his way.

"My baby, Mama missed you." And the lights came on. Ambica was there, right in front of him, her face close to his face. He could not believe his eyes. But when he did, embarrassment hit him for being a sissy in front of the woman he loved. It angered the man in him. He pushed her aside and walked inside the room, taking a few deep breaths, regaining his composure and letting his nerves settle down.

Ambica handed him the bottle of water. He opened the cap and emptied the entire bottle.

"Sorry Veer, didn't mean to scare you. I wanted to surprise you. I am really sorry." Tears swelled in her big deep eyes and within no time washed away the anger and embarrassment of the lover boy. He hugged her tight and she hugged him back tightly. He could feel the warmth of her body. He kissed her neck and she moaned. VVS held her face, tenderly, as if holding a precious trophy, and kissed her head, her forehead, her temples. She closed her eyes and his lips planted hot kisses on her eyelids, warming them. VVS pressed her close, crushing her breasts to his chest. He could hear her heart race like a chugging train. He loosely held a strand of her hair and looked deep into her eyes. Then spotting the faintest invitation in the depth of her eyes, he bent over and kissed her ear lobes, lightly licking them as she moaned his name. Without even saying a word, they sank into red and green thick carpet. Passion and sweat flowed in unison.

Lying in the huge, king-sized bed now, VVS kissed her head again. She snuggled close to him and placed her head on his chest.

"I cannot believe that you…I mean we are here."

She giggled. "One of our clients was a sponsor of the vintage car rally which was held here today. My colleague,

Sameer, was supposed to travel and coordinate the PR, but he fell ill. So, I took the initiative and volunteered for it. I was missing you too much. So, during the first half of the day, I was at the event. Once it got over, I packed the journalists off to Delhi and came to see you." She kissed his chest. He kissed her back.

"Did you miss me?" she asked

"No, I was missing Chaitali."

"What? You rascal!" she bit his chest. He screamed. They both laughed.

"Shut up," she chided him. "Tell me how much did you miss me?"

He kissed her head again. "More than I have missed anyone in this life."

She giggled again.

"How is your work? Is Amanda still screaming at you?"

He pointed towards his laptop. "Bless technology! She is not even aware that I am not in Gurgaon. I take all my calls, using the MCS and am always on mails, courtesy my Blackberry," he winked.

"But what about the campaign you were supposed to handle?"

"Oh! the Contact Center one? This time, Amanda has decided to handle it herself."

"What? That's not fair. How can she do this?" Her voice lost control.

"Baby, you are overreacting. In a way, it is good. Let her do all the work. Before launch, it has to come to me. So what is the hassle? In fact, this morning, she has sent the final creative to everyone. As she has done it, we can have no issues with it."

His phone vibrated. It was the lawyer. He looked at her and she smiled. "I know it could be an important call. Please carry on. Can I use your laptop?"

He nodded as he took the call. She got up from the bed and wrapped a towel around her and disappeared towards the washroom.

***

Ambica stayed back for another day and then went back to Delhi.

VVS met up with Yudhveer and requested him to pressurize the cops again. Yudhveer told him that once the bail comes up for hearing, it would be granted as he had taken care of everything.

Finally, the strike got over and after pulling a lot of strings, here and there, Harsh's bail came up for hearing the very first day. As promised by Yudhveer, the bail was granted. Again, time was not on Harsh's side. By the time the release order was typed and sent back for signature, it was 5 pm and the judge had left for the day and was supposed to get back only after the weekend.

VVS was getting frustrated. It had been ten days since he had come to Udaipur. Now even Sandy wanted him back. There was no way he could stay back any longer. Yudhveer assured him that there would not be any more hitches in the release. VVS told Harsh that he had to leave due to some important work. After doing all this for him, VVS sensed that he still did not seem to be very happy.

He packed his bags, patted his horses, kissed them and left for the airport.

***

As soon as he landed at the new T3 terminal, the sheer magnitude of place, along with the surge of critical mass-made him miss Udaipur. The Maharana Pratap Airport of Udaipur was calm, cozy and almost cute. One could just stroll down to the airplane. But then Delhi had its own charm—Ambica. He was so happy to be back to his love, his life, his everything. From Udaipur, he had bought her a silver trinket, a silk scarf, a silk *kurta* and a pair of *Udaipuri jootis*, the size for which he did remember to take on a sheet of white paper by tracing her feet on it, while she was there.

When he reached his apartment, both Ambica and Chaitali were there. He thanked Chaitali for all her help and gifted her a hand-made silk top along with an antique silver bracelet. Chaitali thanked him and excused herself, as she wanted to go and watch a movie. The moment she left, he hugged Ambica.

"I am so glad to be back with you!" he kissed her forehead.

She did not respond.

"Everything ok?"

"Yes."

"Hey, look what I have got for you." He went and opened the bag and pulled out a few packets. While she kept on telling him that the *jootis* were nice, and the *kurta* and the trinket were cool, he could feel her mind wavering and wandering. He did not force her to tell him the reason, as he knew the inkling of slightest pressure would make her get in her shell. He wanted to sleep for a while and then prepare for the week ahead. It had been quite some time and he was eager to get back to CommTech—back to coffee, Monaco and Good Day biscuits.

***

Change Management

VVS's joining day could not have been worse. The whole CommTech office, seventeenth and the sixteenth floor, was in a state of confusion, fear and shock. The dreaded list had been released and was supposedly sitting with RC. No one had any clue about its content, names to be precise. It was largely believed that the accounts department already had the list as they were asked to prepare the full and final settlement account for the names on it. This assumption had put Abhishek under tremendous pressure. His messenger, mobile and ESN just kept on pinging and ringing. Finally, he had to change the status on his messenger to, "Don't pray, 'cause now it's too late."

There was a GIS at twelve noon to be chaired by RC. It was supposed to be a turning point as it promised its own share of revelations.

Today, the boisterous Aditya was tamed down and even the 'cool as cucumber' Manish was a little ruffled. Sandy's team members—Kaustav, Payal, Shubha were very apprehensive. For some reason, the Pirates of the Caribbean were very confident—Shelly to Neel, Edgar to Sandy. Even amidst all the fear and quandary, Shelly, who worked out of the Gurgaon office, was busy shooting terrorists on Delta Force, on his laptop. His face did not display even the slightest trace of worry. When someone enquired about the list, the pink-slip and RC's call, in his trademark, complex English, he rambled some religious spiel of there being only one provider and protector.

Following the PRS incidence and Amanda's growing curtness, even VVS was very frightened. He had nothing to fall back on. Unlike Shubhankar, Manish or Aditya—all technocrats, MBAs and into the corporate world with over a decade of technical, sales and project management experience, he was just a plain graduate. Too bad, when he could have walked into an IIM, he was too busy treading on a path laid down by his new-found God, Sandy.

He still remembered that while all his college batchmates were not to be seen, as they were burning midnight oil for CAT, he was busy planning Delhi University Students' Union election for Chandrajeet Thakur. Thakurji, as he was fondly called by his fans and followers, was a powerful student leader with a huge support from the student lobby of Bihar and eastern UP. On Sandy's insistence, he had taken the entire responsibility of managing Thakur's campaign. And the trade-off! An

MBA seat at the prestigious IMT, Ghaziabad, under the ministerial quota. So instead of sharpening his logical reasoning and vocabulary, he got engrossed in analyzing and profiling the students on the basis of state and caste, planning and allocating budget for the entire campaign, writing speeches and campaigning for Thakur.

With his intellect, in no time, he was Thakur's right-hand man. For every important meeting—addressing the students at a girl's college to meeting some minister, he was right next to Thakurji. His proximity to Thakur also gave him a face with the cops and the local shopkeepers. The cops started saluting him; the local shopkeepers would not bill him for his tea and Navy Cut. Sandy felt like a proud father watching his influence grow. The election campaign was heating up and so were the preparations for CAT.

The night when the election results were declared sitting at Bara Hindu Rao, the regular joint of the election campaigning team, Thakurji was found weeping like a child and howling, "I have been cheated. I cannot lose this election. I have been cheated. I have lost the war but not the battle. I will be back." VVS knew that his dream of getting into IMT, Ghaziabad, as a ministerial candidate, was shattered.

Some pep talk from Sandy, who had passed out of the college but was still staying in the hostel, made him put in a week of study for CAT. One could only wish that slinging the bell around the CAT were so easy. But he was determined to succeed. Sitting in the examination hall, nothing made any sense to him, least of all, the Logical Reasoning Section. The fatigue of the month-long election campaign, followed by the week of long, late-night studying, did not help him either.

"Manish is taller than Sohan, Sohan is shorter than Ramesh, Hari is shorter than Manish and, therefore Ramesh is taller than...".

All the four options seemed correct and incorrect. In his mind, he tried to figure out the relation between Sohan, Manish, Ramesh and Hari. It was too complex. He decided to do a role-play. He assumed that he was Sohan, sitting on the chair. Then he stood up a little, playing Ramesh. Seeing him playing Ramesh, standing three quarter, the invigilator rushed to him. He had to be assured that it was nothing but a novel way of cracking the CAT. Once the confused invigilator left, he started the process again—of playing Sohan, then Ramesh. Then he looked at the paper to figure out the next relation. So he stood a little more, straining his knees, playing Manish. In his head, he was calculating it all. So if this is Manish, the standing one, and Sohan was the sitting one and if Ramesh was while I was standing a little...

Fuck it! He moved on to the next question.

"Two trains, which are running in opposite directions, cross a man standing on the platform in 27 seconds and 17 seconds, respectively, and they cross each other in 23 seconds. The ratio of their speed is?"

He put his creative visualization to use again. He visualized himself, there on the platform, with a train coming from his right hand side, crossing him. While the train got half-way, he visualized another train coming from the opposite side, also crossing him. So both these trains took twenty-seven and seventeen seconds to cross him, which meant that twenty-seven seconds minus seventeen seconds would be ten seconds. Bingo! Ten seconds to cross each other. Yes he did it, only to realize that the question had asked something else, which was far too complex and beyond the capabilities of his creative visualization skills.

He then resorted to the last technique—the ace about which Sandy had told him. "Look at all the four options and then meditate. Think of all the four options moving in and out, fading and getting bright and then see which one shines the brightest. The truth always outshines everything else. Therefore, if you seek the truth, the correct answer will shine brighter than the others."

This one was easy and he solved all the questions using the divine formula. He should have been thankful to the IIM guys for not sending him his scores.

No wonder he was sitting at CommTech, waiting and praying. 'Shree Naathji, please, I do not want to get sacked. Please help me,' he sent in his application to be processed and to make it work faster he also attached a tag of 'three fasts and three temple visits in a month.'

"Friends, my heart bleeds. But then being the leader I have to be the one to break this news to you."

The GIS had started and RC was conducting it. The office was silent. Every single soul; but for the outsourced services guys like the pantry, maintenance and the housekeeping staff, was on the GIS. Some of them had put the GIS on speaker phone as they wanted to hear the news, the bad or the worst, as a team. The senior guys—the pirates of Capt Jack Sparrow—were too busy pretending, sitting in their glass cabins, with their headsets on.

"Yes, the dreaded list is here with me. I have the list for India. Thirty-five names are on it. But trust me, these names should in no way assume that they are inferior or were less effective than anyone of us. In their respective roles, they were the right choice. Unfortunately, during the reorganization process, either their roles or their verticals had to be done away with. After this call, I will be speaking with each one of them."

Similar calls were happening all over—Toronto, Sydney, Singapore, London, Frankfurt, Paris, across 50 locations, with the sole intention of laying off people.

"Friends, I would like to take this opportunity to let you know that these are tough times. However, if you ask me, this is also the best time to innovate, create, re-align, re-engineer and to help the company in selling more. This is the time to give in everything to your assignments, as this extra input will decide our fate. There is nothing to worry about or fear. I am still the captain of this ship and will be the last man to leave it. With you, my crew, we shall sail fast and sail good. God bless and take care."

In the name of innovation, creation, restructuring, etc., thirty-five people were issued the pink slip, VVS was safe but Manish was not. VVS could not believe this. After all, Manish was one of the few people who really worked at CommTech, that too from morning till late in the evening.

Also, the way in which Manish, along with the thirty-four others, were asked to leave was very humiliating. It seemed that early in the morning, long before the call, the list was handed over to Abhishek. Before the call could get over, the accounts team had worked out the full and final settlement. After the call, the unfortunate thirty-five employees were called, one by one, by Sumit of the HR department. They were told to surrender their laptops, swipe cards, handsets, corporate credit cards etc., with immediate effect, sign the full and final settlement and leave by the fire exit. They were not allowed to go back to their seats and were assured that their belongings, from the drawers, would be sent across to them the next day. No wonder, with phones taken away, no one could call anyone sitting inside the office.

It was only when Manish reached home did he call his ESN to inform VVS. Guilt accumulated in his heart and soul and VVS knew that carrying the burden for too long would get very tough for him.

***

News and emails were pouring in from all parts of the world, highlighting the callous attitude of the leadership towards employee-related issues. For some reason, the top management was only concerned about saving the incentive of the senior executives, not jobs. No wonder, on the one hand there were mass layoffs, while on the other, a retention packet was worked out for the management.

After two hundred employees got the pink slip in Britain, there was a high level of anxiety amongst the CommTech's employees of France. In a development, about hundred and fifty to two hundred employees appeared for a spontaneous demonstration during a monthly meeting in Chateaufort, between CommTech executives and the consulting firm's staff representatives. In other developments, the rally by CommTech pensioners at Queen's Park was taking on a desperate edge as they faced the consequences of the collapse of the telecom giant. A report by the court-appointed monitor, a consultancy firm, told them that critical medical income, life insurance and disability payments could fall by sixty-five per cent.

At a rally held outside the CommTech corporate HQ, workers argued that the province should preserve the $2.5-billion underfunded pension plan from a similar cut. The management was clear on the pension issue. As a company spokesperson, Albert Randell, said, "This is no time to get in a fight with pensioners. It will only increase legal bills and delay a resolution. We are all in a storm and the boat is leaking. Let's not turn it into the Titanic."

The rally outside the HQ was assuming urgency because seventeen thousand pensioners, long-term disability recipients, spouses and dependents were getting their first look at how deep the benefit support would be cut. It made for painful reading. In a nutshell, the salary earner at CommTech, some fifty thousand people, who followed instructions and did whatever they were asked to; who believed in the faceless leadership and in their obscure emails and big promises made over the never-ending rounds of the GIS, were in for trouble.

***

"Hi, long time?" VVS tried his best to sound neutral and cheerful.

"Yes. How are you doing?" Shubhankar's voice lacked its usual zing.

"I am good. You tell me."

"Nothing much. Just trying to face the world and

this life," he let out a faded snigger.

"I am sure, with your experience, you will soon get a job and, that too, a better one," VVS tried to comfort him and bolster his slacking confidence.

"It's not that easy, *Thakur*. Under normal circumstances, I would have got a job within a fortnight. But once you get sacked things change. No one is ready to touch you even with a barge pole."

VVS felt his guts churn and the guilt pangs spreading their tentacles again, over his heart and soul.

"But you can surely explain the situation to the interviewer."

Shubhankar let out a sigh. "*Thakur*, like you, I don't have any Godfather. When Sandy hired you, he had prepared the entire ground for you. The position was created keeping your qualification in mind. It was a tailor-made role. But when you apply in due course, your CV first goes to the HR team. Someone calls you from there and asks you various questions, the main question being the reason for your leaving."

"And can't you tell them the reason?" VVS enquired.

"Well, I can't. Because if I tell them that my role was liquidated, it would mean that my role had no importance in the company. And if I was heading a role which had no importance, then my skills would not be as per the industry standards. So it would kill my candidature." VVS could see his side of the story. Shubhankar continued with his catch-22 situation, "And If I tell them that I was made a scapegoat, as I got into a confrontation with my seniors, it would go against my man-management skills, especially my reporting line skills. So as you see, I am in a soup."

"Shubhankar, is there anything I could do?" VVS had no clue how he could help him

"Just pray for me that I get a Godfather and that too asap. My financial pool is drying up fast."

***

The C Suits

"Gents, we all know that now CommTech is a Chapter 11 company. But there is still some time before it gets taken over by some other brand. Till then, the mandate from APAC is clear—to keep the sales momentum going. This will not only keep us gainfully employed but also help in maintaining a better balance sheet for our prospective buyer." Neel was as articulate as ever. His lock of white hair, hanging insecurely over his forehead like always, imparted him a suave aura.

The conference room was filled with the think tank of CommTech—Pirates of the Caribbean. VVS was the only exception as Sandy had got him under the garb of taking down the minutes of the meeting. VVS watched the cream of CommTech—all dressed in smart business jackets, crisp shirts and silk ties. Seeing them together, he remembered Abhishek telling him that this could be the last opportunity to save CommTech, as it would be the last chance to slaughter the Pirates of the Caribbean. The thought made him smile. For this big meeting, though he had turned up in his best outfit—a black Raymond jacket, a new white shirt and a wine red tie, somewhere he felt that he was the odd man out. Maybe it was his brand new clothes or his age or maybe the uncomfortable look on his face. As it was a big meeting, there was no way he could have got his Rubik Cube.

"Neel sir, considering the marketing stand-point, doing any activity will not make any sense. Our chips are down." Sandy shared his anxiety, while playing with his Mont Blanc pen.

RC shifted his gaze to Sandy and whispered something. They smiled. Sandy showed him his iPhone. Their eyes lit up and they both exchanged sly glances. Sandy's ability to get along with people flabbergasted VVS. Since his college days, he had a way with people. Right from the canteen boy to hostel warden, parking attendant to the college principal, he could befriend almost everyone. Also, this was the first time when VVS was seeing the much talked about RC—Capt Jack Sparrow of the gang. Rakshit Chauhan *aka* RC was a man in his early fifties. A Sikh, his turban added extra inches to his 5'6"-5'7" frame. Slightly on the heavier side, his gelled beard, impeccably-cut suit and accented English made him look like a true business leader.

"Neel, purely from business perspective, I guess the need of the hour is to focus on customer retention, rather than new acquisition. I am sure you will be in agreement that pursuing acquisition will be like a wild goose chase." RC put forward his viewpoint and adjusted his red turban, which today was coordinated with his red tie.

His stint at CommTech had taught VVS the corporate marketing lingo, which included terms like 'customer retention' and 'acquisition', to name a few. 'Customer acquisition' simply meant to launch schemes or campaigns to get new customers, whereas 'retention' implied to hold on to the existing ones by offering them some product or service upgrade.

"Considering the unexpected dynamics that we find ourselves in, it becomes imperative that we resort to a short-term, focused and aggressive data mining on one hand while on the other..."

Shelly was cut short by Sandy. "Shelly, could I please request you to use English?" There was a round of laughter. VVS did not know if he was supposed to join the guffaw or be silent. He chose the mid-path and smiled.

"Guys, this is not fair. At this stage of my life, you cannot expect a catharsis?" Shelly complained.

"There you go again." Sandy pointed and everyone joined him in another round of laughter. Rohit Dhawan, the Sales Leader for the west region, sat silently, listening to people.

"Edgar, what do you say?" Neel directed his question. Edgar, who was busy punching keys silently, with great dexterity, was jolted out of his zone and looked around with no clue of the happening around him.

"Sir, I am sure he would have been revamping his resume when you barged in." Sandy explained Edgar's blank look. Another round of laughter.

VVS was confused. He could not figure out how these senior executives, who were responsible for the company, could afford to keep their cool under such alarming conditions. Weren't they bothered at all? Or may be, they were being too professional about it.

"Gents, if you ask me, let's have a Channel Partner meet. Maybe the last one we have at CommTech. And Sandeep, this time no Phuket, Pattaya or Colombo, please. I am sick of these places." Neel said emphatically.

Before the meeting, Sandy had briefed VVS that most of the large IT companies sold their products through their channel partners. These channel partners were companies, large or small, which were based in different parts of the country. Going by the transactions with a particular channel partner, they were accorded a status—Tier one, two or three. To any company, channel partners were the most important people within the eco-system. Therefore, every company treated them as VVIPs. Apart from running various schemes, promotions, offers, and incentive schemes for them, every year they were taken to an exclusive event, which was held at some exotic location, to pamper and please them. All this was done under the garb of 'sharing the road map ahead'.

"Neel sir, Sri Lanka was not bad. The *Taj Samudra* receptionist still misses you." Sandy's revelation made Neel blush a little, while RC burst into laughter.

"Sandeep, don't exorcise the ghosts of the past, they can haunt you also." Neel protested in good humor.

The whole room echoed with laughter.

Neel fought hard to control his expression, bringing about an air of seriousness and steering the room back on track. "Ok, that is enough of doing Neel's laundry in public." He turned towards Sandy. "Do you think we can have it in Hong Kong? I love the sea food there. Also, I have promised my son a Nintendo." Neel answered his question as well.

"They retail the top end model for 200 USD," Shelly chipped in

"Is it? That's dirt cheap," Neel's eyes lit up.

"Sir, Nintendo will surely award you with a 'life-time' customer award."

"Didn't get you?" Neel looked at Sandy.

"I mean, if you buy a 200 USD gadget for 10 million, won't you deserve the award?" As no one could get the context, Sandy elaborated upon it. "After all, the channel partners meet in Hong Kong will surely cost CommTech somewhere close to 10 million."

The whole room burst out laughing. Only Rohit was silent. So was VVS.

Maybe laughter burnt too many calories as Shelly looked at his watch and made an offer which no one could refuse. "Guys, lunch? I am feeling hungry."

The next half an hour or so was dedicated to deciding the venue and the menu after RC and Neel flatly refused to eat at the office canteen. VVS just sat there, confused and embarrassed.

***

'Hibiscus'—the conference room on the 17th floor of CommTech Gurgaon office—was the meeting place for further discussions on the channel partner event. The people in the room were the same, *Pirates of the Caribbean* and VVS, with just one addition. A fair, tall, broad, burly man wearing an ill-fitting suit, which was a size too small for him. With a red *tilak* on his broad forehead, he looked like the replica of a stout, well-fed *panda*, who inhabited the *ghats* of Benaras. This man was introduced to the cabinet by Sandy as Bunty Tiwari.

Bunty was seated next to Sandy and was trying to adjust his laptop settings to suit the expensive projector, which was clamped to the center of the table. He was tinkering with the switches at random, hoping that his trial and error method would make the things work. The CommTech cabinet, dressed in their usual suits, ties and sleek, black laptops, were waiting for him to start the show. RC and Neel were having an animated conversation on whether to host the event in Hong Kong or Istanbul. The entire board knew that the choice of venue would depend purely on what they were interested in— buying reasonably priced, top of the line, electronic goods or just sight-seeing.

Bunty was still fidgeting, finding it impossible to comply with the exacting specifications of the new-age projector. Neel looked at him, yawned and got back to RC, discussing the merits of venue. Shelly and Rohit were engrossed in discussing some sales report. Amit, Edgar and Sanjay were watching him, killing time, just like VVS.

"Sandeep, you can't expect us to sit here all day, waiting for this projector to light up." Neel complained in his smooth, accented voice. His small face and whip-like tongue had little symmetry. Sandy nudged Bunty who was still trying to find the missing link between his laptop and the projector. Unlike humans and their relationships, the good part about technology is that either it is compatible or not. Surely, Bunty's laptop and this projector were not meant for each other. Not yet.

"Well, though I would need closer inspection to assimilate the facts, but what I can make out from this vantage point is the notebook is a 2002 model HP NX series. And if I can jog my memory...."

"Shelly, can you make the damn thing work?" RC cut him short.

"Sandeep, why didn't you ask the IT guys to fix this before we got into the room?," Neel was also getting a little irritated.

VVS felt bad for Sandy. After all, he was his boss, senior and Godfather and he could never see him take a beating.

"Sir, can I try?," VVS finally found his voice. Though it took him twenty-odd minutes to decide the tone and the precise sentence which he needed to say before the big wigs.

Sandy looked at him and gestured to go ahead.

VVS finally had a chance to repay some part of Sandy's debt. He moved towards the center of table, where the unholy union of laptop and projector was not consummating. Jai Shree Naathji was playing in his mind and heart. At Web Link, he had fixed many things—computers, telephones, pbax, even servers. He had no clue as to how he had acquired the knack to fix things. Maybe, only if his wife was also a thing, he could have tried fixing their relationship too.

VVS clicked on the control panel and browsed through the setting panel.

Jai Shree Naathji.

Jai Shree Naathji.

If it were a typical Mumbai *masala* movie, no doubt the background score would have been full of gongs, temple bells and blowing conches. The image of Shree Naathji would have danced all over the screen, multiplying every second, and the background score would have worked towards a crescendo. And suddenly it happened. The screen on the projector wall lit up. Maybe, the golden rays of the mystical God did finally find VVS. Like a true filmy hero, having found the long sought-after blessing, he smiled. The cabinet sitting around the table looked at him, for the first time, acknowledging him and his talent. VVS felt elated as Sandy patted his back.

"Sandeep, why didn't you ask this boy to do whatever he did right now at the very beginning?," RC complained.

"Because then you would have taken him for granted. He is Virendra Vikram Singh, my new team member. We all call him VVS. Remember, you were supposed to interview him?," Sandy introduced VVS to RC and the cabinet.

"Yes, I do remember. Hi VVS, good to have you on board. When Sandy told me your full name, I thought of calling in my secy to remember it," he smiled. "But with VVS, I can manage. Welcome on board VVS. Good job," RC seemed impressed. VVS did not know how to react. He just stood there, basking in his moment of glory; glory that came to him in front of the top brass of CommTech, a Fortune 500 company.

"Sandeep can we start?," Neel requested with a sense of urgency.

"Sure sir," Sandy got up from his chair. "Good morning. I am sorry for the slight delay due to the inevitable technical glitches. Thank you for bearing with me. Can we all open the PPT titled, 'Channel Partner Meet 2010', which I had sent across last evening?"

Everyone opened the power point.

"Now, if we look at slide one, it states the objective of this meeting which is to decide on a theme for the proposed channel partner conference. Also, we need to get some indicative cost. For the same, I have called one of the better-known event management agencies, Shownine. Shownine has been empanelled with us for quite some time and has been collaborating with us on key projects. Bunty Tiwari, the MD of Shownine, is here to present his thoughts on CommTech's channel partner event theme and its execution. Over to Mr Tiwari."

All eyes shifted to the man who was the culprit for wasting their time. Thirteen pairs of eyes, directed at him, made Bunty nervous.

"Good morning to you all sirs. Sorry for the troubles with your projector." It was the worst opening line he could have made, after making people wait for more than an hour or so.

"It was your obsolete laptop which was the reason, not the projector," Neel cut him to size.

"Yeah, yeah sure sir," Bunty tried to gain some ground.

"And please, without any further delay, get down to the theme slide please." Neel's curtness was embarrassing to Sandy, as he was the one responsible for inviting Bunty over. Sandy gestured Bunty to skip the initial part and to get to the thematic part. However, Bunty was in no mood to let go of the spotlight. He smiled, "When Sandeep called me for the jobs, I was very happy."

Sandy exchanged apologetic glances with the people sitting in the room. RC took a deep breath and straightened his back for a long session.

"It is the great moment for the company, my Shownine. Now I will prove to the entire CommTech that we are the so much best than all the event companies." Wren and Martin would have rapped Bunty on his knuckles hard and then begged him to switch over to his mother tongue, Hindi. "Mr Tiwari, I would request you to come to the conceptual part of the presentation," Sandy could not hold himself any longer.

"Sure sir. It is in a moment," Bunty smiled. "We know that the CommTech is finished. It is gone." There was an awkward silence. Even VVS could feel the temperature beneath his collar rise. RC got very uncomfortable. After all, as the MD, he had every reason to be so. He stared at Sandy. The smart cookie that Sandy was, he chose to look the other way.

Bunty continued, "No one is buying anything from the CommTech, no one is working for the CommTech.

But the Shownine will prove that it is not fair weather friends."

"Mr Tiwari, could you take us to the creative part of your presentation?," Sandy's voice was stern. No wonder it had the desired effect.

"Sure sir," Bunty giggled like a kid in a candy store.

He put up his hands, as if holding a football. "What do man likes?"

People sitting around the table were caught off-guard. They looked at each other, smiled and passed a sigh of futility.

"Well, Mr Tiwari, it depends on the context of the question and also on personal choice," Neel gave a naughty, sly smile. Bunty could not get either the stupidity of his question or the pun in the response that it elicited. Therefore, with unabated enthusiasm, he continued, "A man like actions—to play, games, cricket, football, volleyball, badminton." The stress of translating his Hindi thoughts to English and then articulating them was making him sweat profusely. His eyes bulged out and his red, flushed face was covered with beads of perspiration. The audience, though confused, enjoyed the show as Bunty went on with his verbal diahorrea.

"But man is bored with this games. He had played them all, seen them all and is no interested. Now he wants the new games, the new excitements."

RC was at the end of his tether, "And what is this

new excitement all about, Mr Tiwari?"

Bunty looked at him and smiled; the smile, which a *Guru* reserves for the blessed moment when he is handing over his most deeply guarded *mantra* to his favorite disciple. Bunty's lips moved and words were lost as everyone in the room looked at each other, in utter shock, disbelief and embarrassment.

"What did you say?," Neel was not ready to believe his ears.

"Grand Pricks!"

Bunty whispered the golden words again, only this time more forcefully.

"It has been in the world, like the America and the England for very long. But for five years, man of Asia have also liking Grand Pricks. It is so popular that now there are TV channels showing it all the time."

"Really?," Neel rolled his eyes in disbelief and amusement.

Eyeballs shifted between Bunty and Sandy. One was oblivious to the glares while the other, of course, red faced. There was a sense of utter disbelief. The statement was so brazen that no one was ready to believe his ears.

Bunty continued his onslaught, "and in time, this bad time, when everything is down for the CommTech, what the CommTech and its channel partners needs is the excitements. To have the same, I will call the new event as the Grand Pricks 2010—full excitement, full *masti*."

Rohit was playing the silent spectator for long. He shifted in his chair and looked at Bunty right in his eyes. He had a soft face but it was supported by a matured voice and experienced body language.

"Mr Tiwari, so, as we understand, you would like to brand this channel event as Grand Pricks. Right?"

After finding someone who was on his wavelength, Bunty nodded with gusto.

"Very well, would you also mind telling us how you plan to take this concept forward across the various touch points."

RC, who was livid, wanted to interrupt, but Rohit stopped him with a polite smile, seeking his kind permission. RC shrugged his shoulders in utter disbelief.

"As the excitement is all about the fastest cars …."

The expression on Rohit's face changed like quicksilver and he interrupted.

"Did you just mention cars?," he enquired.

"Yes, as the Grand Pricks is all about the cars. The red cars, fast cars, sporty cars…."

"Don't tell me that you meant *Grand Prix*, did you?," Neel was flabbergasted.

"That is what I am telling. Grand Pricks," his face beamed. "Don't you find it exciting?"

Sandy took a deep breath. His face was amber red with anger, embarrassment and humiliation. VVS wondered how someone as smart as Sandy could align himself with such an obvious joker.

Everyone smiled while Bunty went on displaying the creative renditions of Grand Pricks!

***

Greased Palms

"Sandy sir, why do we need to work with someone as stupid as Bunty?" VVS had a simple question. But probably it was the simplest of the questions which had the most-layered answers.

"Pour me another one." Sandy was in no mood to discuss Bunty, the fiasco or the embarrassment.

Like a good junior and a team member, VVS poured some rum in Sandy's glass and topped it with Coke—the way he loved his drink since college days. They were seated in a plush Innova, a cab, which was rented from office, of course, for a client meeting. The windows were rolled up and the driver was too busy trying to negotiate the heavy peak-hour Gurgaon traffic. Earlier, VVS was a little scared of doing a car 'O'bar in an office cab, but Sandy comforted him by telling that he knew the cabbie for a very long time and that he could be trusted. Sandy pressed a button, which rolled down the window a little. VVS knew that it was time to hand over a lighted cigarette to him.

Sandy took a large sip, followed by a quick drag. VVS also sipped his concoction, which he had mixed in the cold drink bottle itself—two portions of rum with one portion of Coke and one portion of water. The traffic outside was heavy. Cars were crawling and the impatient drivers, so typical of any metro, were honking like possessed souls. VVS looked out. Most of the drivers were on their mobile phones. Few of them looked blank. Maybe a bad day at work, he assumed. The chaotic stillness around him reminded him of the famous song, 'Everybody Hurts' by REM.

The cab kept on inching forward. They both sat there smoking and drinking. Neither of them spoke.

***

He looked at the envelope, which Bunty had given him, and then at the SMS he had received from Sandy. 'Cl once bunty delivers the pkt.'

A fairly simple SMS. But whatever transpired after that was a little confusing. Bunty had come to see VVS with the samples of the T-shirts and caps for the channel partner event. The samples were horrendous. VVS told Bunty the same. Without wasting a single second, Bunty immediately called up Sandy. VVS took offense to his action but it seemed that Bunty was not bothered. Sandy did not take his call and this agitated Bunty. Before he stepped out, he handed VVS an envelope which had PIN1320 written on it.

VVS sat there, in the Marigold meeting room, trying to figure out the PIN and the number 1320. While he was lost in thought, his Blackberry vibrated. It was Sandy.

"What's up?" he was a little extra sweet.

"Nothing much, I was with Bunty, he has just left. The T-shirt ..."

"Has he handed you the envelope?," Sandy had his own agenda and surely the quality of the T-shirt was not on it. "Yes, he did. Sir, why do we work with such a vendor," VVS asked him again. "He has no infrastructure, no commonsense, nothing at all. I am afraid that he could land us in soup."

"Well, there are certain questions which get answered with time." Sandy was philosophical.

VVS knew that it was the end of the road.

"Now listen to me carefully, open the envelope and see what is there inside."

"Sir, it has an ATM card."

"Good, with Bunty's name on it?"

"Yes."

"Has he given you the PIN."

"Well, sir but…"

"VVS, have you got the PIN?"

"Yes sir."

"Now what you need to do is to go to the ICICI bank, which is on the ground floor, and withdraw ten thousand rupees. Repeat the same transaction three times today, after an interval of ten minutes."

VVS was scared. He knew that the card belonged to someone else. Also, Sandy's hushed tone proved that something was shady. After the hacking debacle, VVS was in no mood to get into any kind of complication with the law enforcement agencies. He knew it well, that if anything went wrong, with a hacking enquiry already going on, in Udaipur, everyone would believe him to be a habitual offender.

Like a secret service agent, alert and looking around for suspicious faces around, he walked down. He took the stairs as he remembered seeing in some movie that a combination of stairs and the elevator was the best way to throw off any trail. He came down four floors using the stairs and then took the elevator. Every other face seemed suspicious to him. He entered the ATM booth and hurriedly inserted the card and punched the pin. When the machine asked if he wanted a printed record of the transaction, out of habit, he pressed yes. With ten thousand in his pocket, and the statement in his hands, he knew that the account exactly had seven lakh and ninety thousand rupees.

"Shree Naathji, please protect me from any wrong doing," he folded his hand, closed his eyes and prayed with all honesty. Once he had withdrawn the three rounds of ten thousand each, he felt exhausted.

"Sir, it's done."

"Good boy."

"Sir, the account has seven lakh and seventy thousand rupees more," he blurted out.

"Who told you?," Sandy sounded as if he had been caught on the wrong foot and was therefore annoyed.

"Actually, I printed the slip and…"

"Did I tell you to print the slip? Did I VVS?" VVS did not like his tone as it sounded outright humiliating.

"You know curiosity kills the cat and now it will kill VVS too." Sandy's tone changed and he burst into laughter, confusing VVS.

The task entrusted to VVS by Sandy was a simple one. To take out the remaining seven lakh seventy thousand rupees in denomination of ten thousand in four lots everyday and to keep the money at his place. VVS was extremely scared of keeping such large sum of money and told Sandy the same. As usual, Sandy was casual and cool and asked him to buy a good suitcase and to stack all the money in it. He also mentioned that it was the payment for the small-time vendors who would need cash during the channel partner event as they would not get cheques issued from CommTech, since they were not empanelled.

***

Walk, Trot, Run

It all seemed just like yesterday. VVS was back from Hong Kong. All that transpired at the channel partners meet—Get, Set, Go—had left him shaken and perturbed. The joy of his first foreign trip was replaced with the guilt of playing pimp to Neel, sleeping with a hooker and seeing a man he looked up to all his life, Sandy, stoop to a level, which was beyond the dignity of any living soul. He wanted to run away from everything, to a place where no one could find him.

But was there any end to feeling like a loser, and running away from every situation? When he was in Udaipur, he cursed the *banas*, the city, the parochial thinking, stuck-up people and dreamt of a life with an MNC, rubbing shoulders with the suave and intelligent. Now, here too, he faced the same demons of restlessness.

Why was he a mis-fit everywhere? He could see people enjoying themselves everywhere—in Udaipur and also at CommTech—having a blast, irrespective of everything. Why was he unhappy at both these places? Where did he belong? What was happiness to him, for him? Was it his own shortcomings that did not let him be happy anywhere, or was it something else?

Was he a failure? Maybe he was. After all, he had failed on every front—as a son, a husband, a junior, an employee—disappointment surrounded him everywhere he went. Was it destiny, his *karma* or a mix of both? He could still not believe that a Fortune 500 company filed for bankruptcy the very day he joined. Did it happen only because of him?

What did the red heart with three piercing daggers mean? Who could cheat him? Rajeshwari? But then he would be too happy if she cheated on him and walked away. Ambica? Why would she? They were together because they liked each other. There was no compulsion, no social pressure. Even if she liked someone, there was no need to cheat, as she was always free to exercise her free will. Who could be the traitor? Sandy? He had already showed his true colors. Who else could give him heartache and tears?

For VVS, six months at CommTech had been nothing short of a roller coaster ride. But for Ambica, everything had depreciated—health, peace, stability, ethos, morality, confidence, just about everything. In Udaipur, he was frustrated but had hope in his eyes; of a world, which was nice, clean and too good to be true. A world which was perfect, with perfect people and perfect emotions. But now, after being a part of his dream world, he could see how wrong he was. Like any other world, this world too had its own share of devils and demons, miseries and pain, even its own heaven and hell.

***

"Hey dude, could you do me a favor? I have sent you a mail. It has two things. One, my PPF account number and another account number in the name of Vimla Kumari. In my PPF account, which is at SBI, Qutab Colony, Gurgaon, please deposit forty thousand. And in the account of Vimla Kumari, keep on depositing forty thousand, for fourteen days."

VVS was bewildered.

"You will be left with two lakh. Right?" Sandy probed.

"Yes sir."

"That is for you. Enjoy."

VVS took time to understand. "Two lakh?"

"Can't you understand English?" Sandy laughed.

"Sir, I mean, I get the PPF part, even the Vimla Kumari part? But why are you asking me to keep two lakh? I mean what am I supposed to do with it?"

"Who is the boss?" the question was straight.

"Well…you." VVS was still apprehensive.

"And don't you know that the boss is always right?"

"I know, sir, but you had told me that the money is for paying the suppliers who were not empanelled."

"VVS, aren't you too naïve to survive in this real world?" Sandy was irritated.

"I mean, sir..."

"Listen to me. This money is for us. Out of the eight, two lakh is for you. Do whatever you want to do—drink, shop, splurge, hump, just about anything. But I would suggest that you save it."

"I mean sir, is this a kick back to give Shownine the channel partner event?"

"No, sweet little baby. It's a token of my smartness. If I can execute a job of hundred rupees in eighty and keep the twenty rupees for myself, would you still call it a kick back?"

"But sir...." VVS was perplexed.

"See if you don't want it, that's ok by me." Sandy was to the point.

"Well..."

Sandy laughed.

"Don't be stupid, take it. These bastards at CommTech will throw us out any day. Then what are we going to do? Don't you think we have a right to ensure a safe future for ourselves? Don't you think, before taking the high ground of morality, we have a responsibility towards our families? If tomorrow, I am chucked out of

CommTech, because that motherfucker Buck and leaders like RC couldn't run the show, why should my family suffer? They have made their millions. Salary, perks, retention bonuses and God only knows what else. Why can't I make a few lakh for a rainy day?"

For some reason, whatever Sandy was trying to explain was not making any sense to VVS. Though the logic was sound but the heart was not ready to comprehend or accept. Finally, the man in VVS succumbed to the charm of her lady love as the money promised him an opportunity to please her, to make her smile, to see her eyes shine. He decided buying Ambica something nice, maybe a nice pair of diamond ear studs.

"Thank you for the money sir."

Sandy laughed again, "You ass, don't forget to do what I have told you."

***

"What's up *Thakur*? How was your Hong Kong trip?" Ashu sounded as joyous as ever. A new shiny job had added more spark to his tone and ever-exuberant spirit.

"It was good."

"How many whores did that bastard Neel hump this time?"

VVS was scandalized as he had no clue that everyone knew this secret.

"And how many hookers did the marketing team book this year?," Ashu probed further. VVS felt like an idiot. The entire world knew about it, except him. Why didn't someone tell him? But then he knew that even if someone tried telling him, he would never have believed as corporate guys were Gods to him—straight, upright, knowledgeable, tech savvy and a role model.

"Hey! *Thakur*, all well? Hope you are not depressed because during the past four weeks, when you guys were busy preparing for your channel partner event, we snatched every single order from CommTech. Wake up little *Thakur*, wake up." Ashu mimicked the famous song.

"Well Ashu, I don't know if I am supposed to feel good for you, or bad for CommTech." VVS's confusion was justified.

"You know *Thakur*, you are a genuine guy and that is why I like you."

"Thank you sir for liking me but I hope this liking won't get too sweet for my comfort." VVS just wanted to give him a feeling that everything was fine. "No way. This world can surely do with just one couple, Shah Rukh and Karan." Ashu laughed and VVS smiled.

"Listen, we are sponsoring the premier of *Kaminey*."

"Not bad. I am sure your marketing team could never have found a better movie to describe you guys so aptly." VVS wanted to sound normal.

"Sure sure. And you know if CommTech's marketing team sponsored a premier, it would be of the Living Dead." Ashu was quick to counter. They both laughed.

"*Thakur*, 26th, 8 pm at PVR Saket. Done?"

"Sure, can I get someone along?"

"Not bad. So finally you did manage to sink your fangs into some girl?"

"Shut up, Ashu."

"No, I mean, good going. After all, horses and women are so much alike. Aren't they?"

***

"Neel, things are not looking any bright here." RC sounded concerned

"I know. Whatever we are doing on the sales front is just a short-term measure and is sure to backfire, sooner or later." Neel was blunt.

"See, for me and my cabinet, with Crompton, I have negotiated a retainment bonus. He has agreed to pay us twenty per cent of our gross. So, that will keep us warm for the time."

RC adjusted his turban. Today, it was solid orange with orange and black spotted tie.

"What does the scenario look like?" Neel sounded casual.

"Not too good. I was on a call with Buck. He thinks

that with a change of guard, my chair could come in the line of fire. Therefore, he was suggesting that I move to a global or an APAC role as it would be safer. We all know, during the initial months, the new buyer will be focusing more on country-level roles and getting them right for the sales to stabilize. Global roles would be tampered much later."

"Hmmm, so what do you think?" Neel probed.

"Well, surely, he has a point. He has offered me the post of Global Director, Voice and Data Applications. The role is more of a facilitator's and I will not be directly responsible for any numbers. Though it would not have much power and budgets, but then, under the present circumstances there isn't much any which ways. Moreover, it will be a safe position, which will give me all the time to pursue my golf along with spending some time with my family too. I am seriously contemplating either taking it up or taking this offer from another US-based company which is into a similar product line."

Neel nodded his head and brushed his lock of white hair with his hand.

"What about me?" He looked at RC.

"I have spoken with Crompton. He will take you as Head, Service Delivery for APAC. Go and have some fun in Singapore." They both laughed.

"And who will step into your shoes?" Neel quizzed.

"Well, Rohit seems to be a fine choice. He has been heading the west region for long and has been achieving his targets quarter after quarter, for almost seven years now."

"He is also young and ambitious," Neel added.

"And will go for the bait straight away." RC completed the chain of logical thinking.

They both smiled.

RC adjusted his orange turban. "He is a really nice chap. You know Neel, for all these years, ever since he was just a manager whenever I was in Mumbai, he always came to pick me up from the airport."

"Right. I guess it's your turn to reward him." Neel gave his patent, sly smile. "Too bad he won't be able to enjoy his new chair for very long. But then, is there anything permanent in this world?" RC tried justifying his hidden agenda with philosophy.

***

Manish's chair was still empty and the sight always depressed VVS. He had called him up a couple of times, but he never answered his call. VVS knew that for someone as methodical as Manish, everything, including life, was a project, which needed effective project management. Therefore, getting a pink slip would have been a huge blow to his confidence as it questioned his project management skills. VVS thought of paying him a visit, but then he did not want to encroach upon his personal space. But without fail, everyday, he prayed for him and Shubhankar. He was sure that Shree Naathji would help them find a better job.

Amanda was getting more and more aggressive. But surely, she had a method to her madness. She was the only one in the entire CommTech system who was fighting hard despite knowing that the battle and the war, both were lost. She worked for sixteen hours a day, gathering all facts and figures, going through each and every lead, making notes, following up plans, approving each and every cost, planning for every region and marketing prime. Her calls got shorter and more demanding. Every time she fixed a call, people got uncomfortable as she asked straight questions and expected straight answers. She had no personal life and expected the same from her team.

Rohit, along with his team, was putting in every bit to swing the sales number in their favor. Irrespective of the Chapter 11 situation, like a true fighter, he wanted to give his best. However, the results were not so encouraging and for the first time in his seven-year career, he failed to achieve his sales target.

Sanjay Singh quit silently. He did not even bother telling anyone. Aditya was aggressively looking for a job, but due to some reason, nothing better or even decent was coming his way.

***

The hall was packed with people. Ashu was kind enough to receive them—Aditya and VVS—at the entrance. They were sitting in the sixth row, corner seat, loaded with popcorn, coke and hot dogs. VVS was missing Ambica. Too bad, she had an important client meeting. He knew that she would have loved the buzz. He also knew that Ashu and Aditya would have got incredibly jealous, if they saw her. After all, she was everyman's dream and desire rolled into one and her beauty could have burnt a hole in any mortal's armor.

There was still time for the movie to start. Senior functionaries of Sailnet were busy ushering in their guests. Most of them were either clients or channel partners. Missing Ambica, VVS excused himself, came out of the hall and dialed her number. He could hear her mobile ring, but there was no response. He typed an SMS, telling her that he was missing her.

He came inside the hall and walked up to his seat. As he sat down, Ashu leaned towards him, "You see that tall guy in black suit, standing near the front row?" The guy, in his late thirties, was quite attractive and exuded charm and confidence. "He is Angshuman Dhingra, Head Marketing, Sailnet, a very powerful man. He is looking for guys to strengthen his web and CRM team. If you want, I can put in a word."

"Thanks, but no thanks." VVS refused the offer politely.

"Are you a jerk? CommTech is sinking. It's high time you stepped out."

"Ashu, don't be crazy. I can never leave Sandy sir. And you please don't get emotional about it; we will talk about it later," he stuffed some popcorn in Ashu's mouth. He choked on them and cursed him.

While they laughed, VVS's eyes caught some movement near the hall's entrance, which grabbed his attention. He saw a woman who looked exactly like Ambica. He could not believe his eyes. Her resemblance to Ambica was uncanny and it freaked him. She had the same height, the same hairstyle, the same smile. She was holding Angshuman Dhingra's hand and was talking with him. But then his eyes caught something else. She was wearing the same silk *kurta*, which he had got for Ambica from Udaipur. He strained his eyes, to be sure. Yes, it was the same *kurta*—wine red with golden motif. VVS did not know if it was a dream or a nightmare. He took out his phone and redialed the number. He could see the woman look at the flashing screen of her mobile, disconnect it and then put it in her bag.

"Can you see that woman?" Ashu was again leaning towards him. VVS was too lost to react. Ashu was persistent. "The woman who is standing next to Angshuman is his new-found passion."

Words made no sense to VVS. Rage blinded him. Even in the month of December, he was sweating. His veins strained and he felt his temples would burst.

Ashu moved closer to his ear. "Now, with this incentive, I am sure you will send me your CV. You horny *Thakur*. The whole Sailnet knows that he is bonking her. Who knows, even you might get lucky with a woman like her one day."

The sound of the slap was so loud that even amidst all the commotion, it stood out. Everyone turned towards the source of that whip-like sound, Ambica too. Ashu yelped out of sheer surprise and pain while VVS stood there, looking towards Ambica, with vacant eyes. The image of the Tarot card; a red heart with three daggers stabbed across it flashed before his eyes and the words of the Tarot reader 'expect worry and tears' reverberated in his ears.

***

The balcony, the Aravali range, the chair, the table, Ambica, VVS, everything was the same. It was only time that had changed. VVS sat there, silently, smoking. His drags were long, to support his introspection. Ambica stood there, admiring the mystical Aravali bathed in the slow descent of night. She looked up. It was a clear night. The stars were bright and many.

"Veer, I am not going to give you any excuse or pretend being the angel that you think I am." VVS acted indifferent.

"I am a very ambitious woman. And I want to do as well, if not better than men. I know, being the nice soul that you are, you will never even ask me for an explanation, but I owe you one. I've owed you one for a very long time."

"Ambi, why even get into all this? Let it be. I do not want to know anything. Whatever you say or do will never make me the man that I was."

"Veer, contrary to what you think, nothing was planned. It all just happened."

"Ambi, please don't give me your destiny story. Did destiny tell you to cheat me, play with me, take me for a ride and then dump me?"

"Veer, you are overreacting."

"Am I? How would you have reacted?"

"Veer, I know that you have every reason to be hurt and angry. But trust me, whatever I did, your happiness and future were always a priority for me." She walked towards the empty chair and sat down and placed her hands on VVS's hands.

"I am sorry for hurting you. I know, God will never forgive me. But whatever I chose was the best way out for everyone." She looked at him and could see tears in his eyes. He grabbed the Rubik Cube and started fidgeting with it aimlessly. She continued, "Some three years ago, after I joined this PR agency, I started servicing Sailnet. Sailnet was one of our largest clients. There, for work purposes, I used to interact with Angshuman. He headed the marketing division. That was the time when I was going through a lot of trauma in my personal life. My husband was not ready to divorce me and was forcing me to get back with him. My parents wanted me to consider his offer as they thought that every marriage came with its own set of compromises. They believed that if I moved in with him, things would be normal. Somehow, I knew that love was like a free-flowing river or air. It has a life and a mood of its own. It is something natural. It happens or doesn't. One cannot force oneself into or out of it. When you are in love, the whole world assumes a new shade, a new hue and when you walk out of it, the same shades change. For me, living with someone without love was impossible. I was so confused and tired of my life. Without even my knowing or realizing it, Angshuman became my lifeline, my support system. He counseled me, showed me the way and gave me a reason to smile—to be happy and feel good about myself again. Before I could even articulate my emotion, I was in love with him. Being a sane man, he understood my feelings and shared his own demons with me. He told me that even he was going through a bad marriage and was on the verge of filing for a divorce. After both of us knew of each other's situation, we were very clear that if we wanted to stay with each other, we would have to get married. For the same, it was important to be single again. This meant getting our respective divorces in place."

VVS looked at her. She continued, "Getting a divorce is a very taxing process, both emotionally and financially. My parents disowned me, leaving Angshuman as my only source of hope. Unfortunately, life always walks ahead of us. For various reasons—competition, shrinking market and recession, Sailnet started losing market share. Angshuman came under a lot of stress and fire. He tried whatever he could, but things did not look up. Our divorce cases were also in the court. Work pressure was driving him insane. His bosses, sitting out of California, were breathing down his neck. He slipped into depression and almost had a nervous breakdown. I did not want life to turn its back on me again. I did not want to lose him; my future, my happiness again. I knew if I lost it this time, it would be gone for good and forever. To preserve my happiness, my future, my love, I was willing to do anything." Her eyes looked determined.

VVS was still watching her. He knew that subsequent to this revelation, everything between them would be over, as if it had never been there. But he still could not take his eyes off her. She looked so angelic. God was so partial while creating her. Her bell-like voice was still so soothing. Even with her integrity under question, how valiantly and with so much dignity, she was trying to present her side of the argument. He felt so good to have been with her, as a part of her life, even if it were for a short period.

"And then you came looking for an apartment, and finally moved in. When you told me that you had moved on to the brand side of marketing, I had no clue what it could mean for us. One day, generally, I told Angshuman. I still don't know how and why it clicked in his mind that if he could lay his hands on the marketing plan of CommTech, maybe he could do something to boost his sagging fortune. He looked at me for help. Too afraid to lose my future and love, I agreed. From that day, I became extra sweet with you. I started taking more interest in your work, especially the PRS campaign. Like a simpleton, you told me everything about it and like a blinded lover, I passed it on to Angshuman. He saw a new lease of life and internally started selling the idea of capturing the market share of CommTech, which was a low-hanging fruit. To make all this happen, he did numerous rounds of presentations to his bosses and finally they agreed. So one day, while you were showing me your final PRS campaign, I copied the whole thing and handed it over to Angshuman. After some tweaks, Angshuman presented the campaign internally and was appreciated. So before CommTech could do it, he launched the same product, in the same market. Sailnet managed to capture a massive market share. With just one campaign, he was back with a bang."

VVS could not believe whatever she was telling

him was true. Still like a lover boy, he sat there listening to her.

"While I was doing all this, the guilt was killing me. I knew, I wanted to get married to Angshuman, but I was getting drawn towards you. It was not your looks, or your style but your simplicity. The way you trusted people, the way you shared things. You showered all your love on me. I could see you getting torn between Rajeshwari and me. And then, I saw that you chose me and I got afraid. Not for me, but for you. I never wanted to hurt you and break your heart. I knew that if I did, no amount of time would be able to heal it again."

VVS did not know if he should hate her for her devilish ways or love her for her candor.

"Owing to the success of the PRS campaign, which was so unexpected, people at Sailnet started looking up to Angshuman for everything. He was their new star. His bosses also got a big pat on their back and they wanted Angshuman to perform the same magic every time. This again put him under stress. He got desperate and got crankier by the day. He told me to find out about your new campaign. I refused but he insisted. I felt extremely miserable, both for you and me. I wanted to tell you but then Angshuman's career was at stake. I was so confused. I could not sleep for nights, trying to find a logical way out. I could not figure out if I was in love with him, then why was I getting drawn to you? If he was the one who loved me, then why was he forcing me into something, which I did not want to? If I loved you or even liked you, why did I cheat you by stealing your campaign? Too many questions just kept churning inside me. I also knew that if I did manage to steal your next campaign, you would get sacked. For sure, I did not want it to happen. But seeing Angshuman getting so desperate, I was forced to do it. He actually begged me to do it and when I told him that you were not in town, he gave me a ticket to Udaipur. I felt like an object, a bait, which was dangled before you, by him, to solve his needs. In Udaipur, the sole purpose of my visit was to steal the campaign. It is a different story that when I boarded the plane, my only objective was to see you. For some reason, I missed you, your face, our conversations…just everything about you and me. Angshuman kept on calling me and reminding me, what I was there for. He kept on bringing up our future and projecting an image where our future depended on my theft. When he saw that his pep talk was not working, he begged me, even cried. I was swayed by his tears. That evening in Udaipur, when I asked you for your laptop, I copied your Contact Center campaign. I was so perplexed and torn between both of you. But in my own way, I did what I could. I spoke to Angshuman that in reparation for all this, he would absorb you in his team. No wonder, he readily agreed to it."

VVS had no words. He was still fidgeting with the

Rubik Cube. Perplexity was plastered large on his face. He lit a cigarette. With nicotine dissolving in his blood stream, he felt a little better. He looked at her. She had tears in her big beautiful eyes. She shifted in her chair and looked towards the brightly-lit sky.

"You know Veer, Sailnet is releasing your Contact Center campaign tomorrow. I know, saying sorry would mean nothing, but...."

VVS kept the Rubik Cube on the table and got up. "Ambi, it might sound a little weird, but every relationship is like a building. A building under various stages of completion—the foundation, plinth and the consecutive floors. If you look around, people are drawn towards each other for different reasons. Some go for looks, some flip for intelligence, many for the money, some even dig fame and glamour.

"So, if a relationship is based; say on looks, once the look factor wears away, it starts running into trouble. Or let's say if it is built on money, it will evaporate the moment some richer guy or girl steps in or if your own fortune dwindles. Then there are a few relationships that are built on faith, where faith is the basis of all future conversations, interactions, liking and love. I thought that our relationship was built on faith. Therefore, I assumed that with each passing day, it would keep on getting stronger. And then finally we would reach a point where our faith would make us surrender. That day, the compartments of expectation, the difference between you and me, the class divide, the age conflict, the thought gap, all would be consumed by the holy fire of love and we would be one. This oneness would be our new identity, our life force. We would need no one, but each other. We would be each other's mentor, guide, lover, friend, inspiration, support and just about everything. But when the same faith has been trounced under the feet of ambition, greed and conflict, I see no way ahead. By the way, even if you had asked me to mail you the Contact Center campaign, I would have. At least, it would have saved you all the trouble of coming to Udaipur." He got up holding the Rubik Cube and walked inside.

***

It was a long and torturous night. The fuchsia pink walls looked garish and it hurt his eyes. The room felt suffocating, as if there was no oxygen in it. He opened the window, letting the cold December air in, finding some warmth. Everything seemed to be out of its place, the dressing table, the wardrobe, the bed—just about everything. He pulled out a cigarette and looked at it, as if weighing the pros and cons. He finally decided against lighting it and tossed it away.

He tried to focus, or maybe, just lose track of everything. He picked up the Rubik Cube but got agitated with every single move he made. He looked at the wall clock. For sure, he was losing the sheen. He concentrated on it, trying to figure out his next moves and the subsequent ones. The harder he tried, the more jumbled it got. He looked at the wall clock again. It had been more than ten minutes and he was no closer to solving it. Out of sheer exasperation, he threw it, back on the writing table.

It was well past midnight. He was feeling lost and lonely. It occurred to him, during all these months, she had been the centrifugal force of his life. Right from morning till late in the night, his whole life revolved around her. Her thoughts, her conversations, her company, her eyes, her smile, the cozy moments, the tenderness—every single minute had her touch and memories. He could not fathom a life without her, rather even a single moment without her. The mere thought of not having her in his life made his hands and feet go cold and numb. It was a feeling, which was very alien to him. He hated himself for it. Beyond feeling cheated and betrayed, he was in a state of stupor. He could not come to terms with the fact that he had been used and now with his role over, the time had come for his effective disposal by snapping all the ties. How could she do it? Was she such a great actor that she could emote and control even the rising temperature of her earlobes, the spreading amber color of her cheeks, the changing colors of her eyes, or was it all just a figment of his fertile imagination?

How could a girl in love with someone else even think of doing things that she did with him? Was she nothing but a good face, hiding all the filth inside her? How could she let him touch her, feel her, caress her when her heart, body and soul belonged to someone else? Whom did she cheat more, Angshuman or him? Would Angshuman be aware that on the pretext of taking the campaign, she had actually slept with him? Every time she kissed him back, was she really kissing? Every time she climaxed, was it all made up? Could this be a part of a pre-decided agenda, between her and her successful corporate honcho boyfriend or did she indulge in the carnal drama just to satisfy the woman in her? How could she be such a… he tried to find the apt word and the only word which came to his mind was 'WHORE.'

He felt so nauseated thinking that all this while he was kissing hands, which were kissed by Angshuman regularly, kissing lips which were sucked by her boyfriend, delving inside her, a place which Angshuman frequented every now and then. He ran towards the washroom and threw up. His eyes flooded and he let them spill over, finding a release, as he sobbed. Lying in his bed, with tears streaking his pillow, he wanted to call up Rajeshwari and confess that he had been a fool for not respecting her; as a woman, as a wife. He wanted to tell her everything—Sakshi to Ambica, Hong Kong to Gurgaon. He had realized that he always failed in judging people. From Sandeep Khandelwal to

Ambica, Harsh to Amanda. He felt like an idiot, with no place to call his own, no shoulder to cry upon.

What a waste of time and dreams, he thought. All these years, he had dreamt of a world, a life, only to realize that his dream world was just a visual delight with no substance. It just floated in thin air, with no roots, no ground, and just a pin could end it all. All his life he dreamt of a love worth dying for, only to discover the price tag attached to it was too steep. Why did everyone, every situation around him let him down? Did he expect too much or were his expectations unreal? Why was he such a misfit everywhere?

Should he find solace in the present, giving up his resistance, accepting things or should he seek what he aimed for? But then, what did he seek? He had no clear-cut answers. Ambica's face kept on haunting him. He still could not believe that she had used him. How could she be so mean? Did emotions mean nothing in this world? Was logic bigger than love? Was there no place for love at all? The questions were unending.

He got up and pulled out the small bag, which had the money he had taken out from the ATM. He counted his share; two lakh of hard currency and packed it in a shoe-box. He knew what he was supposed to do. But did he really know the answer to the bigger question which haunted him.

***

"Are you out of your mind?" Sandy was stunned.

"No sir. But I have decided that I will tell Amanda everything and will accept that it was due to my negligence that the campaigns were leaked."

"And she will get your ass kicked out of CommTech. Dude, don't even think this to be heroic. It's life, not a movie where the heroine falls for the honest hero. That bitch is looking for an opportunity to hide her inefficiency."

"Sir, on the contrary, she is the only leader who is effective within the entire CommTech system. At least she is fighting and giving this fight her best shot."

"And how many leaders have you interacted with? Please tell me Mr Virendra Vikram Singh?" Sandy's temper soared.

"Enough to know that they are all a bunch of nincompoops."

"You JCI 3 level creature. Do you have any clue what leadership is all about? Have you ever managed a single man in your life, leave alone a team or an organization and you are telling me what effective leadership is about?"

"Sir, you are right. I'm a JCI 3 level employee. No wonder, JCI stands for Job Complexity Index. At JCI 6, your level, I understand that your's is truly a complex one. Of course, playing a pimp to one's boss is not something everyone can do," VVS's voice was composed, yet razor like. "How dare you? You call yourself a *Rajput* and this is how you pay me for all my love and affection?" Sandy was livid with rage and hurt.

"Sir, I am a *Rajput* and I am very proud of being one. That is why I appreciate values like integrity, honesty, character and valor. And that is the reason why I refuse to be a part of this circus which is nothing but a whole lot of muck and sleaze."

"Where was this *Rajput* when he begged me to get him in here? I created a position for this asshole of a *Rajput*. You mother fucker. You were rotting in some shady web company in Udaipur. And now, when you are out of that hell, you think you can give me this preposterous *Rajput* theory? You thankless piece of shit!"

"Sir, I am grateful to you for getting me this job. Trust me, if it weren't for the gratitude, I would have killed you with my own hands for taking me so far away from what I was or wanted to be."

"How dare you threaten me?" Sandy was trembling with uncontrollable rage. "I am not threatening you, just making you go through some introspection. If you look at me and my despicable state today, you will realize that you are the one who is to be blamed. Since my first day in college, when you took me under your wings, instead of being my inspiration, you just gave me false aspirations. You know sir, I would even go to the extent of branding you as a pervert who initiated this eighteen-year-old into a world, which you knew would ruin him. Would you have ever made your younger brother or your son follow the same path of self-destruction? Answer me sir. Then, why did you do it to me?"

Sandy was silent. "Though you kept telling me always that you knew the precise role of a senior. But in reality, you just wanted to control this gullible mind, to suit your vested interest. Back then, I thought that all my batchmates who avoided you were losers but now I can see, how smart they were, as they knew that you were just bad news." VVS was in no mood to stop.

"I am going to send my resignation to Amanda, not you. From now on, I refuse to work as your junior Mr Sandeep Khandelwal. You are nothing but a pimp and a fixer. I have deposited the money in the account of Vimla and trust me I will never tell anyone about it. But don't ever try to cross my path or else...."

The call was disconnected and VVS walked out of the phone booth.

***

Around noon, there was a sudden wave of murmurs, travelling from one end of the office floor to the other. CommTech India had received a mail from RC inviting every single employee to join his call at 2 pm. With the fear of the dreaded list still there, everyone dropped whatever they had on their hands—Facebook, surfing on *naukri.com* or *monster.com*, planting crops on Farmville, playing video games, nurturing the artist deep within by doing Coffee Art or even printing a dozen copies of resumes.

Every individual, every group had a different theory. But each one of the clusters had some unison at one point—something big was coming. The past few weeks were a little tough as arbitrary expenses like phone bills, cab bills, travel bills, entertainment bills had been clamped. Going by the JCI level, expenses were fixed. With immediate effect, it also put a clamp on all travels and made it mandatory for everyone to seek prior travel approval not only from their respective line managers but also from a level above. Telephone bills for sales team was fixed at twenty-five hundred per month and for everyone else at one thousand. The cost cuts were as obnoxious as cutting down on paper tissues, hand-wash and even toilet paper rolls.

Everyone felt the pinch, but most of the employees were old wood and really had no place to go. They were obsolete, even in the CommTech system, so an outsider hiring them was well beyond any question.

"I apologize for inviting you on this call at such a short notice. I also appreciate your effort and regret the inconvenience caused by it. I won't take much of your time as I know you would be using it better, winning every single customer for CommTech. Due to personal reasons, and when I say personal, I mean family reasons,

I have decided to step down," RC paused for a moment, maybe trying to gauge the sentiment. There was silence. Every single CommTech office across India experienced the same effect. Pin drop silence.

"I would take this opportunity to introduce you to your new leader, leader for CommTech India, Rohit Dhawan."

Still there was silence.

"Rohit has been with CommTech for seven years and has set a new record by meeting his targets quarter after quarter, year after year. For three consecutive years, he was also the CommTech Hi-Flier. I need not mention that CommTech Hi-Flier is the most distinguished award within the CommTech system. Rohit will take over in a week's time. With a strong understanding of CommTech culture, the transition will be a smooth one. I am sure most of you must have worked with Rohit during his tenure at CommTech. I would expect you to give him the same support and love which you all so selflessly bestowed upon me."

"RC, I have a question." A confident and honest voice made everyone on the call sit up. Every head had just one question. "Who could this guy be?"

"This is Virendra Vikram Singh, a JCI 3 employee, who is so junior that you would not even have heard my name."

"Virendra, this platform is to make an announcement,

not to ask questions. If you have any send them to me. I will request RC sir to see if he can answer the same," Sandy's voice was shaky and scared.

"Sandeep, please let the young man clear his doubts. It is young men like him who will take CommTech to the next level. Go on young man." RC played the role of a seasoned player.

"Why did CommTech go bankrupt?" VVS's voice sounded so confident that it made even RC nervous.

"Well VVS, I guess that's too late in the day."

"Yes it is. But why is it too late?" VVS thundered. "Because, before CommTech filed for Chapter 11, it was you, your boss, his boss, the entire management of CommTech which had gone bankrupt. Bankruptcy of thought, leadership, honesty, morals and ethos. Come to think of it, CommTech a hundred-year old brand and in just five years, you, the highly-qualified management team of CommTech, ensured that from USD 214 at the NSE, it got delisted from the stock exchange."

The messenger box on VVS's laptop screen blinked. 'VVS get off the call now.' You SOB, don't roger me along with you. Get off now!'

But VVS was a possessed man. "Everything was in place, the systems, the processes, the forms, the accounting, but for honest people who ran the entire thing. I come from a very small organization. It had only six employees. But there was someone to own up to everything, to put a hold on every wasteful expense, to keep an eye on every movement. Here, it's like a picnic, no one to take care of anything, no one responsible for anything. You go to HR they give you an email ID, you go to the Admin they give you another, you go to the accounts, they give you a form. Can't we even spare two minutes to listen to a fellow worker? Are we so busy playing FarmVille and downloading movies?

In Gurgaon office, there are six printers, the large ones cost ten to twelve lakh each. Not to forget, three operators to handle them. After this how can any line manager pass the vouchers for buying individual desktop printers? Shouldn't the manager who passes this voucher be sacked? Can't anyone see? The bigger printers are used for printing personal projects, family pictures and what not. Can't the HR department, which is largely restricted to handing out the joining docket and mailing the holiday list find one honest man who can be made accountable for at least the printers? Is that such a big task?"

"VVS, this is not a six-man shop. This organization has over fifty thousand people," RC interrupted.

"And not one who is honest?," VVS's query was an innocent one. "Isn't it shameful and unfortunate? CommTech spends a fortune organizing sales workshops, training workshops, for the managers and what not. Don't you think we should first have workshops on how to be nice humans? Didn't the management think that it was important to have nice and honest fifty thousand people first rather than fifty thousand smart managers who would get too smart for their own good?"

Hundreds of messenger boxes were blinking on hundreds of laptop screens.

"He has a point."

"But who the fuck is he?"

"I swear, he has the balls."

"What is he trying to say?"

"Is he insane or what?"

"Bitter but true."

"Capt Jack Sparrow must be getting furious."

"So would be his pirates."

"Hey, he sits in the bay next to me."

"Do you know him?"

"He is a shy guy."

"Boss, he is my friend. We call him *Thakur*. Trust me today he will rape RC."

"You sack poor people, who gave their entire lives to this company, claiming downsizing to be the reason. Yet, for your own self, you work out hefty retainment bonuses? The purchase guy is making money in buying laptops, chairs, even appointing cab vendors, the procurement team also has the same agenda, the sales guy fudges numbers to get his bonus, the marketing guy takes kickbacks to push a shoddy vendor, the accounts guy charges money to arrange for fictitious bills and to clear them. Despite all the checks and multi-level clearances, everyone here is making money. Why? Because they all believe that the leadership is doing the same. You could argue that it's not true. But if it's not why didn't you sack the guy or the team that was responsible for the multi-million dollar bid fiasco which cost the company some 500-odd millions? Why was it swept under the carpet? Why was no one taken to task for his blunder? RC, you are the leader for India. How many people do you know by name? Tell me. I can tell you that my local MLA, who is not even high school pass, remembers each and every name in his constituency which has some fifty thousand-plus voters. If he can, surely an IIM topper like you can remember at least five hundred names. But you don't want to as you think that life and work starts and ends with your cabinet. Have you ever met a normal employee, apart from your cabinet members? Have you? I waited for you the entire day, anxiously, as I was scared and apprehensive to meet the great IT leader RC, only to be told that he found having *cholle-kulche* to be a better investment than meeting me who could have been his fan for life?"

Messenger boxes continued flashing on every screen.

"This guy is right."

"I wish we could have told Capt Jack Sparrow the same earlier."

"Is this guy out of his mind? He will be thrown out."

"Sandy, ask someone at the Gurgaon office to stop this bastard."

"Sandy, your career just got over."

"Shelly, get this mother fucker off the phone."

"But Sandy…"

"RC wants it."

"All this is due to the ineffective leadership."

"Buck is a fraud."

"So are his H mails."

"Shelly, go now."

Shelly came out of his cabin and called up three more people from the adjacent bay as he was afraid of going there alone. They rushed towards VVS's bay. VVS saw them and he stood up, with his headset on, and like a true blood of a *Rajput* gave out a war cry, "Shelly, don't even think of doing what you have in mind. Today, I won't hesitate to even kill you to complete what I am here for." His no-nonsense warning sent a shiver down the spine of guys on the call. People from adjacent bays got up to locate the source of the war cry. Though none of them ventured out to stop VVS.

VVS continued looking at Shelly. "You belong to a martial race yourself and you know that when a *Rajput* sounds a battle cry, it's impossible to stop him."

Shelly froze in his tracks, so did the three guys. All

stood there in the long corridor, looking at VVS but not daring to move an inch further.

"RC, don't you know that when your sales team should have been out in the field they were busy having a game of cards at the guest house? What action did you take against the employee who had the audacity to submit a bill for thirty-five thousand rupees against tea and snacks? None I am sure. Why? Because you always assumed that you are bigger than the system. No wonder, you had the channel conference in Hong Kong just to buy a Nintendo. It made you feel powerful, almost like God. Every leader at CommTech assumes the same.

You know RC, I was hired for the role of Brand Manager despite the fact that I had no clue of the role or the function. The honest soul who tried to raise this issue of insane hiring by bringing it to the notice of senior leaders like you, he was systematically flushed out of the system. Why? Because amidst crooks, his honesty stuck out like a sore thumb. No wonder, even during the austerity drive, the CEO himself was using the company jet to travel from his home to office. Just because he is doing it, therefore, every single leader is running his own show. Think of a situation where every employee starts emulating the CEO or you. Don't you think this company would have filed for Chapter 11 long back? You should thank your lucky stars that it didn't."

"I had come here with dreams in my eyes. Assuming

that I will learn, I will work, I will grow. But then I realized that I was learning, but only how to cheat and fool people, that I was growing but away from the truth, I was working but on things which were not important to anyone. We all will find jobs. But did we ever think about CommTech? Didn't we all kill it just because we were too greedy? The day we will introspect; we will find ourselves guilty of a million murder. Murdering hopes, dreams and aspirations of thousands of people. I lost everything I had come here with. The only thing this city gave me, her, and I lost her too. I don't know about you, but I feel completely bankrupt, and as a man it's a terrible feeling to cope up with. Let us hope that we are able to live with this pain and take life forward, if there is any."

***

Team CommTech,

Today, I am pleased to announce that we have entered into sale agreements for our Enterprise Solutions Business with Sailnet for US$375 million.

This is further proof of the considerable value CommTech's businesses have in the marketplace. You have built the Enterprise Business into a strong player and a valued asset in the industry. If successfully completed, this transaction would provide additional clarity for our Enterprise customers, partners as well as employees, a number of whom we expect will have the opportunity for employment with Sailnet.

Again, the most important contribution you can make during this time is to continue your unrelenting focus on serving our customers and maintaining ongoing operations. Your work now will contribute to realizing the value of these businesses as well as preserving innovation and jobs to the greatest extent possible.

Thank you for all you are doing for CommTech.

Buck Howard

***

Curtains

CommTech, the hundred-year old legacy brand, could not even touch the 500-million mark, thanks to leaders like Buck, Sue, Crompton and others. However, all these leaders made pot loads of money through their retainment bonuses.

Buck resigned.

Thousands of people were rendered jobless. With worldwide recession, most of them could not find a job. Many of the laid-off employees filed for claims. Many are still confused over their PF status.

Nobody heard of VVS again. *Daata* and *Dadosa* assumed that being the coward that he was, he would have committed suicide. *Bai ji* still believes that he is alive and would return some day.

Rajeshwari became indifferent and almost stone-like. She moved back to her parents' place.

After a heated altercation, Ambica told Angshuman that she could never marry him as she loved someone else. Despite knowing this, Angshuman was keen to marry her.

He believed that with time and a new city, Singapore, where riding high on his success he was supposed to take over as Marketing Head, APAC, everything would be normal. But she stayed back, in the fuchsia pink room, cherishing the memories.

Capt Jack Sparrow joined another medium-sized IT organization. Most of his pirates joined his gang again.

The sexual harassment case against Neel was swept under the carpet and he was made the Country Head for Sailnet, India.

From being the Country Head, Rohit was shifted to head the Enterprise vertical. He tried his best to manage his Country Head chair but Neel proved to be too smart for him.

Sandy, being the master fixer that he was, in no time gave up his marketing hat and donned the PR one again. He now heads the PR function for a large-format IT organization.

With the two lakh rupees, which Shubhankar found in his mail box, he started off his own systems and process consultancy along with Manish.

Amanda went back to Australia.

Crompton, who is still the President for APAC, was heard of filing for a claim, against the very company that employed him; the very company that he and his senior and skilled team of highly-qualified management professionals had put into bankruptcy.

Harsh got bail and now waits for the cops to submit their *challan*.

Everybody found a new job, a new career, a new life. Everyone but for CommTech. The gentle giant just stood there, feeding everyone, running thousands of households across the world. Never complaining against any act of atrocity. Just selflessly giving away whatever it could till the last day of its existence. And then one day, almost silently, the bluecolored board was pulled down from every building, every door, and replaced with another one—a new and a bright red one.

***

Characters

Rawla Akehpur

Virendra Vikram Singh aka VVS	:	The protagonist
Daata	:	Father of VVS
Bai ji	:	Mother of VVS
Dadosa	:	Elder brother of VVS
Rejeshwari	:	Wife of VVS

Udaipur

Harsh	:	A bana from Udaipur and friend of VVS who gets VVS involved in cyber hacking
Sukhram Meena	:	SHO of the Ranibagh police station and the officer investigating the cyber hacking case
Deepak and Rajan	:	The Baniya brothers, owners of Om and Mewar Travel
Yudhveer	:	The journalist and Chaitali's contact in Udaipur

CommTech

Abhishek Saxena: Prime, Payroll

Aditya : Account manager and VVS's friend, a part of his office gang

Allan : Marketing head, ASEAN region

Amanda Wither
: Lawrence's successor

Amy Slater : Head,Marketing Communication, APAC

Ashu : Group manager and VVS's friend

Bunty Tiwari : MD, Shownine and the event manager for the channel partner event

Jane Lui : Marketing head, Greater China

Kaustav, Payal & Shubha
: Sandy's team members

Lawrence Kilam
: Sandy's boss and Head, Marketing & Communication, APAC

Manish Kumar: Project Manager and VVS's bay mate

Neelesh Dang aka Neel
: VP, Enterprise and a part of RC's cabinet

Nick Doe : VVS's boss at the time of his joining

Rakshit Chaheil aka RC
: MD

Sandeep Khandelwal aka Sandy
: VVS's college time senior and his boss at CommTech. Also a part of RC's cabinet

Sanjay Singh : Leader, SMB, a member of RC's cabinet

Shailainder Bajwa aka Shelly
: Head, Sales, North Zone, Ashu and Aditya's boss and a member of RC's cabinet

Shubhankar : Prime-Systems and Processes and a part of VVS's office gang

Sue Flaherty : Chief marketing officer and Lawrence's boss

RC's Cabinet :

Rohit Dhawan, Amit Kukreja, Shailainder Bajwa aka Shelly, Sanjay Singh, Edgar Augustine, Sameer Roko, Prashant Kulsherstha, Keshav Khurana, Animesh Mishra, Digvijay Bhamri, Neelesh Dang aka Neel and Sandeep Khandelwal aka Sandy.

Gurgaon

Ambica : VVS's apartment mate, ladylove, life force and a PR agency executive

Chaitali : VVS's apartment mate and a journalist with a leading news channel

Rajesh : Head, Panache, the advertising agency of CommTech

Angshuman Dhingra

: Head, Marketing, Sailnet

Glossary

A

Abala nari : A helpless woman

Aanda-bread : Egg and toast

B

Bai ji : Mother or any elderly woman in Rajasthani language

Bana : A suffix used after the name of the boys belonging to some of the martial clans of Rajasthan

Baap : Father

Beedi : Rolled tobacco leaves with tobacco stuffed inside

Bigha : Measurement of land in northern part of India, a part of the revenue system

Black label : One of the variants of Johnny Walker scotch

Bollywood Thakur : The archetypal portrayal of village landlords in Bollywood movies

C

Chunni : A piece of cloth used by rural woman to cover their heads and bust.

Cholle-Kulche: A typical north Indian food of white flour bread and boiled chick-pea, served with diced onion, chilly and lemon.

Challan : An official document produced by the police in court against the convict

D

Daata : Addressing father or any elderly man, respectfully, in Rajasthani language

Dabish : Police raid

Dadosa : Elder brother, in the state of Rajasthan, India

Daroo : Liquor / alcohol

Delta Force : A popular, first person shooting, video game

Dilliwala : Resident of Delhi

Dupatta : Long scarf worn by women around their head or shoulders

F

Filmy : Larger than life, melodramatic connotation

G

Gaon wali biwi: Wife hailing from a village background

The Geeta : A Holy book of Hindus

Ghagra-choli : A traditional Indian embroidered, long skirt and blouse

Ghat : River bank

Gora Saheb : Address reserved for the British officers by the Indians during the Raj period

Gyaan : Knowledge, wisdom

H

Harami : Bastard

Haata : Government approved drinking place

Haldi Ghati Battle
: The famous battle fought between the forces of Maharana Pratap and Akbar in the year 1576

Haka : An exercise done during hunting of animals specially tiger, to bring it out in the open by beating of drums and cymbals

Haveli : A palatial residence

Haramkhors : Lazy, good for nothing people

Hukum : An address reserved for people in power, generally means My Lord.

K

Kunwar Saheb: Son of a village thakur

Kaminey : Title of a Bollywood block-buster which means unscrupulous

Khamaghani : A salutation used in the state of Rajasthan, India, which literally means 'Heartfelt pardon if any error was caused un-intentionally.'

Kuldevi : Ancestral Goddess

Kurta : Long shirt worn by men or women

Kurti : Short shirt worn by women

Kurta-pajama: Long shirt and loose fitting trousers

L

Laal Maans : A spicy, mutton dish of Rajasthan

Laddoo : A kind of Indian sweet, especially prevalent in North India, always round in shape

M

Maa Ambe	An Indian Goddess, a form of Shakti—power, she rides the tiger and has been attributed with getting this earth rid of many powerful demons.
Maata	Mother
Machaan	A raised platform used in hunting
Masala	Spicy
Masti	Enjoyment
Mujra	Dance and song performed by the nautch girls
Monster.com	A popular job search site
Murki	Ear studs or ear rings worn by men in Rajasthan

N

Nimboo-paani	Lemonade
Naukri.com	A popular job search site

P

Phirangi	Foreigner, especially Caucasians
Pandaa	Priests in Hindu temples
Peeli daal tadka	Yellow cooked lentils, a popular dish usually an accompaniment with boiled rice

R

Rawla	Home of the village chieftain, Landlord, in Rajasthan
Rajput	A gallant, noble martial clan of north India

S

Saafa	Turban worn in the villages of north and west Indian states

Sandhya Vandan : Evening prayer

Saheb : Sir

Shikar : A hunting expedition

Shakti : Power

Surya Vanshi : Descendants or belonging to the clan of the Sun God

T

Thakur : A title used by the Landlords of old times

Thikana : Domain of a Thakur, typically one or more than one village

U

Jooti : Traditional hand-made footwear with embroidery work

Y

Yaar : Buddy, a friend

Z

Zari : Gold and silver thread used for embroidery